"*Entwined* is wholly entertaining and wholly unique, a gorgeous fantasy filled with romance, humor, and a gas lamp glow. H. M. Long doesn't miss."

HANNAH F. WHITTEN, *New York Times*-bestselling author of *For the Wolf*

"*Entwined* will sweep you off your feet to another time and place, filled with sparkling wit and breathless adventure. Ottilie is a heroine like no other!"

SUNYI DEAN, *Sunday Times*-bestselling author of *The Book Eaters*

"A cheeky heroine, a unique magic system, and a compelling world make *Entwined* an exciting start to this action-packed duology by H.M. Long. I eagerly await the second installment!"

GENEVIEVE GORNICHEC, author of *The Witch's Heart*

"Intriguing, heartfelt world-building"

CAITLIN ROZAKIS, *New York Times*-bestselling author of *Dreadful*

"Ottilie's search for salvation becomes a battle between safety, love, and the dangerous truth of who she truly is. Perfect for readers of Sarah J. Maas and Rebecca Yarros, this spellbinding romantic fantasy brims with rebellion, sisterhood, and the perilous cost of freedom."

KATHLEEN KAUFMAN, author of *The Entirely True Story of the Fantastical Mesmerist Nora Grey*

"Fans of H.M. Long will find everything they adore here—characters you root for; unique and gorgeous magic with the perfect dose of darkness; a cinematic sense of place; ambitious, breathless action. Add Gilded Age fashion, sword fights, rebellion and romance, and *Entwined* is a fantasy adventure as engrossing as any in the canon. I emerged from reading this in a breathless daze, desperate for the sequel!"

HANNAH MATHEWSON, author of *Witherward*

"*Entwined* is H.M. Long's best work to date—and that is saying something! A lush, Gilded-Age-inspired world sets the stage for a story that is just as witty and charming as its protagonist. In *Entwined*, Long once again demonstrates her deftness at creating indelible, believable characters that capture the many facets and depths of what it means to be a strong woman. This book is utterly entrancing, effortlessly engaging, and a roaring good time. I, for one, already cannot wait to get my hands on the sequel."

MJ KUHN, author of *Among Thieves*

"With a whip-smart heroine on a dangerous quest to recover an ancient artifact, a light-based magic system that is cinematic in visuals, and a whimsical voice and construction reminiscent of Miyazaki's *Howl's Moving Castle*, *Entwined* will delight and surprise readers. H. M. Long stuns again with this Gilded-Age-inspired fantasy that explores the framework of discrimination and othering that arises when different classes of people are systematically placed in separate boxes. Long has a sharp instinct for grounding readers in a realistic, historic setting while cleverly weaving the fantasy elements every SFF reader craves. It was impossible to put down."

GABRIELA ROMERO LACRUZ, #1 *Sunday Times*-bestselling author of *The Sun and the Void*

ENTWINED

*Also by H. M. Long
and available from Titan Books*

THE FOUR PILLARS
Hall of Smoke
Temple of No God
Barrow of Winter
Pillar of Ash

THE WINTER SEA SERIES
Dark Water Daughter
Black Tide Son
Red Tempest Brother

ENTWINED

H. M. LONG

TITAN BOOKS

Entwined
Print edition ISBN: 9781835411384
E-book edition ISBN: 9781835411438

Published by Titan Books
A division of Titan Publishing Group Ltd
144 Southwark Street, London SE1 0UP
www.titanbooks.com

First edition: March 2026
10 9 8 7 6 5 4 3 2 1

This is a work of fiction. All of the characters, organizations, and events portrayed in this novel are either products of the author's imagination or are used fictitiously. Any resemblance to actual persons, living or dead (except for satirical purposes), is entirely coincidental.

© H. M. Long 2026

H. M. Long asserts the moral right to be identified as the author of this work.

No part of this publication may be reproduced, stored in a retrieval system, or transmitted, in any form or by any means without the prior written permission of the publisher, nor be otherwise circulated in any form of binding or cover other than that in which it is published and without a similar condition being imposed on the subsequent purchaser.

A CIP catalogue record for this title is available from the British Library

EU RP (for authorities only)
eucomply OÜ, Pärnu mnt. 139b-14, 11317 Tallinn, Estonia
hello@eucompliancepartner.com, +3375690241

Designed and typeset in Bookmania by Richard Mason.

Printed and bound by CPI Group (UK) Ltd, Croydon CR0 4YY

For Grama Janet

A NOTE UPON: THE ENTWINED

Regardless of their freedoms or station in the societies which The Vigilant Lady Traveller may encounter, the Entwined are defined as those who are not human, whether they be Adepts or Affinates, of the Moon or of the Sun. They are mages, those who wield magic sourced from the presence or absence of light.

The extent of an Entwined's powers varies from mage to mage, with Affinates being the weakest of their kind. All, from Adept to Affinate, possess tattoo-like threads which appear on their throat, shoulders, jaw, or temples when exposed to their corresponding quality of light or darkness. But while Affinates have no direct access to that power, only an inclination of personality, Adepts are powerful, dangerous, and guarded closely by their Guilds.

The Vigilant Lady Traveller should meet all Entwined with caution and remain alert for visible threads, whether they should appear a travelling companion, a new acquaintance—or an old.

FROM THE VIGILANT LADY TRAVELLER:
A GENTLEWOMAN'S GUIDE TO THE WORLD

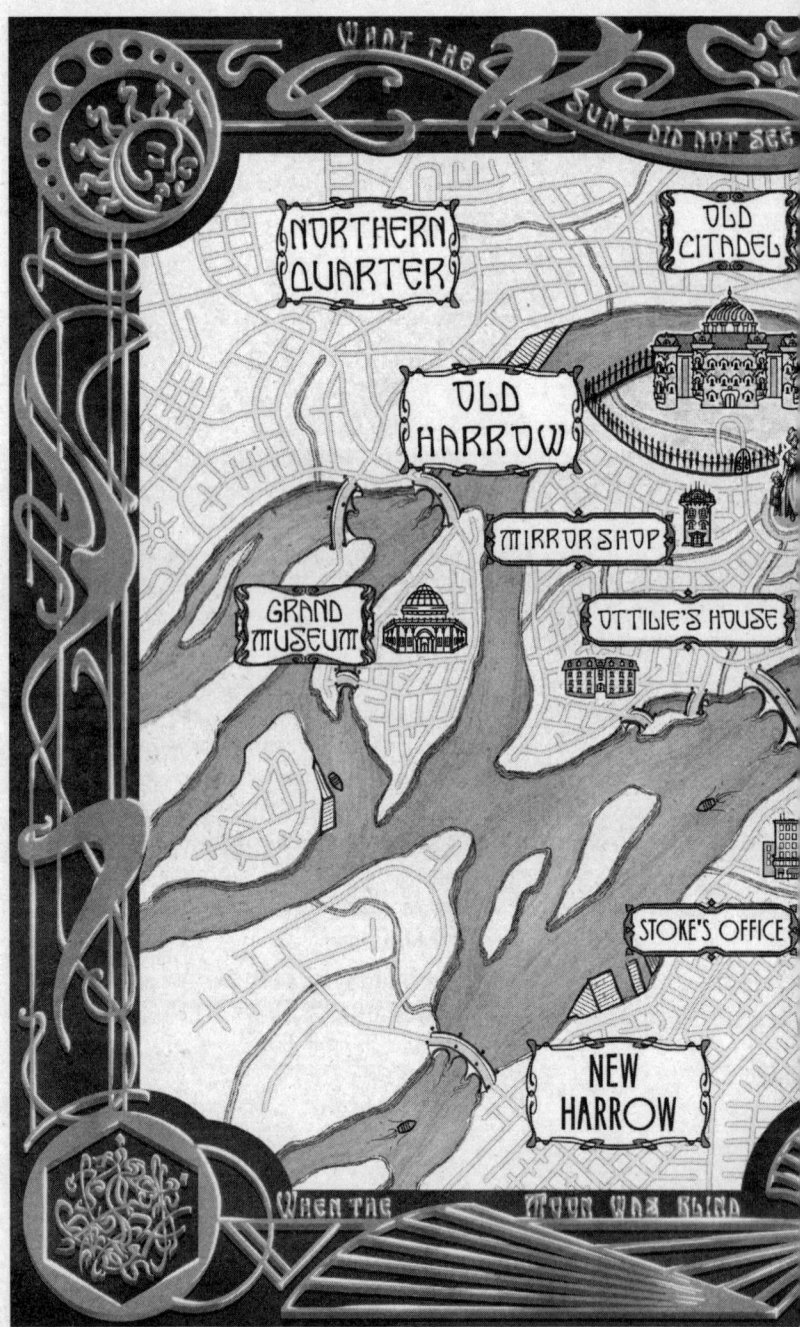

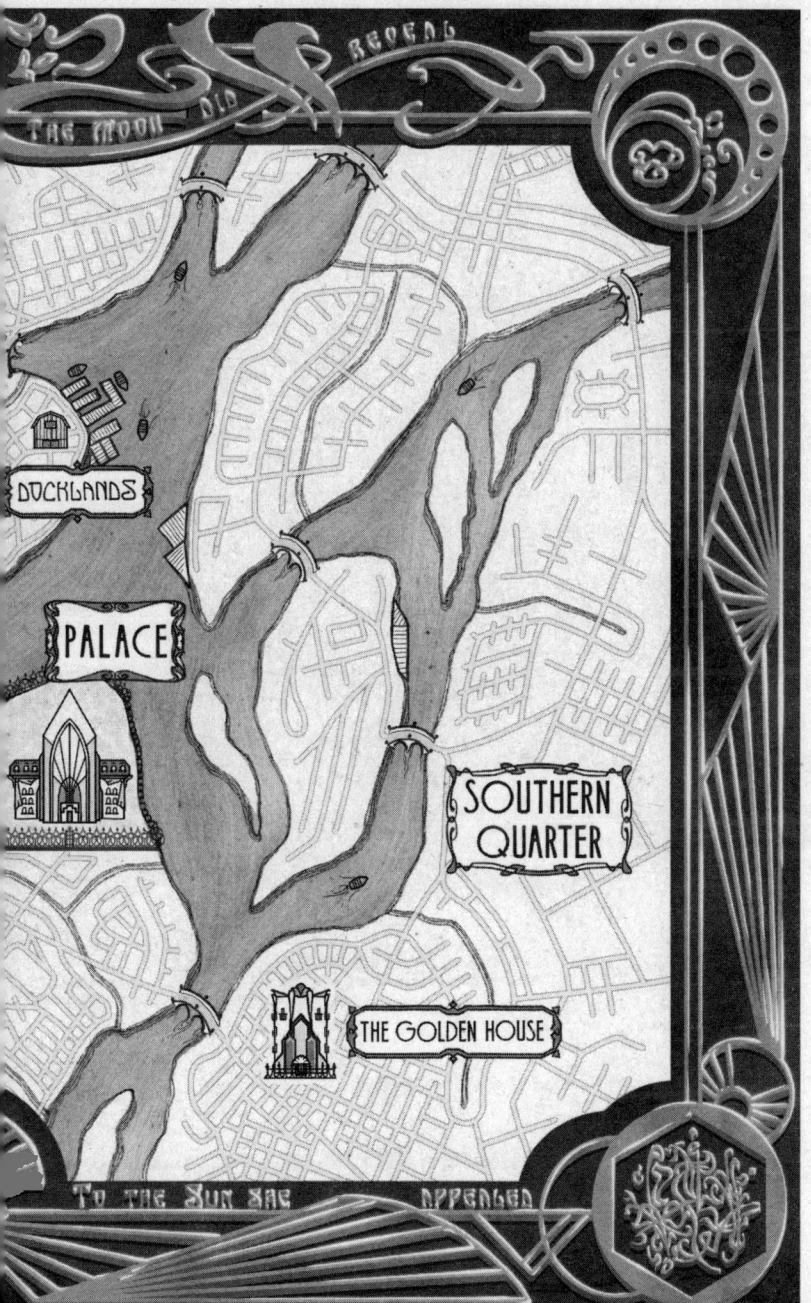

CHAPTER 1

The smuggler was, in my not uninformed opinion, certainly a mage. His eyes were too keen in the night, his movements too quiet. When he cast a long look across the black gloss of the river, I could have sworn I glimpsed silver markings on his throat, between his high collar and unruly reddish-brown beard—silver that appeared only in the thin light of the moon perched above the warehouses and chimneys at our backs.

A lone mage in a disreputable line of work. Worn, laborer's clothes. No Guild ring on his finger, no partner in sight, in a city that would string a mage from a lamppost without the slightest provocation.

A Separatist? A Rogue?

I discreetly tilted my head, feeling the reassuring brush of my high collar, and stopped before him.

"Mr. Harden?" I inquired.

The smuggler flicked his cigarette into the water beside the quay, where it joined a lapping line of refuse. "Who's asking?"

"Miss Fleet, associate of Mr. Stoke. You have an item for us?"

"Ah. Illing's girl." Mr. Harden appraised me down the length of his nose as the wind gusted between us, cold as the coming winter. He had a fine nose, I noted, statuesque, in a face that looked to be perhaps thirty. "Your boss is late."

"He will be along presently," I assured him. "In the meantime, you may show me. Where is it?"

The smuggler shoved his hands into his pockets and rocked back on his heels, nonchalant and self-assured. "I'll not be doing that. What are you, to our dear Detective Stoke? 'Associate' being rather vague, you understand. Daughter? Secretary? Bodyguard? Lewis sends his regards, by the way. I offered to pass on a kiss, but he declined. Now, if you'd like to send him one, I won't be back south for some time, but a good, solid kiss will keep."

"I am the detective's secretary," I interrupted. I considered him dryly for the span of a few lapping waves before the thought of Lewis made me ask, "Did Lewis seem well?"

The way Mr. Harden eyed me made me feel utterly transparent. I suspected Lewis had told him far more about me, about *us*, than he'd told me about Harden—first and foremost, that the man was a Guildless mage.

I trusted Lewis, but that did not sit well.

Mr. Harden said, "As well as anyone is, down there. Times are not what they were."

I pressed my lips into a thin twist of agreement.

The sound of footsteps drew our attention down the riverside. There, a shadow separated from an alleyway and moved purposefully towards us, walking stick carried brusquely in one hand.

"Harden," Mr. Stoke, my employer, greeted the other man. In his late fifties with a well-tended moustache, slightly melancholy eyes, and a decidedly average frame, his voice was his most notable quality. It was low and smooth and gentle, turning Harrow's clipped, bitter dialect into a soothing rumble. "Good to see you again. I've your money, and apologize for my tardiness. Where is it?"

"Detective." Harden tugged his forelock. "Follow me."

With that he moved off down the walk, his strides long and easy. Mr. Stoke and I followed, falling into step with one another.

"You should have waited for me," Mr. Stoke murmured, keeping his gaze on Harden's back. "Do not tell me you walked at this hour."

"I took a hackney," I soothed as Harden stopped by a large warehouse door, barely a pace from the river's edge and shadowed by block and tackle for unloading the long, narrow riverboats.

Mr. Stoke's lips momentarily flattened into a line. "Please wait for me, in the future."

Future. The word burrowed under my skin, stinging with guilt, as we followed Harden into the warehouse and the light of a pungent oil lamp. If electricity had reached this quarter of the city, the warehouses' owners had yet to take advantage of it.

The space was large and vaulted, evidenced by the echo of our footsteps, but so dark and packed with crates, bundles, and barrels that I could not see far. I eyed gaps and shadows, all too aware of how many enemies could be hidden just out of sight.

"This is it," Harden said, dividing my attention. He wove his way to a long worktable, gouged and smoothed by decades of use. A nondescript crate sat atop, with a waiting crowbar. "The latest spoils of revolution. Lewis assured me this is what your patron requested."

My employer fished into his pocket for an envelope and relinquished it. Harden glanced inside, then tossed the envelope on the table and shoved the crowbar under the crate lid.

He pressed down, encountered resistance, and tried again with a muttered curse. My gaze slipped to his throat as he adjusted his grip, but the silver threads I had glimpsed under the light of the moon had faded in the lanternlight.

I startled as the lid yielded with a crack. Harden sniffed in apparent satisfaction and stepped aside to allow us to peer into a nest of raw cotton.

I pulled off one glove, revealing the simple engagement ring on my fourth finger, and brushed the top layer away. As I did my fingers skimmed the surface of something below—hard wood, smooth and carved.

Images assailed me. Other hands, touching, placing.

A bright sky, and a dark chamber hewn in stone. A familiar face with a short moustache, neat sideburns, and the canvas-clad helmet of a soldier. Lewis. My heart startled in my chest, but long practice kept my expression passingly curious.

The object I touched was now discernable as the top of a box. A symbol stared up at me, complex and arcane.

"Miss Fleet, if I may?" Mr. Stoke murmured.

I stepped back. The man took my place and lifted the box from its nest, revealing it to be a perfect cube, its wood pale and sapped of color. Its sides were the length of Mr. Stoke's large hands and carved with circular symbols, like the top. There was no visible opening, though I noted the suggestion of joints. A puzzle box.

"Well." Harden looked unimpressed. "If you're satisfied? I've other business to be about."

Mr. Stoke nodded, shifted the box under one arm and shook Harden's hand. "A pleasure."

"'Course," Harden said. "Glad to help a man such as yourself. You know how to find me if you've more such... mutually beneficial opportunities. I'll be about Harrow from now on. But I can make arrangements."

Mr. Stoke nodded, touched his hat and made for the door, gathering me with a glance. I fell into step, pulling my glove back on and watching the symbols on the box disappear as the detective wrapped it in cloth.

"The same goes to you, Miss Fleet."

Harden's voice made me pause in the doorway. The breezy autumn night swept around me, stirring my skirts and smelling strongly of river, mildew, and coming rain.

Mr. Stoke continued a few steps before he glanced back.

"Pardon?" I looked at the smuggler with blooming irritation, but that shifted to unease as I met his gaze. He did not leer as I expected, but there was assessment in the tilt of his head, and a hint of knowing in his eyes.

"You know how to find me if you've any business opportunities," he clarified. "I'm very good at finding things, as you know. Moving them, discreetly. And hiding them."

Lewis had most certainly told him too much. I returned the man's smile, thin and false, and hastened to catch up to Mr. Stoke.

We did not speak as we wove through the series of alleyways and yards back to the main street, both of us sequestered in our thoughts and watching the shadows. We deftly avoided a patrol of city watchmen, standing quietly in the shadow of an awning as they passed, and reached the main street just as church bells began to toll fourth hour.

"Your landlady will not be pleased with me," Mr. Stoke observed as he glanced up and down the street for a hackney. There were none in sight and by unspoken agreement we began to walk. "Occupying you at such a disagreeable hour."

"My landlady can stuff it," I declared. I did not add that, regardless of my bravado, my landlady had begun threatening to lock the doors at midnight, and thus force me to abandon whatever unholy pursuits kept me out at night.

Mr. Stoke frowned. "Perhaps I should speak to her. I can reassure her that you are respectfully employed."

"Sir, we have, just now, met with a Silver to retrieve antiquities smuggled out of The Sarre. I am unclear how that constitutes respectful employment."

"We were hired to recover a possession for a respectable council lord," Mr. Stoke corrected, but there was a hollowness to his tone, and after a moment, he frowned. "Though, I will say, I have had my moments with the morality of this particular endeavor of ours, Miss Fleet."

He seemed as though he wanted to say more, but the sound of wheels caught our attention. Mr. Stoke stepped out into the street, one arm raised to hail a hackney.

"I will speak to your landlady, Ottilie," he informed me, shifting back to our original conversation. "You are too dear to me, I will not permit the possibility of seeing you cast out onto the street. Or snoring on my sofa."

I produced a laugh, but guilt reared again. "Please, there is no need."

"All the same. Hello, good man."

The hackney stopped and the driver, a small man with a large hat, greeted us in turn. By the time we settled inside, Mr. Stoke, perhaps noticing my distraction, had set aside the conversation. He sat the bundled box onto the bench beside him, rested his walking stick over his knees, and commenced looking out the window.

Perched across from him with the skirts of my walking suit rumpled, I followed his gaze as the city began to pass by. More people appeared as we left the warehouse district—night workers, drunks, whores, and the displaced. Fires burned in alleyways, surrounded by silhouettes. The public houses were hushed and their windows dim, the boisterous companies of the early night long gone. The lampposts were unlit and neglected, serving as little more than posterboards for chaotic layers of flyers and bills.

And, in the worst of Harrow's traditions, gallows.

I felt the warmth leech from my face as a crowd came into sight, preceded by the jostling light of torches and lanterns and the clash of voices. The hackney driver bellowed to clear the road, but was largely ignored. Thus the carriage slowed, and Mr. Stoke and I were treated to a clear view of events.

A rope had been tossed up over one of the lamppost's sturdy arms. At one end, a noose was wrestled around the throat of a wiry woman, her shrieks rising above through the shouts and cheers. Half a dozen men seized the other end, jesting and jostling for the privilege, and before Mr. Stoke could draw breath to shout or I could close my eyes, the rope tightened and the woman swung. Her shrieks abruptly silenced and the crowd roared as she kicked and struggled over their heads.

The hackney sped up, our driver taking advantage of the crowd's sudden press closer to the dying woman.

Just as we passed the lamppost, someone leapt up and grabbed the woman's legs. The sudden weight snapped her neck. I saw the panicked light leave her eyes as we trundled away—eyes that, though they saw nothing more in this world, gouged into mine.

Markings appeared on the woman's throat, around the noose. Soft, glinting copper tendrils, like ivy, crept into wakefulness as her life faded. For a few terrible moments they stood out, pulsing with the beat of her dying heart.

The crowd roared in approval, their bloodthirsty cries only increasing as the woman's Entwined threads faded back into her now swollen, reddened skin—marking her death.

Then we were through. Mr. Stoke slumped back on the bench, his expression pale with shock and a resigned, bitter rage. I sat straight on the edge of my own bench, staring back at the hanged woman without truly seeing her.

Instead, I saw myself. I saw my sisters. I saw that helmeted soldier, resting the carved box in a nest of cotton. I saw threat and danger, and felt a hot rush of desperation.

"It's getting worse," Mr. Stoke observed grimly. "Did you see the police in the crowd?"

"No," I said tonelessly.

"There were several. They did not try to stop it. No one did."

"They are too afraid," I observed. "Or they agree, or they do not care. Apathy is a deadly thing."

"Indeed." Mr. Stoke swore under his breath and pulled his hat from his head, slapping it onto the seat next to him. His dark hair, gradually lightening with an influx of grey, was mussed. "This cannot continue, Miss Fleet. Such cruelty, such brazen violence. This is not the city I grew up in."

"The city you grew up in was ruled by Entwined," I commented, though my mind was tumbling away from him, the hanged woman, and even the city itself. The guilt that had beset me earlier at Mr. Stoke's talk of the future was gone, replaced with singular determination. "From what I hear that was no better. The problem, I fear, is not with the differences between humans or Entwined, but that which we share—prejudice, and avarice."

Mr. Stoke was quiet for a time, resting one hand on the box at his side. "That's insightful, Miss Fleet."

The words were my mother's, plucked from a speech she had given to the Continental Guilds when I was a child, but I could not admit that.

"Thank you, sir. Should I send word to Lord Stillwell, to retrieve the artifact and settle accounts? For tomorrow evening, perhaps." I looked back out the window, noting the quality of the darkness. I would have enough time to get home before dawn, and the twilight that heralded it, but only just. "Or rather, that would be today."

Mr. Stoke looked discomforted, even a little appalled that I had moved past the hanging so quickly, but whatever he saw in my face tempered him. "Yes, thank you."

I nodded stoutly. "Very good, sir."

A Note Upon: The Entwined of the Moon

Entwined of the Moon fall into the following classes of mage: Silver, Twilight, Starlight, and Sightless. Their abilities respond to moonlight, or the absence of light entirely.

Entwined of the Moon are, quite rightly, considered to be more dangerous than their daylight counterparts, from the Silver's affinities towards physical violence to the Moonless's ability to wield shadows.

The Vigilant Lady Traveller must not hesitate to distance herself, or defend herself, in the presence of such mages.

From The Vigilant Lady Traveller:
A Gentlewoman's Guide to the World

CHAPTER 2

I was many things: sister, daughter, and faux fiancée. I was secretary, swordswoman, and connoisseur of scandalous novels. But I could, in no way, claim to be a mountaineer.

Only a flailing grab for the balcony saved me. With my foot tangled in my skirts and my woeful climbing skills stretched far beyond their limits, I toppled from the wisteria and clutched at the rail like a drowning sailor. The wisteria gave a rustle of protest, showering my face with dead leaves, curling seed pods, and plaster dust as I hauled myself onto my balcony.

My landlady, true to her word, had locked me out of the building in protest to my wayward ways. My home was situated on one of the octagonal courtyards signature to Old Harrow, with apartments to every side and several deep archways leading out to the streets, each barred by ornate gates. Balconies, like the one I had so gracelessly deposited myself on, marked each of the six stories. They were decorated by elaborate railings and fine, curling moldings clung about with ivy, climbing roses and thankfully, rampant wisteria.

On a summer day the courtyard was lovely, faced with pastel plasters and blessed with the warm sun on the patterned paving stones. But here on a dark autumn night, dead plants rustling and the only light from the occasional illuminated window, my nerves frayed.

Dawn was nearly upon me, and I needed to be in the shelter of my room before true twilight.

I stood and dusted off my hands, flicked stray bits of hair from my eyes, and removed the wedge that held the balcony door open just enough to let in a small calico cat.

Tiny paws hit the floor and the cat in question came to twine around my legs. Bending, I scooped him up and planted a kiss between his ears. "Hello, Hieronymus. Heavens, you smell of cigars. Climbing in the neighbors' windows again?"

Hieronymus forced his head into my hand, demanding a scratch.

"Well," I said, complying and setting him down on the bed. "We will not be here much longer. As soon as Mr. Stoke is paid, you and I will be off to meet Lewis."

Matters, of course, were not that simple. But I chose to remain focused on the tasks closest to hand. Claim the bounty, add it to the savings stuffed into my mattress, and board a ship. Meet up with Lewis and take on the new identity he had secured as his contribution to our alliance.

Then I would be free. I would still need to keep my collar high, but I would be far from Harrow's dangers and the Harren Guild's searching eyes. I would be free to pry the ring off my finger and go my own way, to live, at last, without looking over my shoulder.

The thought of the Guild and my ring made me glance at the dressing table as I unpinned my hat and cast it onto the unmade bed. There, a framed portrait of Lewis stood amid scattered cosmetics, brushes, and books. Handsome and mustachioed, his hair neatly parted and combed with his cap under one arm, he stared stoically out of the frame in sepia tones. A tactful application of paint concealed the pins on his high collar that marked him as a Guild-loaned mage, one of the tithe the Entwined gave to the Lusterless human government in an attempt to keep the peace. My landlady already had a low opinion of me—she hardly needed the ammunition of a supposed human engaged to an Entwined. But the reputability of having a fiancé at war had secured my rooms, modest and cluttered though they were.

I left the balcony door open to the cold as I discarded my outer clothes on an overburdened chair, pried off my corset, and sat on the narrow bed in my chemise and drawers. I curled my bare toes against the draft and quickly shook out my hair, finger-combing it into a plait while I watched my reflection in the mirror. Hieronymus curled up beside me.

Twilight began to seep across the worn wood and oriental carpets of the floor. It ran up the papered walls and my legs, skimmed the lace hem of my drawers, and passed up my arm to the shoulder. When it reached my neck, I leaned a little closer to the mirror, turning so that my throat stood out stark and pale in the gloaming.

There, under my skin, dusky threads began to entwine me. They moved like smoke, awakening from the nape of my neck and spreading out, out around my throat and shoulders.

They did not stop there. Unlike Harden's silver threads, or those of the hanged woman, mine went further—they trickled out from my hairline, smoky trails winding across my temples.

But here, alone in the quiet of my room, there was no one to see but the mirror, a placid cat, and Lewis's staring portrait.

I arrived at Mr. Stoke's office just after noon with a paper-wrapped bundle of pastries, dark circles under my eyes, and a haze of anxious anticipation.

Mr. Stoke had yet to arrive and my footsteps echoed in the wood-panelled foyer. To either side were doors, one leading to my small office and the other to Mr. Stoke's larger one. Both were dark, with shutters and curtains drawn.

A note was pinned to my door. I plucked it off on my way in and unfolded it as I bit into one of the pastries in a burst of cinnamon and sugar.

I froze. Where I expected to see Mr. Stoke's bold, blocked handwriting, I instead found a flowing script.

Meet me at the Ciciley House, tomorrow, four o'clock.

Your adoring sister, Pretoria

I bolted into Mr. Stoke's office and spun, taking in every familiar feature, searching for anything out of place. I saw disorganized bookshelves and a plain desk stacked with open letters and waiting documents. The worn old sofa of dark wood and pale green velvet, site of many afternoon naps. An aged grandfather clock, its steady ticking counterpoint to my rapid breaths.

The shelf, with the safe hidden behind it, appeared undisturbed. Relief washed over me along with a flush of curiosity.

Perhaps I should ensure the box was still there. Perhaps I should examine it, just to be sure. Nothing of value was safe in Pretoria's vicinity, and if the box was gone, all my plans would collapse.

I had just set down my breakfast and begun to pull off my gloves when the main door clicked and Mr. Stoke's voice broke the stillness.

"Ottilie? I tried to pick up a hansom at Glaster Square but it's cordoned off. I haven't a clue why—have you heard anything? Ottilie? Miss Fleet?"

I plastered a smile on my face and turned as he entered the office, half concealing the note behind my opposite forearm. "Good morning! I bought pastries."

"And there are still some left?" Mr. Stoke pulled his hat from his head, quirking a brow at me. "A great sacrifice. Making amends?"

"Well, yes. I was late too, if I am honest." I moved to open the windows and turn up the radiator beneath, forcing myself not to stare at the bookcase.

"Never mind. What of that letter?" Stoke asked as he settled in, shrugging off his coat and sitting down at his desk. He nodded to the paper in my hand—not well hidden, after all. "Anything I should know about?"

"No, no." I cleared my throat. "My sister was here. Rather, she is coming to town, that is all. I will meet her tomorrow."

Stoke pulled off his jacket. "Which one? I thought they both married and moved overseas."

It was not entirely a lie. The Guild had assigned my sisters and I carefully chosen spouses, selected for the propagation of the most powerful Entwined offspring to add to their quiver. Only Madge had submitted to marrying hers and had, upon her wedding at twenty, thrown herself into her propagational duties. She had, last I heard, produced four Adept children in eight years. Considering Entwined rarely conceived more than twice in a lifetime, this was remarkable.

I, meanwhile, had turned my intended not into a husband, but an ally. Captain Lewis Illing and I, despite being thrust together by the Guild we despised, had forged a mutually beneficial alliance. Together, with our combined skills and contacts, we would escape the Guild and go our separate ways.

Pretoria's actions towards her Guild match, meanwhile, were altogether more complex, and I would do the reader an injustice to unfold the entirely grisly tale at this juncture. However, let it be said that in the wake of her Separatist lover's execution, her fiancé had vanished. She had then faked her own death and thrown herself into a life of crime overseas with a contingent of other Rogue mages.

Officially, Pretoria Rushforth was dead. Unofficially, she was the largest thorn in the Harren Guild's foot, and many of the Continental Guilds as well.

"Victoria," I lied to Mr. Stoke, citing her false name. "My sister Victoria. She intended to surprise me, it seems."

"I see. Oh, I have something for you." My employer raised a finger in sudden thought and fished a stack of letters from the pocket of his coat. His eyes were abnormally tight today, I realized. But perhaps that was fatigue. "I've one of these for you. I saw the postman on my way in. Wait a moment."

He thumbed through the stack and produced a letter. A coy, but somehow false grin touched his face as he pointed to the top one. "I know this handwriting."

The sender's hand was angular and swift, elegant in a

windblown way. There was no return address, but it was obviously from Lewis.

My heart lightened as I accepted it. "Thank you."

"No matter. Best that those letters come here, away from your landlady's prying eyes." Mr. Stoke scratched at one cheek. "How is your Lewis, by the way?"

I paused, a little startled at the inquiry. Mr. Stoke's definition of a private life was exceedingly broad, and he rarely inquired about my fiancé beyond logistics surrounding the artifact we had located for Lord Stillwell.

"He does his duty, writes his poetry and never sleeps. Same as always."

"Is his poetry any good?"

"He's Bronze, sir. I should hope so."

"So long as he does not use his abilities to woo you."

"He would never do that," I assured my employer. Bronze Entwined, with the ability to imbue written words with uncannily visceral images and emotion, were often considered manipulative by humans. But as I said, Lewis would never manipulate me in such a way—not simply because such manipulation was beneath him, but because he had no apparent desire to woo me.

A frown ghosted onto my lips and I decided to change the subject.

"Sir, the box we retrieved last night, is it in the safe? Or did you take it home with you?"

"In the safe," he said distractedly. His attention had been caught by another letter, but I could not read its typewritten face before he slipped it into a drawer. "Did you ring Lord Stillwell's?"

"I will now," I replied, glancing at the bookshelves. "May I examine the box? I saw it so briefly and I confess... I am curious."

"As am I, Ottilie, as am I. But satisfying our curiosity would be inappropriate," Mr. Stoke said, giving me a distracted but genuine, rueful smile. "The pay will be high enough to console us, I'm sure."

"Of course," I relented, unable to resist giving the bookcase one last, nervous glance. "I will make the call now."

By the time the afternoon began to wane, my stomach was as empty as the pastry box and my head so full I thought it might rupture. I scrawled in ledgers with uncommon industry, posted payments and bills, and, desperate for more distraction, reorganized files in the dusty cabinet, dating all the way back to Stoke's retirement from the Heddon Street Constabulary.

But my concentration was fickle, my mind flickering between Pretoria, the artifact, and my impending departure. Lewis's letter sat next to my typewriter, waiting to be read in privacy this evening. I did not intend to leave, however, until Lord Stillwell's man had come to retrieve the artifact and I had been paid.

Just the thought of the money made my pulse race. It would be enough. Finally, enough. There would be new identities for Lewis and I, and with them, new lives. There would be no more coalsmoke in my lungs or watching my kin hang from lampposts.

I would need to buy Hieronymus a travelling basket. I scribbled a note to myself to that effect and shoved it into my pocket.

I had quite forgotten about it again when, at six o'clock, Mr. Stoke poked his head into my office. "Ottilie, why don't you go home early today?"

"Stillwell's man will be here soon," I reminded him.

"Yes, but you needn't stay. I've asked enough of you over the last few days and you are clearly preoccupied."

"I would like to be here. I can take notes," I tried. *I need my money.*

"If there are notes to be taken, I'm sure I'll manage," Stoke said with amusement. "I should accustom myself to it, after all. You won't be with me forever."

For one petrified moment, I thought he knew. I thought he had figured out I intended to slip away, abandoning him without a word.

"Sir..."

"Go home," Mr. Stoke urged me, more gently this time.

"I'll see the artifact delivered safely. Also, you should know, I've decided to take a holiday. I'll leave tomorrow and leave your pay in the safe. And I will ring your boarding house when I'm back in the city."

I parted my lips to protest, but something in his eyes, something in his expression—there one second, gone the next—gave me pause.

"Is everything all right?" I asked.

"Of course." Mr. Stoke laughed, a sound genuine enough to make the muscles in my shoulders relax. He spoke faster now, as if he had found his stride. "I doubt I'll be back before the end of next week. After that, I've a few letters from potential clients we can peruse and see what we think."

We. Anything I might say in reply was suddenly lost in a resurgence of guilt.

Rubbing at the corner of one tired eye, I finally nodded. "All right. Good evening, sir."

"Good evening, Ottilie."

CHAPTER 3

A Note to the Reader:
Lord Stillwell and the Landsdown Relics

Eavesdropping on Mr. Stoke's meetings with clients was something of a hobby of mine, and the day Lord Stillwell strode into the office, three months before my present narrative, was no exception. Thankfully, the council lord and old acquaintance of my mother did not recognize me as he passed my office—how could he, when he cast not a glance at Mr. Stoke's homely secretary, in her simple shirtwaist and tweed?

Lord Stillwell had promptly sequestered himself in the office with the detective. At first there was laughter, a few comments about the weather and the click of lighters as they fell to their cigars. They knew one another from their youth, I gathered. A military connection, then. Mr. Stoke was deferential, but the ease of their conversation conveyed mutual respect.

Then came a stretch of silence, and Mr. Stoke's deep voice rumbled, "How can I help you, my lord?"

I pressed my ear to the crack of the door, breathing softly and steadily.

"I hear you are adept at locating items, and have connections in The Sarre," Lord Stillwell said. "As you know, I was forced out when the Seaussen and the rebels seized the colony. My home was pillaged—nothing irreplaceable, save several antiquities I had recently acquired for my private collection. Rebuilding that collection is of the utmost importance to me. Most went to Seau before we sealed the borders again, but not all. Some remain in the colony, including the item which I would like you to secure."

A rumble from Mr. Stoke.

Stillwell went on, "The endeavor must be discreet. And requires a certain... circumnavigation of more official channels."

I heard the creak of a chair. "May I ask why?"

"Please trust me when I say it is better you do not."

"I see." Mr. Stoke's tone was polite, but there was a dubious undertone I shared. Our occupation frequently necessitated treading the line of morality, but neither of us did so casually.

There was a rustle of paper and a further exchange of lowered voices. I held my breath altogether and managed to hear, "Five thousand, for its return."

I covered my mouth to smother a giddy curse.

I ensured that I was out of sight as Lord Stillwell left, then hurried into Mr. Stoke's office. He looked up at me, his eyebrows raised.

"You heard?" It was not really a question.

"Of course." I cast myself down in the chair across from him with a rumple of skirts and reached for the paper on his desk. I scanned it as the detective spoke, noting a sketch of a simple box and a brief of the object's history. "'*Numbered among the Landsdown Trove discovered by P. Landsdown in 1897 at the site of Keforey Sarre,*'" I read aloud. "I'm familiar with the Landsdown Trove, but only in name."

"A collection of artifacts, largely carved of Incarnate stone, Stillwell informed me," Mr. Stoke said. "More valuable than diamond, aside from their historical value."

"Then there is something inside the box, presumably carved of this stone?" I asked, glancing at the sketch again.

"Stillwell did not comment on that, but it would seem reasonable." Mr. Stoke nodded. "Is Lewis still in The Sarre?"

"Last I heard, yes."

"Would he be willing to help? I would prefer not to go to south, myself. I would be something of a fish out of water."

I nodded. Mr. Stoke had never left Harrow, much less the City States of Arrent to which it belonged. "Absolutely."

Mr. Stoke sat back with a satisfied air and laced his hands over his stomach. "Well, this has turned into a rather fine day, Miss Fleet. A fine day indeed."

A NOTE UPON:
HARROW AND THE CITY STATES OF ARRENT

The City States of Arrent, with their capital of Harrow, were freed from the rule of the Entwined in 1890 and united by the efforts of Grand General S. R. Baffin. They represent a haven for humanity, a land in which the Entwined have been firmly regulated to the keeping of the Entwined Guild and are restrained within broader society.

The Vigilant Lady Traveller may rest at ease in regards to the dangers of the Entwined in Arrent, knowing her dignity, person, and virtues are held in the highest esteem.

FROM THE VIGILANT LADY TRAVELLER:
A GENTLEWOMAN'S GUIDE TO THE WORLD

CHAPTER 4

Present Day

The streets of Harrow were still bright and busy as I left the office, adjusting my hatpin and fighting back a wave of frustrated exhaustion.

My need to leave Harrow loomed before me, still out of reach and yet closer than ever, and all of it too momentous to contemplate. I wished I were already back in my apartment, sequestered beneath blankets and silencing my overburdened mind with a generous supply of chocolates and the kind of novel that would have made Pretoria cackle and Madge bristle with indignation.

The thought nearly made me smile. That, I determined, was precisely how I intended to spend the rest of the evening. As soon as the sun was up, I could face the future. I would return to Mr. Stoke's office to retrieve my pay from the safe, then go right to the docks and book passage out of Harrow. I would meet with Pretoria to see her one last time, turn down whatever her latest scheme was, and with any luck, I would be at sea before Mr. Stoke returned from his trip.

I would already be on the path to freedom.

And I would not have to say goodbye.

The city bustled around me as I wove through pedestrians, avoided carriages and the occasional bugling motor car. I caught the end of a tram heading uphill towards the hub of Communion Square, riding like a coachman on the backboards until the conductor approached to extricate a fare.

I landed lightly back on the cobblestones before he could reach me and walked over the rise to the square, the beating heart of New Harrow. The tram diverted in front of me with a warning cling of its bell, electricity snapping on the lines and wheels grinding in their well-worn grooves as it passed storefronts, cafes, and fine hotels.

There were people everywhere. Every shop seemed to have placed tables outside, every café was bursting with patrons, and policemen and soldiers were out in force.

The reason for all this rapidly became clear. The opening bars of a rousing song soared above the retreating rumble of the streetcar, and the passive clamor of humanity became a roar.

Thousands of people gathered in the center of the square. Many waved white and green flags of the City States, while bunting of the same colors girded temporary barriers and ran between lampposts.

In the center of it all was a stage, where the orchestra sat. I stopped, watching as a man joined them above the heads of the onlookers, lifting his military cap as they thundered again. His uniform was a bold, rich blue, trimmed with gold braid and glistening with pips and medals. His hair was an admirable chestnut, refusing to grey despite progress into his fifties. It was slicked back with not a hair out of place, and his moustache and sideburns were perfectly trimmed.

I felt my mouth dry. When a woman jostled past me, I hardly noticed. When a young boy tried to sell me a newspaper, I ignored him, not out of any ill-will, but because my mind simply refused to move past the sight of the man on the platform.

"Good people of Harrow!" Grand General Baffin, Arrent's conqueror and king in all but title, called over the square. A cavalry saber hung at his hip, light and of impeccable craftmanship. It was no ceremonial sword and, if the papers were to be believed, had seen a great deal of use. "What a pleasure it is to return to you. There truly is no finer city on this island, no more industrious and admirable folk."

The crowd cheered.

"You will have, no doubt, heard of my recent exploits in The Sarre," Baffin continued. "But this news, I tell you, is fresh. We have evicted the Seaussen and their allied rebels! The Sarre is free, once more a nation unto itself, with the generous guidance and support of our great nation. Hand in hand, we move forward!"

This time I had to cover my ears against the assault of noise. I retreated towards the wall of a nearby café, my skin prickling with gooseflesh. This *was* news, and whether it was for good or ill, it constituted a drastic shift in the situation abroad. There would be reorganization in The Sarre, changes in personnel, and Lewis might be affected.

I thought of the letter in my pocket and nearly reached for it, but Baffin was still speaking. He recounted the valor of the Arrentian troops and the cowardice and immorality of the Seaussen, who had so fiendishly stirred the Sarren people to rebel against their Arrent-allied monarchy, and forced the flight of Lord Stillwell and many other Arrentians living in The Sarre, tearing them from their homes and possessions. Little was mentioned of the violence and displacement brought upon the locals themselves, but that was no surprise.

"You should move along, Miss Secretary," a voice said in my ear, accompanied by the scent of something strangely metallic. "Quick, like."

I recoiled as the smuggler from the docks, Mr. Harden, shouldered past. He crossed the tram tracks and vaulted over one of the barriers without looking back at me, sidling wolfishly into the crowd in a long coat with popped collar.

He was not alone. I picked out a half dozen, a dozen, two dozen figures weaving through the crowd and passing the barriers with equal focus. Some carried satchels, others wore heavy coats.

My eyes rounded.

A sound like a gunshot cut off Baffin's speech and a flare arced into the sky. Fizzling red and orange rained down.

Chaos broke loose. Shouts and screams tore through the air as more flares went off, blinding and deafening. It was so loud, so overpowering, that when the bomb exploded, it was almost obscured.

Someone crashed into me. I slammed into the wall and muffled an exclamation as a stampede broke out, men and women shoving past one another with confused abandon. A man fell, bellowing, and rolled to avoid thundering feet. The newspaper boy I had ignored hit the wall next to me, eyes wide and terrified as his newspapers scattered, ground, and slid under the feet of the mob.

The terror in his eyes cut through my shock. I grabbed him by the arm and, sheltering him with my body, dragged him through the door of the café as the patio was overrun, tables and chairs toppling and porcelain shattering.

"You can't come in here!" an aproned man protested, already trying to shove us back out the door. The café's staff and a handful of patrons pressed towards the back of the establishment, as distraught as the crowd outside.

"Oh, shut up!" I shot back, shoving the newsboy further inside. I turned on the door and slammed it closed. "Help me!"

He braced the door next to me as more panicked pedestrians tried to get in. The door half opened, slammed again, and shuddered. A panicked woman met my eyes through the glass, but just behind her, I saw another woman, her face hidden beneath a hood, pull something from her pocket.

A grenade.

There was a crack and flash. The front window of the café shattered in a hail of glass and I dropped, covering my head.

Bitter smoke filled the room, searing and thick. A second blast went off, this time close enough that I felt a flush of heat. More smoke came then, carrying the more natural scent of burning wood and cloth. And hair.

From there, my memory skews. The café burned, that much I recall. I fled through the kitchens with other figures and stumbled into a shockingly empty street. Only the prone forms of a few wounded remained amid shattered glass, toppled tables, and fluttering, charred bunting. I did not see the newsboy again.

Ears ringing and mind numb with shock, I did not flinch

as a hand took my arm. I had the vague impression of a man in a long coat, guiding me out of the way as a fire engine clattered past, its half dozen horses prancing and shaking their manes amid wafts of smoke.

"What is happening?" I asked him, my voice sounding terribly far away.

"Stay out of the street," Harden replied, his voice equally distant, and distorted by the ringing in my ears. I felt a hand slap my cheek, firm but gentle. "You hear me? Are you hurt?"

"You." I recoiled, some of my sense returning. "You're a Separatist!"

"Aye." He frowned and searched my eyes as if he suspected I had hit my head. "No Guild, no government, all of it. You look like you need a drink."

"You are a terrorist," I accused, anger sparking. "How will this help us, you fool? You attacked the Grand General! You attacked innocent people!"

"Us?" he repeated. His gaze dropped to my collar, then lifted back to my eyes and narrowed. "Ah, well, I was right. What are you, then? Not a Glim, I see, and certainly nothing so lowly as a Silver."

"Get away from me," I hissed, jerking from his grasp.

"Oi, you!" a voice bellowed. "Leave that woman alone!"

Harden backed away, already half running, and shook a finger at my face. "They'll find you out, secretary. Join or run, you hear me?"

With that he was gone, streaking away down the street with three policemen on his heels.

I stared after them, the shock of the attack now merging with the horrible understanding that I had given myself away. After years of keeping my sorcery a secret, I had revealed myself to the worst class of my brethren. A Separatist.

There was no help for that now, though, and I had to get off the street. I moved, glass crunching beneath my boots. I walked. And, eventually, I sank down on my bed in my apartment, wiping blood and soot from my face, and pulled Hieronymus into my lap.

It was not until the twilight of dawn awoke my threads, drawing me from an exhausted slumber, that I remembered Lewis's letter.

I fumbled blearily in my pile of cast-off clothing. The cat watched me archly through one narrow eye, then returned to sleep.

I found the letter and leaned towards the balcony doors to catch the growing light. Beyond the glass, wisteria pods rustled and one of the neighbors began their habitual morning concert, the low strains of a cello drifting through the courtyard.

I squinted. The paper was gritty, warped, and smudged, but I had received letters in worse condition. The words mattered less than Lewis's magic within them, and my own magic, ready to amplify it. There was a reason the Guild had paired Lewis and me.

I brushed my fingers across the paper. My skin began to prickle with gooseflesh and my threads, already standing out smoky grey against my skin in the twilight, grew cool.

Letters and words, scribed in Lewis's angled, swift script, faded. My room too slipped away as the paper recalled the last thing it had seen before the envelope closed for the long, solitary dark of the journey across the sea.

Lewis sat at a writing desk, pen scratching while a sea breeze buffeted the sun-bleached tent around him. The tent flap was open, letting dawn light pour over his shoulders and ignite his glistening bronze threads, visible just above his collar.

Lewis looked weary and sunbaked, but healthy. His officer's tie was loosened for comfort but only just, and the corners of his eyes, thick with blond lashes, showed premature lines of concern.

He tugged absently at one ear as he wrote. On the paper before him, between his worn khaki pith helmet and a forgotten cup of tea—its flower-patterned, delicate porcelain out of place in this make-shift world—words flowed from his pen, glistening as bronze as his threads before they dried, black and dormant, into the page.

At the same time, back in my room, my magic waned. My surroundings returned to me, and with it, another wash of dawn light.

For a moment two magics were suspended in the play between beams of pink dawn and the last grey shadows of twilight—Lewis's dawning sorcery of the written word and my twilit gleanings of memory.

Then the twilight yielded. My threads retreated beneath my skin and with them, the height of my power gave way to its usual, more passive existence. Lewis's magic, however, continued. His words sculpted images before my eyes and emotions in my chest, lending vivid detail to the thoughts and events he had succinctly penned.

The letter was dated for three weeks ago.

> O,
> Forgive the briefness of this letter. I am being transferred. The Seaussen have been driven south, but I was injured in the push and have been loaned to the Settlement Office in Sarre Grand, to sit at a desk and recover.
>
> If the opportunity to move up our timeline comes, take it. I can no longer stand this place. Wait for me at the place we agreed. I will meet you soon.
> L

In my mind, I glimpsed the intention behind his words; the violence of the recapture of the Sarren capital of Sarre Grand, its ancient stone buildings blurred by smoke and mosaicked streets filled with running soldiers and flashing rifles. I saw Entwined officers, gathering in private conference. Then I saw the Sunrise Isles—our intended meeting place. A Harren foreign stronghold clung to the skirt of one of the smaller islands, ramparts armed with pivoting artillery and her waters studded with warships.

The real world returned to me in a rush of clean daylight, the crackling of a gramophone through the walls, and the chatter of children leaving the courtyard with their school bags. The cello clashed with the gramophone and a child laughed.

'If the opportunity to move up our timeline comes, take it.'

The opportunity had come, in the form of a stack of money currently waiting for me in Mr. Stoke's safe.

All I needed to do was retrieve it.

CHAPTER 5

A Note to the Reader:
Regarding My Engagement

The first time I met Lewis was the day of our engagement. It was an impersonal encounter, a joint gathering hosted by the Guild Academies.

Over a dozen couples were presented that night, the heads of the Guild calling our names and joining our hands beneath glistening chandeliers, to hearty applause. They made it all as grand as possible, with a lavish dinner and ball, soft music and warm candlelight and all the windswept beauty of Old Harrow. They lavished us with wine and the finest costumes the Guild's considerable vaults could buy.

It was calculated, the whole of it, to make us feel valued, lauded—to instill in us the weight of our upcoming task.

"Miss Ottilie Rushforth," the headmistress called.

I stepped forward out of the line of other young women, my hair perfectly swept up, the heavy beading on my bodice glistening. I turned in place, the long drape of my gown tugging into an elegant swirl about my legs, and looked down to the line of waiting young men.

My expression was set, my posture one of dignified ease—skills that I had learned over eleven years in these glittering halls. But beneath my skin, my blood thrummed.

I was, at that point, uncertain at the notion of a Guild husband. I rebelled against the expectation of it, the insistence upon duty and fidelity to an organization that had stolen me from my mother's side and kept me contained within stone walls.

I heard Pretoria's voice in my mind, roiling against the confinement of the Guilds, prior to her escape. I remembered the face of her lover, Emeline, frozen in confused horror at the moment of her execution, and my chest burned with rage.

But there was a power to this moment, a weight of respect and responsibility that left me unexpectedly stirred. Madge's influence came with that feeling, bolstered by the pride in her eyes as she watched me from the assembly with a baby in her arms and two children clinging to her skirts of rose and powder blue. They were beautiful children, well-behaved and calm.

And already marked by the Guild, with their emblazoned little sashes of ebony silk. Adepts. Full mages.

The rush of my blood sounded loud in my ears.

"Mr. Lewis Illing," the headmaster of the men's academy boomed.

A man with perfectly combed dark blond hair stepped forward. He wore a neatly trimmed moustache and there was gentleness in his resigned hazel eyes. He was not the tallest or the broadest among the men, but he filled out his uniform well and his bronze threads, tricked by the candlelight, glistened every so often.

Lewis walked down the line of mages and, with one arm crooked behind his straight back, offered me his free hand. I took it—a brush of warm skin—and we proceeded to one side. There we took up station next to one another, watching as the next couple was named.

We let go of one another's hands. I resisted the urge to fidget. My mind churned, searching for something to say, but everything felt mundane. This man was to be my husband within the next year. We were expected to copulate, to produce children, to serve the Guild side by side for as long as the Guild saw fit. What if I hated him? He was handsome, but that meant little. He might have a temper, or unbearable habits, or unsavory expectations.

That was when his fingers brushed mine. It was a small movement and his head did not turn, his eyes did not leave the proceedings, but one of his fingers hooked through mine in a small, nearly imperceptible gesture of comfort.

"We shall be good friends, Miss Rushforth. Allies." His voice was soft and genuine, and I could not help but believe him. "Pretoria sends her love."

CHAPTER 6

Present Day

I unlocked Mr. Stoke's office door and entered, pulling off my gloves and unpinning my hat as I adjusted to the dark. Papers rustled beneath my feet, and the world froze.

The offices were a disaster. Books had been torn off the shelves, the desk emptied, and the grandfather clock smashed. My desk was fully overturned and papers had been scattered into the foyer where I now stood, interspersed with keys from my brutalized typewriter.

The only thing intact—or almost intact, rather—was a cup of coffee I had made Mr. Stoke before I left last night. It sat right where I had set it on his desk, the papers around it stained in scallops of brown where the liquid had overflowed.

I rushed in and jerked the curtains back, the scrape of rings nearly lost in the thunder of blood in my ears. Two terrors beset me—that the flood of light would illuminate Mr. Stoke's body, and that the safe would be open and ransacked.

Light spilled across the carnage. Blood—no, a broken inkwell. A body—no, a toppled chair. A further snowfall of papers. The bookcase still stood against the wall, though its books had been hurled about the room.

A figure unfolded from the shadows. He was in his thirties, dressed in a three-piece suit of fine grey tweed, with a bowler hat and respectable moustache.

I lunged for Mr. Stoke's desk, jerking out the drawer where he stowed an emergency pistol. The drawer was empty, save for a scattering of thumbtacks, which unhelpfully stabbed my scrabbling hand. I cursed and jerked back bleeding fingers.

"Miss Fleet, I presume?"

I looked up the length of a long-barrelled pistol. The make was familiar to me—I could not remember the name, but Lewis carried one similar.

The intruder's narrow chin drifted slightly to one side. In his other hand, he held up the small revolver that should have been in the drawer, then returned it to his pocket. "There is no need for violence. I am here on behalf of Lord Stillwell. Where is the artifact?"

"Mr. Stoke handed it over last night." Now that my initial shock had passed, I was more indignant than afraid. It was all I could do not to look at the bookshelf with my money, my hard-won freedom, supposedly in the safe on the other side.

The stranger eyed me, as if he expected I might burst into hysterics at any moment. I almost wished I would—a normal secretary might, I imagined. The more in control he felt, the less guarded he would be.

But I was too distracted to be properly afraid. When I held his gaze, he stepped back into a broad stance and clasped one hand on his opposite wrist, gun pointed to the floor.

"Let us begin again. My name is James Wake, and I am here on behalf of Lord Stillwell. Your employer, upon meeting with me last night, failed to produce the artifact he was contracted to recover. He said he would do so this morning, but"—he gestured meaningfully around—"he did not show."

I slowly straightened, pulse thrumming against my collar. So, the box *had* been taken from the safe—it was the only explanation I could think of, just then. And now Mr. Stoke and I were facing the consequences of Pretoria's theft.

For it had to have been Pretoria. The timing, her habits—it all lined up. And for Mr. Stoke, perhaps the consequences had already been dire.

Silently, vehemently, I cursed my sister.

"Are you injured, Miss Fleet?" Mr. Wake prompted, his

gaze lingering on a few small cuts from the riot that paste and powder had not been able to conceal. His eyes were grey, cool and stony.

"I was caught in the Communion Square bombing," I said. "Where is Mr. Stoke?"

"As I said, he did not show," Mr. Wake replied, his thoughts inscrutable. I was not sure he had blinked since the conversation began. "Fled, I presume. Either evading the repercussions for his negligence in losing the item, or perhaps *with* it? Did he, unwisely, field other offers for its recovery?"

I shook my head firmly. "No. No, he would not do that. Mr. Stoke is a good and dependable man."

"You may not know your employer as well as you believe."

"Granted, but you know him a good deal less."

His eyebrows twitched up at that. He changed tack. "You did not seem surprised when I told you the artifact is missing."

"Well, obviously something is amiss." I waved at the ransacked room. "Let me be frank. There is no use in suspecting me. I had nothing to do with either disappearance, and my chief concerns are finding Mr. Stoke and the artifact."

And getting my money, a practical voice in the back of my mind whispered.

A knock sounded on the main door. Both Mr. Wake and I went quiet, the ensuing silence so loud it rang in my ears. Or perhaps that was the lingering effects of explosions the night before.

There was a second knock, then a third. At last, the visitor departed and a shadow passed across the window.

As soon as they were gone Mr. Wake, pistol in hand, moved to tug the curtains closed.

A faux twilight rippled across the room, thickening the shadows and making my threads prickle. I resisted the urge to tug up my collar and brush at my temples, to check for traitorous threads.

"Did you discover nothing of use in your pillaging?" I inquired, gesturing again to the room.

Mr. Wake, half his face dimly illuminated now, gave me a wry look. "You could have the decency to be somewhat afraid of me, Miss Fleet. I've lain in wait for you for several hours, and I do have a gun."

I held one hand into a sliver of light. There, it trembled slightly.

"Satisfied?" I asked. Without waiting for him to answer I went on. "I would make a better ally than victim, Mr. Wake."

"Somehow, I believe you. However." He raised the pistol again, and the thin congeniality we had mustered fell away. "Here's the situation, Miss Fleet. We—you and I—serve someone, someone who has our loyalty. But yours is misplaced. I can only conclude that your Mr. Stoke has fled the city, with or without a very valuable artifact belonging to a very powerful man. I am left with nothing to show my employer except a secretary with the personality of an aged mule."

As insulted as I was, my breathing was beginning to shallow, my head starting to cloud. All of a sudden, I recalled the tightness around Mr. Stoke's eyes yesterday as he sent me home, as he spoke of getting out of the city.

What if I had misread him? What if that had not been sadness on his face, but guilt? And what if, as I had plotted to abandon him, he had already been on the path to abandoning me?

The whys—those I could not answer yet—but the sting of betrayal remained.

"I do not know what happened," I said, sounding as troubled as I felt. "I assure you, I do not. But I will find it for you. Consider this... situation... only a small delay in delivery."

Mr. Wake nodded slowly, considering my request. He settled his weight into his heels in easy confidence. "Very well. Meet me here this evening, and we will discuss what you've managed to uncover. I am sure I need not warn you about involving the police or higher authorities."

I huffed. "They would hardly be helpful."

"Indeed." Mr. Wake looked amused, again. He pushed the brim of his hat back with the mouth of his pistol and smiled at me. "I will see you this evening. Good day, Miss Fleet."

He departed without looking back. The door closed behind him, leaving me transfixed in the half light as I waited for his footsteps to fade and his shadow to pass the window, beyond the curtain.

That was when the shaking took over. It rushed down my limbs and through my belly like a winter chill, turning my guts to water.

I started for the bookcase, but my legs would not move. I bent forward, pressing my face into my hands and dragging air into my lungs. One breath. Two. Three.

I should run. I should ignore all of this and go into hiding. I could stow away on a ship, start again in another city, and buy my new identity in another few years. Lewis would forgive the setback, would he not?

But the thought of so much wasted time and effort was crushing. And if Pretoria was involved and Mr. Stoke endangered, I could not walk away, however much I wanted to. I would regret it forever.

I gathered myself. I locked the front door and closed the curtains fully. I did not bother to light a candle, taking the time to let my Entwined eyes adjust to a sepia world of shadow and texture as familiar to me as the light of the sun—the sight of the nocturnal classes of Entwined. I unfastened the top button of my collar so I felt a little less strangled. Then, flexing my hands, I drew a deep, steadying breath and rested one finger on the cold cup of coffee on Mr. Stoke's desk.

Ottilie Fleet might be an overwhelmed secretary, without family or friends in a city divided by prejudice and violence, but that identity was giving way. And the woman beneath, the elusive Entwined Adept soon to leave Harrow to build a life?

She had work to do.

A Note Upon: Eventide Mages

We continue our discussion of Entwined classes with a note upon one of the most rare and unsettling varieties— that of the Eventide, or Twilight, mage.

Eventide mages may access the memories of a person or object via direct physical touch, reading them as The Vigilant Lady Traveller reads this very guide! Their power is present at all times, as with other varieties of Entwined, but is the most potent just before sunrise and just after sunset, in twilit moments, as their name suggests.

The authors of this guide recommend exercises in modesty as the best defense against such mages. Bare skin, as the Vigilant Lady well knows, invites all varieties of trouble.

FROM THE VIGILANT LADY TRAVELLER:
A GENTLEWOMAN'S GUIDE TO THE WORLD

CHAPTER 7

Power seeped down my arm, through my wrist and into the pads of my fingers. My body stilled and my senses narrowed, forgetting the rattle of carriages in the street outside, the voices of passersby and the distant roar of automobiles. I sensed only my connection to the cup and my threads.

Though the reader may already be familiar with the nuances of Entwined power, I feel a short explanation would not go amiss, particularly at this juncture in my story.

There are three levels of Entwined power, dictated by proximity to the quality of light which triggers one's inherent magic. The first is the general, passive power accessible to an Entwined at any time of day or night. As an Eventide—bound to twilight—that allows me to see the most immediate history of an object or living person or creature, within, say, a day or two.

The second level comes to me in simulated twilight, like the room as it was now or at the warehouse with Stoke and Harden. With that I may see anywhere from a week to a few months in an object's past, depending on its environment during that time—the more memories the object has gathered, the shorter my reach.

And finally, there is the power of true twilight. In those sparse moments just before dawn and just after sunset, I can reach years, if not decades, into the past of nearly anything I touch.

The same may be said of all Entwined classes, diurnal or nocturnal, from Silvers to Glims and Moonlights. Three levels of power, and three alone.

To return to the matter at hand: Recent memories seeped from the cold porcelain cup and into my mind. They were fragmented, non-linear, and evasive, as is common with inanimate objects.

Still, I felt the cup shake as someone jostled the desk. Luke-warm coffee spilled over my fingers, though in actuality the cup remained still and my hand was dry.

I moved my touch to the wood of the desk. Now I heard Mr. Stoke shout, his voice coming to me through a thin wall of memory. I glimpsed his assailant, pressing him down into the desk with a pistol under his jaw—each point of contact thinning the chain of memory.

His attacker was Mr. Wake, his hat fallen away and auburn curls hanging into his eyes from a middle-part.

"*Then where is it?*" Wake demanded the detective. His voice was low and deathly calm, chilling in a way that he had not used with me. "*Who took it?*"

"*I don't know.*" Mr. Stoke's chest rose and fell with shallow breaths, but he was admirably composed. "*I'll find it for you. I'll find it and—*"

There were more voices, unidentifiable and obscure, then silence. Events had separated from the wood of the desk, and therefore I could not see them.

The world slipped back to speed. Moving more quickly now, I crouched to plant a hand on the floor, but brief footsteps and thick-soled boots had, as usual, left little for me to glean.

I moved on to the bookshelf and set my open palm upon it. I found nothing but stillness. The shelves had not moved recently, and before that they recalled only Mr. Stoke placing the box inside. If anyone else had moved the case, they had worn thick gloves or used other methods to ensure they left no impression.

One more weight on Pretoria's side of the scales, then. She knew the nuances and limits of my sorcery better than anyone else.

I crouched down, setting aside skewed stacks of files until I uncovered a knot of wood at the back of the shelf. I pried it out, revealing the latch.

I glanced at the window, then again to the office door. There was always a chance Mr. Wake would come back. I had to be fast. I lifted the latch, grabbed the shelf and pulled.

The bookcase swung out. There in the wall, right where an old fireplace used to be, sat the safe.

Three deft turns later, I heard a soft click. I pulled the door open and peered inside. Files. A small strongbox where Mr. Stoke kept cash, which was now painfully empty. There was nothing else. The canvas-wrapped artifact was truly gone.

I closed the safe and bookcase once more and sat against the wall, staring across the dim room and trying to sort my thoughts. If Mr. Stoke had fled and left me behind, there *had* to be a valid reason.

I glanced at the clock out of habit, but it was still gutted and mute. I lifted the curtains to peer outside, and found the angle of the sunlight across the roofs and chimney pots indicated that it was nearly noon.

The day was passing. I needed a safe place to think, gather my thoughts, and pass the time until I confronted Pretoria.

I gathered my things from my destroyed office, cast one last glance around the quiet building, and left.

I spent the noon hour at a café by the river, occupying a secluded spot in the warmth of the sun and the cool of the breeze. I could see in nearly every direction, tucked between one outer wall of the café and a potted shrub, but only the most observant passersby might see me.

I scattered a few notebooks on the round wrought-iron table and stared at them, pen in hand and cup of tea growing cold. I made a list of factors, random elements to the story that I could not piece together yet. I recorded all I could remember of Wake, and every fraction of memory I had gleaned from the office. I made a timeline of events, with gaps and questions and possibilities. And I made a list of my options on a small paper, kept from the breeze by a spoon.

All the while, the river flowed by. On the far side lay Old Harrow and a great clocktower, its façade and clockface decorated in the windblown, wave-washed style of Old Harrow and its former Entwined rulers. There, dancing women in gold and pastels and drapes of gossamer were captured behind elaborate clock hands, glinting in the sunlight.

A quarter past the hour sounded with one sweet note. The water rushed beneath, grey-blue beyond a white stone balustrade. This was the nicest part of the river, with the industrial docks and their smoke and unappealing barges far out of sight. Here, instead of dockworkers and fishmongers, fine ladies twirled their parasols, and men sat under shoe-shiners' umbrellas. Nurses from the tall, graceful homes up by the palace—the palace where the Grand General refused to reside, preferring a town house among his subjects—guided pink-cheeked children by the hand.

Here, today, it was hard to imagine bombings and hangings. Here, life waltzed determinedly on.

It was as I contemplated this foolishness, eyes focused on the middle-distance over the river, that I saw Madge.

The world retreated until all I could see was my eldest sister. She strode along the riverside on the arm of an older, grey-haired gentleman with a vicious-looking walking stick. The man wore a short collar, his bare throat exposed to the light. That was shocking, both on the level of fashion and common sense, but it was Madge's throat that captured me.

Above the Guild medallion that both she and her companion wore, Madge's fine Golden threads twined in the daylight. They framed her strong, square-jawed face and entwined her neck, exposed to the stares of the crowd. She made no attempt to hide them from the light, wearing no collar and only a silken scarf, low on the collarbone, in a cursory salute to modesty.

Madge. Madge was here. I had not seen her since my engagement, before Lewis and Pretoria had helped me escape the Guild. She looked older, her cheeks a little thinner, her lips a little tighter, her waist a little broader. But her eyes, they were the very same—the chill, haunting blue of my deadly, indomitable eldest sister.

I was not the only one who had marked her. The crowd parted like water around a rock. Madge watched them go, her gaze roaming face to face from beneath the brim of her grey, feathered cartwheel hat.

People turned away. No one in their right mind wanted a mage with golden threads to remember their face. Then she might paint them, stealing a memory, an emotion, a piece of themselves, as unwilling payment.

This, naturally, was a distortion of the truth, propagated by the Lusterless's—humans with no threads or magic, as termed by the Guild—general fear and ignorance of Entwined powers. In truth, Madge *could* steal memory and emotion, locking it into uncannily lifelike portraits, but only if her subject was physically present as she painted.

Some exposed themselves to her power willingly, secreting away their pain and sorrows and regrets into portraits of unparalleled beauty and poignancy. Others, like those bound to a chair at the Guild's command to have a specific memory or tendency erased, might not be so enthused.

My nerves, already overtaxed, jangled. I dropped my chin so the brim of my hat shielded my face and watched the hem of Madge's forest-green walking suit pass out of sight. Only then did I raise my head a fraction, reach for my pen and scrawl on my list of random, uncategorical factors:

Madge is in Harrow.

CHAPTER 8

A Note to the Reader:
An Account of Multiple Abductions

The Guild came for my sisters and I many times. Due to my mother's occupation, we were frequently abroad, and this served my mother's goal of evading the Guild Inquisitors quite well. Therefore, I was six years old by the time an Inquisitor managed to cross our path for long enough to steal Madge.

We were on the temperate, windy coast of Oanse at that time. My mother was smoothing a rocky agreement of some dull nature between Oanse and the Guild, and her then husband, a distractable Copper with no interest in the offspring of his wife's previous unions, allowed the Guild right into our rented seaside manor while she was away at court.

I remember the moment well. The three of us were engaged in domestic training under our governess. Pretoria and I were embroidering. Madge was drawing, as usual, in the light of a glassless window, the salt breeze stirring the ends of her tight blonde ringlets. Our governess was, ostensibly, preparing our next lesson (in actuality, she was flirting with a local shepherdess over the edge of the balcony).

A door slammed off in the house. Pretoria pricked her finger in startlement and, cursing, threw her embroidery on the floor. I glanced from it to her in horror—I enjoyed embroidery, in all honesty, and was quite taken with my own pattern of flowers and birds in flight.

The parlor door opened. A woman stood there in a travelling gown of reddish tweed, tightly buttoned and fitted like a glove. There was a medallion at her throat, and a briefcase in her hand.

I sensed immediately what she was. It was in the way Pretoria's eyes shot to the balcony as if she intended to escape, and the slow way Madge rose from her stool, folding her hands before her skirts in acquiescence.

Between the Inquisitor's high, laced boots and my silk slippers, Pretoria's embroidery lay discarded on the floor. *Help me*, it read in careless stitches.

(I wish I could laugh at that particular aspect of the memory, but even these many years removed, I cannot.)

At four years my senior, Madge was already two years past the age when Guild parents were required to submit their Entwined progeny. Pretoria was several months short of that ominous birthday which would make her a candidate, and was spared only by that technicality.

Before my mother returned, Madge was gone, bundled into a coach and off on a ship. The way my mother wailed when she learned the truth—it is scarred into my mind. It was a shattering, a breaking. A tearing of the soul. She immediately orchestrated our transfer and left her negligent husband behind.

They came for Pretoria at the appropriate time, three months later. My mother was present, in a lofty, sprawling apartment in Castenfal, on the Continent. She saw the Inquisitor in the dining room, while a maid bundled Pretoria and I out the back door and took us for a walk. This walk ended at a cable car, which deposited us at a mountain chalet for several weeks until my mother could risk retrieving us. Bribes paid, excuses made, she had bought us another season. Another scattering of precious months.

I was not there the day my mother's scheming finally failed and Pretoria was whisked away. I returned from a walk with one of the maids to find her sitting listless on the floor beside Pretoria's bed, the veins about her eyes burst from strain and tears, and chunks of her hair scattered across the floor.

I had thrown myself into her lap and cried the tears she

no longer could. She simply held me, another third of her soul broken upon the floor. Her grip was loose, gentle. She did not speak.

By the time the Guild came for me, my mother had begun to come unhinged. I saw it in the increase of her flirtations. I saw it in how constantly she rejected her latest assigned husband, refusing to beget any more children for the Guild to steal. She drank too much, laughed too loud, and began to send me away for longer periods of time, as if she had already lost me.

The Guild took me on the precise day of my eighth birthday, at dawn. I looked for my mother as a maid led me down the stairs—I had heard her voice in the hall—but she did not come. She did not say goodbye. The last I saw of her was her hollow-eyed face in an upper window, little more than a flash before the carriage door closed.

The red-tweed Inquisitor, this time a man, offered me a small smile.

"No tears, there's a good girl," he said, leaning forward to pat my knee paternally. "Partings are hard, I know. But your sisters are so excited to see you again, little Miss Rushforth. Chin up. There now."

I waited until I was alone in my cabin aboard the steamship to cry. I cried as my mother had, as she had taught me to. And I swore that I would never be like her. I would never let the Guild take my children. I would never turn away and not say goodbye.

Because there would be no goodbyes.

A Note Upon: Starlit Mages

Starlit Entwined, whose trademark threads awaken beneath the light of the stars, exert governance over time itself. Thankfully rare, Adepts possess the ability to slow or pause time in their own vicinity. In Affinates, this ability manifests in admirable and civilized qualities such as punctuality. But in Adepts, it enables these mages to move unseen, to pass beneath the very noses of their victims. Thus it is, naturally and most commonly, utilized by the criminally minded.

*The Vigilant Lady Traveller may be glad of one thing, however—the Starlit mage cannot turn **back** time.*

From The Vigilant Lady Traveller:
A Gentlewoman's Guide to the World

CHAPTER 9

Present Day

Ciciley House, the teahouse where I was to meet Pretoria later that day, was attached to the Harrow Grand Museum of Ancient History. It was on an island on the west river and graced by Old Harren architecture, her grand triple domes of green copper presiding over the lower roofs of the finest businesses and galleries and bursts of burgundy trees.

Leaves blew across my path as I ascended the stairs of the museum. Pretoria was not due to arrive for an hour, so I stalked lavish halls of statues and paintings, stared into the blank eyes of mummies, and stood in the shadow of the great Illiope Façade—stolen brick-by-brick from a contested island in the South Sea.

I had seen it all a hundred times before, and not simply because the museum was free to the public, and I had little coin to spare for other diversions.

The place drew me. Artifacts, ruins, the weight of history—it always had affected me. A trait of my kind, they said. The vast layers of memory that lingered on dry wood and painted stone, carefully restored jewelry and rusted weapons, drew an Eventide Entwined like a warm fire on a cool night.

Most items were out of my reach, contained behind glass, and their history so long and layered I could see little without the aid of genuine twilight. But I trailed my fingertips across the Illiope Façade when none of the guards were looking, collecting whispers. Impressions. The *feel* of a world beyond Harrow, beyond my own.

The façade ended at the *Weapons of Antiquity* hall. Beneath a ceiling thick with moldings of mythical creatures at amorous play, I stared at the sword with which the last Entwined Queen, Alessandra, had been beheaded twenty years ago by General Baffin. I had no desire to touch that particular item, nor glean its memories.

The sight soured my already somber mood, so I wandered into the *Ancient West* wing. There I perused displays of Ummani art as tied to my childhood as my father's laugh or my mother's scolding, and my uneasy soul settled somewhat. As much as we had travelled in my youth, following my ambassador mother's lead, Ummi was where our home had been, and its comfort all the more valuable for the rare occasions we were there.

It was here, as I sat under the reconstructed ceiling of an Ummani gazebo, all intricately carved and painted wood and memories of a bright, airy coastline, that Pretoria appeared.

"Hello, Tillie."

My head shot up. She sat beside me, as settled and calm as if she had been there for the last half hour—which, in Pretoria's case, she possibly had.

As a Starlight Adept, she had evidently detached herself from the flow of time in the broader world, arriving hidden in plain sight and settling in while I stewed, unaware.

It was my own failure. A childhood full of unpleasant surprises and spoiled secrets should have taught me to expect such things.

Now I hissed between my teeth, fighting between rage and an irrational, melancholic gladness at seeing her. "You hag! Where is the box?"

Pretoria arched her finely plucked black brows at me. "Pardon me?"

"The artifact you stole from Mr. Stoke's safe," I snapped, ignoring a host of observations and memories as I looked at her face. She had scarcely aged, her fine brown skin—a gift from her father, my mother's second husband—as smooth and unblemished as it had always been. "And the money."

Pretoria shifted her hips so her honey-hazel eyes could search my face. "You are inordinately angry with me, and for no reason! I have no clue what you are on about."

"Did you rob Mr. Stoke?"

She recoiled, so taken aback that I almost regretted the accusation. "Rob Mr. Stoke? No! He's been like a father to you. I would never hurt you so."

Indignation and suspicion tinged my anger. "How would you know? You have been— well, the last postcard was from Lorva. Who were you and your henchmen—"

"And women," Pretoria interjected, deadpan. "We are very modern."

"—robbing there?"

"You really have a low opinion of me."

"Do not forget you dragged me around the world for two years, I know how you live." I began to tug off my gloves, keeping our gazes fixed on one another. "Did you steal from Mr. Stoke?"

"Piffle!" she scoffed. "What would he have worth stealing?"

My glove came off and I seized her exposed wrist. Before she could so much as gasp, I pulled memories from her flesh like words from a book.

One, I saw Pretoria following me through the museum. Two, Pretoria hanging off the end of a tram, high-laced boot poised beneath mustard-colored skirts, ready to step off in a busy street. Three, Pretoria practicing a disarming smile in the mirror. Four, breakfasting late at a hotel. And five, rising from a bed with not one, but three dozing paramours.

Pretoria's nails dug into my wrist so hard my fingers convulsed. The remembrances broke off and I found myself bent forward with my arm wrenched behind my back.

I may have trumped my sisters in blade and firearms at the academy, but Pretoria, I painfully recalled, had more than earned her stars in hand-to-hand combat.

"Tori—" I wheezed into my knees.

"How dare you!" Pretoria pushed me further forward.

"How dare you break into Mr. Stoke's office!"

"How dare you read my memories!"

"You are not stable, Pretoria!" I shrieked.

She bent forward so that I could see her, puffed out her cheeks and blew a raspberry at me, the expression a drastic contradiction to her lace collar, pearl earrings, and perfect chignon. "Me? Horsefeathers. Madge is the unstable one, you skulking little toad, even Mother agreed on that. Now, I am here to help you, if you will listen. Will you?"

"My arm..."

"I shall release you if you swear never to do that again."

I let out an exasperated whine.

"Swear it!"

"No!"

"Fine." Pretoria released me suddenly. "I should be grateful for an honest answer, considering your entire life is a lie. You must have gotten very good at it, deception and secrecy."

"I have had to earn my living. I could not simply run away like you, Miss *Castell*." I threw back the name of her most common false identity and shrunk away, clutching my arm and eyeing her like a fox might eye a wolf. My hat was askew, yellow silk flowers dangling in the corner of my vision.

"Oh piffle! I did not mean your name. What is a name anyway? A passing fancy." Pretoria shook her head in exasperation, then, resettling herself, added casually, "By the way, I am Russel this time around. Castell is too well known... I am considering having her die in a mysterious accident as my true self did. Or something tragic. Saving a child from a fire, I should think. I do love a good redemption."

"Pretoria, did you steal from Mr. Stoke, that day you left me the note?"

"No," she said, and this time I almost believed her. "But I am probably acquainted with whoever did. And like I said, I came here to help you."

"Help me with what?"

Just then, a shadow peered inside the gazebo. I stilled and Pretoria turned the male intruder a slow, unruffled glance.

"Ladies," a faceless museumgoer said in apology, glanced around the room without much interest, and moved on.

"Did he hear us?" I hissed.

"No," Pretoria returned, not bothering to explain why. She had likely had us in a continuous skew of time, separating us just slightly from the flow in the rest of the museum. It was, to her, the most banal of magics, and she had probably done it without even noticing.

"I see," I said coolly, reaching up to fix my hat. "Let us go to tea. I am starving, and peevish, and in need of something strong. Then you are going to answer all my questions."

Soon we occupied a corner table in the museum's café. Above us spread a ceiling that depicted the fall of empires and mythological scenes in signature art styles from the last four centuries, from round-bellied and downcast pre-imperial processions to smooth-lined and largely naked interpretations of Old Harrow, and the geometric, bold lines of New Harrow. A great chandelier of stained glass illuminated all, permitting the two dozen diners to consume their tea and cakes—and in the case of a table of boisterous Kessans, heavily laced coffee—in a wash of warm light.

"I do love it here," Pretoria commented as she eased her willowy frame into a chair. Her gown was a lively mix of oranges and yellows, draped in a style that echoed her father's Ummani origins while nodding to current Harren fashion. "Now, tell me what it is you think I have stolen?"

The waiter appeared, giving me a moment to think as my older sister ordered me a pot of tea and: "Cake and coffee, like those Kessans. I do enjoy the Continentals, so exotic."

The waiter nodded politely, no doubt classifying the both of us as decidedly un-cosmopolitan, and vanished.

Once he was gone, Pretoria looked at me promptly. "So?"

"You stole an artifact from Mr. Stoke's safe. Now he is missing and *I* am to take the fall for not delivering it to its owner." Fatigue beset me like a shifting breeze and I added, "And Madge is here."

Pretoria's pleasant expression faltered. That glimpse of the woman beneath her mask, the same betrayed sister that I, too, harbored in my heart, told me she had not known. "Smudgey?"

Pretoria's use of Madge's childhood nickname—earned from years of charcoal-smudged fingers as she studied her art—nearly upended me. "Yes. I saw her by the river with a handler, or her current husband. He is an Adept, in any case. I did not recognize him."

"Odd. Perhaps he is an import. Did she see you?" Pretoria asked, lowering her voice slightly as the waiter produced our order and departed again.

I shook my head.

"A small mercy." She selected a slice of thick chocolate cake and deposited it on her plate. "She is very possibly here for you, you do realize that? You are making quite a mess of living incognito, Til."

I reached for my tea and downed half the cup, ignoring the burn and buying time to gather my patience.

Pretoria contemplatively licked chocolate icing off a tiny fork. "I doubt it was me that drew her. I have befriended half of the Continental aristocracy and only been recognized once. But you? I barely had to lift a finger to find out where you live, work, the fact that you have no friends or sensitivity for fashion—"

"Hush!" I cut in, leaning forward across the table. "Be serious. Where is the damn artifact?"

"Impatient as ever." Pretoria primly took up a forkful of cake, but stopped short of eating it. "And I see you have expanded your vocabulary to the base."

"Please be serious," I hissed. "If you do not give the artifact back, you may find me floating in the river by next week. And if the Guild has caught wind that either of us are here... Pretoria, we are in grave danger."

Her chin lifted and, all at once, she was perfectly sober. "I know that, little sister. I know that very well."

There was memory in her eyes, painful and sharp. She did not need to speak Emeline's name for me to know it was her my sister thought of then.

Pretoria went on, "That is why I left a comfortable position in Lorva just to come fetch you. See how much I love you?"

That took me by surprise. "Fetch me?"

A hard note entered Pretoria's eyes. "Yes. You should not be on your own, not in a city full of Zealots and the Guild's watchful eyes. Even on the Continent people talk about Grand General Baffin's hatred of Entwined, and prophesy of escalation, particularly as he now has the wealth of The Sarre back at his disposal. So, come work for me. I have never met a safe that your ilk could not crack. And the Continental Guilds are so political nowadays, they rarely cause us Harren defectors any trouble. A bounty hunter here and there, nothing to fret over."

I bristled, at first in response to her mention of Baffin, then her invitation and her casual mention of bounty hunters.

"I know there will be more than that. As if theft wasn't enough!" I leaned forward across the table, delivering my words in a hiss. "You have some scheme, some brick to lob at the Guild, and you will drag me into it."

Her eyes seemed to glitter then, distant bright stars in a pool of night sky. "I would keep you safe."

"I do not need you to keep me safe."

She did not speak, did not so much as flinch, her gaze remained locked on my face. The moment lengthened, and in that stretch of time, I saw so much in the depths of her eyes. I saw passion and courage, rage and determination. I saw a thousand wrongs received, and a thousand more waiting to be returned upon her wrongdoers.

It stirred me in a way I could never pin down. Was it guilt, for not sharing her conviction? Was it discomfort, at the boundaries she was willing to cross to achieve her goals? Or was it simply jealousy, because she had something to devote herself to, something that drove her and fuelled her and filled her eyes with an intensity that bordered on the divine?

I had never felt such a way. I suspected that I simply did not have it in me.

I was not made to reshape worlds. Pretoria was. Madge was. And I? I was forever tugged between the two, forever in their shadows and hoping that someday, I might find my identity in their absence.

"Pretoria," I began again. "I am not working for you, not in Lorva or anywhere else. You are a thief."

"My occupation is far more nuanced than that, as you yourself said. But I can see you care not for the details, so I shan't tell you. Ottilie, you have had two years of independence, and how did you fare?"

I lifted my chin. "I have done very well for myself."

"You have managed not to die or starve," Pretoria corrected. "But if there is anything a proper fugitive learns—and I thought I had taught you—it is not to stay too long in any one place. But you have been here two years, running about with that shoddy detective, dancing on the train of Lord Stillwell's robe. He might recognize you from all those diplomatic functions with Mumma and our papas, and then where would you be?"

I stared at her. What if she *was* right? What if I had been here too long, and that was why Madge had turned up?

"I know you are waiting about for that mopey Bronze to come back from the war," Pretoria continued, lowering her voice again. "But like I said when you and I parted ways, Lewis has a soft side, but he is uncommitted. He is discontent with the Guild, enough to help you escape, but he himself will not leave. He is a smuggler but pretends not to be a thief. He is a fiancé but will never be a husband, using your engagement to avoid any other. I am sorry you fell for him, dear. I did not intend that."

I raised my chin, emotions cloistered. "I have no desire to marry him. He is not why I am still here."

Not precisely, anyway.

"Then why?" Pretoria asked, genuine emotion slipping into her voice. "You are an Eventide Adept, my dear, one of a scarce dozen in the City States. No matter how hard you try, no matter where you attempt to make a normal life, the Guild will find you. If Harrow does not kill you first."

I nearly told her then. Desperate to defend myself and prove my independence, I nearly admitted that I was in the process of fleeing, that Lewis had arranged for new identities and as soon as I was paid, I would be gone.

But I did not.

"Do you know anything about the artifact?" I asked, low and steady. "Anything at all?"

"No," she replied, matching my expression and tone. "I did go by the office to leave my note, and I did snoop to see what you and that detective have been doing, but the results were so dull that I left within... say, a quarter hour?"

The server, about to stop by our table, saw the intensity of our exchange and abruptly diverted his course.

I stabbed my cake too hard, trying again to decide whether I believed her. This was Pretoria. She had sent me Lewis to ensure I was not paired with a proper Guild monster and she had arranged my rescue, but I had left her and settled in Harrow for a reason. She spent her time flitting from country to country, from crime to paramour to gods knew what else. Emeline's death had unbalanced her, and for that I could not blame her. But I wanted a steadier life, one without choking collars at my throat or bounty hunters on my heels.

The Guild had driven Pretoria into a world of shadows, and she had become its queen. But I was not my sister.

"You look as though you are about to cry," Pretoria broke into my thoughts. "Or vomit; they are similar expressions for you. Let me help you and your Mr. Stoke. Let me prove myself to you. And who is this cretin that has threatened you? I shall pluck out his eyes and replace them with lemons."

I cringed and scrubbed my forehead. Nearby, the table of boisterous Kessans pushed back their chairs and began to depart.

That was what I should be doing. I should get up and leave, leave Pretoria and this city before Mr. Wake came for me, Zealots strung me up or the Guild dragged me north in chains. What else could I do, alone and without any leads?

That was not quite right though, I realized. I had yet to investigate Mr. Stoke's house.

"I need time to think," I said at length. "When can I see you again?"

"Tomorrow?" Pretoria offered, lifting a large, indelicate bite of cake to her mouth. "I am at the Hotel Cherron. We can breakfast in my rooms, and you can meet my husband."

I choked. "Your husband? Pretoria."

Pretoria popped the bite of cake into her mouth and gave me one of her disarming, double-eyed winks. "Yes, you heard me correctly. He is very handsome," she said around a mouthful of chocolate. "Now where is that waiter? Sir!"

CHAPTER 10

Mr. Stoke lived alone in a narrow rowhome on one of the nicer streets of New Harrow, where the classical pillars, smooth curves, and many arches of Old Harrow yielded to straight lines, star motifs, and steel-hearted brick buildings.

A group of children thundered past as I approached, chasing one little boy with a ball and screaming like a troop of monkeys. They toppled their way around a corner, passing a disgruntled older woman perched on a stool. The woman eyed me as I followed the children, merging onto the next street and diverting down an alleyway behind the houses.

Criss-crossing laundry lines dripped onto my hat as I unlocked the door of Mr. Stoke's cellar with a key I had quietly procured in case of emergency. I descended uneven stairs into the murk and, after an intimate encounter with a series of cobwebs and a needlessly large spider, I dusted myself off in Mr. Stoke's kitchen and closed the cellar door.

The kitchen was small, little more than a countertop and table and plastered walls. The bread was stale, the icebox warm, and the woodstove cold. There were no recent memories to be gleaned, and the older fragments I glimpsed were dull, daily things.

Mr. Stoke had not been home in days, that much was

evident. In the study, I discovered memories of smoking cigars, and found a pearl-handled revolver and box of bullets which I commandeered. Upstairs, the bed was neatly made. Mr. Stoke's clothing was ordered in his wardrobe and a photograph of his sister—who died of influenza as a child—was set upon his desk.

That sight filled me with a troubled kind of relief.

Mr. Stoke would never have fled without such a treasure. He had not abandoned me.

But that left only much, much darker options. I sank onto a chair between his desk and the window and stared across the room, letting the quiet seep into me.

My solitude was overwhelming. I thought of Mr. Wake, waiting for me this evening, of Pretoria and her offer, and Lewis, still so far away. I resented his absence and let myself molder in that for a time.

When I took hold of myself once more, I returned to the kitchen. I made myself a cup of tea and sat at the kitchen table, setting out my notebooks and taking up a pen.

A rustling snared my attention. I instantly dropped out of the chair, knocking my hat askew and crouching in a position that Pretoria would, no doubt, have described as toadish.

I caught a shush of paper against metal, a clack, then quiet.

Belatedly, I remembered the revolver and slipped it off the tabletop, secreted six bullets inside, and slowly rose to my feet.

The hallway was quiet and the front door closed. But there on the mat lay Mr. Stoke's mail.

I snatched the letters up and hastened back to the table, shuffling through the stack as I went. I recognized nearly every name, marking Mr. Stoke's usual correspondences. A cousin in the countryside. A lady friend who Mr. Stoke insisted was not a lover, but whose letters always put color in his cheeks. And so forth.

One letter was out of place. A Dr. Maddeson, Professor of Philology at Harrow University.

I opened it with no little trepidation, conscious of just how critical this missive could be.

I was not disappointed. There, in typewritten text, this Dr. Maddeson addressed several questions about the symbols on a certain box. Familiar, wheeled symbols which Maddeson had sketched across the bottom of the page by hand and identified as Old Sarren.

Clearly, Mr. Stoke had an interest in the box beyond retrieving it for Lord Stillwell.

I needed to speak with this Dr. Maddeson. Perhaps he had seen Mr. Stoke after his supposed disappearance.

But it was far too late to go to the university, and I did not want to learn the repercussions of failing to meet Mr. Wake. The day was fading, and my threads would soon twine.

I finished my tea and dozed on Mr. Stoke's sofa until the nearby church sounded nine bells. Full darkness had settled over the city—the dangers of the dark were lesser, I believed, than those of active threads.

The night was cold enough to threaten frost and the streets deserted save for a retiring lamplighter with his stilts resting on one shoulder. His shadow stretched long over the street as I set off at a brisk pace, burying my chin in my collar and keeping watch for a hackney.

None appeared, but my body warmed with the exertion and my overburdened mind calmed. An influx of courage came with it, and I found my shoulders relaxing, my steps slowing as I passed over Pointer's Bridge and into Old Harrow.

Soon, I passed the intersection of Old Harrow's canals. On an island in the center sat a statue of the Entwined Lady Honoria Grey. Robed, with her hood cast back and a modest gown visible beneath, she stood with her arms around two children—one human, the other Entwined with golden threads. Despite being a mage, her reputation as a mediator between Entwined and humanity had kept her likeness standing, even now.

I moved on, into the narrow, cobblestoned intersection of Glassmaker's Square. There was nothing square about the space, wrapped around the belly of an ancient watch tower that had been overrun by the rebuilding efforts after the revolution. Foundations of red stone were swallowed by the Almany Cathedral with its lording belltower and a face of moons and stars.

A sensation of being watched crept up the back of my neck. Careful not to look behind me, I crossed the square, passing through the shadow of the clocktower, and glanced in the window of a nearby shop.

I blinked in momentary distraction. Instead of seeing my shadowed reflection once in the glass, I saw myself a dozen times, in every size and at every angle. Some reflections were stable, while others spun lazily—suspended on long chains from the ceiling.

The reason why was quickly clear. Over my head, the shop's sign stretched.

Mundey and Mayfair, Mirror Makers.

The footsteps continued, but more slowly. There, in the window and a dozen refractions, I saw a new figure enter the square. Wearing a long coat and a fitted cap, he did not look left or right, but straight towards me.

Feigning calm, I set off up the steep street beyond the mirror maker's shop.

Footsteps drifted after me, echoing faintly against the close-packed buildings. It was not immediately clear whether they followed me directly, but I was not about to take the chance.

As soon as the road turned, cutting me off from sight, I diverted into an alleyway and broke into a run. Another turn, a low archway—more pre-imperial ruins, swallowed by new buildings—and I found myself in a tiny courtyard.

A courtyard with no exit. I spun, staring up at row upon row of windows and criss-crossing laundry lines towards a circle of open sky. The moon had slipped from behind the clouds, bathing me in silvered light and banded shadows.

There. Stairs. I mounted them lightly and ducked into an open-air hallway, startling a plump cat and passing right through the building, onto a bridge over the next street.

I swept the street with a glance before skittering across and onto a section of preserved stone wall. I followed the ramparts until they ended at a large, locked gate.

"Miss Fleet."

I spun. Harden stood behind me, head cocked to one side in the moonlight. The tips of his silver threads flashed, just above his collar. "You've no sense, have you?"

"Why are you following me?" I cocked the revolver in my pocket. The sound was impossibly quiet, damped by wind and wool, but Harden still noticed.

"A little sense, then," he amended. He paused, and after a moment seemed to come to a decision. "I'm not. Following you, that is. Well, I wasn't, until I saw you wandering in the night like a fool."

I stiffened. "This is hardly Dockside and you are not responsible for my wellbeing."

"I'll leave you to it, then." He shrugged and started to leave. He tossed over his shoulder, "But you should stay on the main streets. I'm heading that way, if you happen to have gotten yourself lost."

I took a reflexive step after him before catching myself. "I am not lost, but if I was, it would only be because of you."

He kept walking.

"Is there another way off this wall?" I called.

He gave me a flat look and, with the air of someone aiding a particularly inebriated friend, gestured to one side.

I flushed. There, shadowed but obvious from this angle, was a staircase leading down. I had walked right past it.

Reining in my pride, I trailed after him through a warren of alleyways, side streets, and courtyards until we reached a main road again. A man and a woman passed beneath the low light of an ill-tended gaslamp, ignoring the jeers of a drunken man sitting in the center of the street in a toddler's straight-legged pose.

I let out a long breath. "Thank you, Mr. Harden."

He shoved his hands into his pockets and regarded me with an expression that was considerably more forgiving than before. It was during that look, likely the most unguarded I had seen upon him, that my mind and body elected to inform me that he was, objectively, an attractive man. There was a stateliness in the hard lines of his face, an echo of the statues

I had perused at the museum hours before. There was stolidness to his posture that spoke of self-assurance and competence—even if he applied that competence to throwing bombs in public squares.

I looked away.

"Mayfair!" the drunk in the street called, waving broadly. "My dear, dear friend!"

"Mayfair?" I repeated.

Harden gave a long-suffering sigh and strode towards the drunk. They spoke, too low for me to hear, as he helped the other man to his feet and guided him to the sidewalk. There he deposited the drunkard in a doorway.

"Don't sit in the street, Stewart," Harden commanded.

Stewart gave an overly serious salute. "Aye, sir!"

"Mayfair?" I repeated a second time.

"He thought I was someone else. Let me walk you the rest of the way home. Why are you looking at me like that?"

"I am weighing the dangers of escorting a bomb-lobbing Separatist to my door with those of walking home alone," I said frankly.

"We did not set those bombs or throw the grenades," he said firmly. "We only fired the flares. Credit for the bombs must go entirely to Incarnadine and her Zealots."

I hesitated as he started walking. The Zealots were a human organization devoted to the eradication of the Entwined, and they were not picky about how they went about it—slander, framing, murder.

Hangings.

"What are you saying?" I hurried to catch up. "The Zealots framed you?"

"Yes. We do not bomb innocents. And I was not following you."

I was not sure I believed him on either point, but a little of my caution drained. I frowned, recalling the events and the mirror maker's shop.

"Mayfair. I see... You were going to the mirror shop and I happened to be there. Harden is your alias, for criminal enterprises."

"Emrys Harden," he corrected. His face caught the light of a nearby lamp and my heart stuttered in my chest. His gaze was direct and perceptive, and though I could not see his threads in this light, I knew they twined.

For the first time, his being Entwined struck me as a bridge between us, rather than a barrier. He knew what I was, if I recalled the events after the bombing correctly. We were kin, in a distant way.

"All right, then. Emrys Harden is a smuggler and Separatist," I observed. "And Mr. Mayfair is a mirror maker?"

Harden-Mayfair abruptly took my wrist—his grip round like a manacle, barely touching my skin but solid as iron—and tugged me into a doorway.

I pinched my lips closed, smothering a startled noise, and surveyed him with my back to the doorpost.

"You are a Rogue Adept," he stated, enunciating clearly, though his Harren accent was strong as ever. "What is *your* real name, Miss Fleet? What threads are you hiding?"

I did not bother denying it. "It seems we both know something we should not. Shall we blackmail one another? Betray one another? Or agree to simply forget and move on with our lives?"

He glanced out into the street at distant voices, sniffed, and frowned. "I'd be more forgetful with a drink in my belly."

I paused, searching for his meaning. "Are you asking me to bribe you with alcohol, or have a drink with you? I will do neither." I held up my left hand and pointed to the outline of my engagement ring, beneath my glove. "Lewis. I am engaged to your colleague, Lewis. Also, I require sleep. It is very late."

"Colleague? The man's a brother to me," Mr. Harden scoffed. "You misunderstand. I know of your and Illing's arrangement. You're no more lovers than me and Stewart."

"That is good news. Stewart seems like the unreliable sort and I would feel obliged to dissuade you," I quipped, to conceal a rush of conflicted feelings. Not only had I not known how close Lewis and Mr. Harden were, but Lewis *had* apparently told him our engagement was a façade. What else had he said?

I opened my mouth to ask, but caught myself. This line of thinking would not do, and I needed to silence Mr. Harden. I could think of no other way to do so save murder, which seemed a rather brash escalation. And considering Lewis's lack of interest in me, what harm was there in taking a drink with Harden? His attention was unexpectedly appealing, and a pleasant distraction from the looming threat of meeting Mr. Wake.

"A drink, then," I relented.

He smiled, slow and genuine and warm, and I felt a flush rush from my cheeks all the way down to my toes.

I pinched myself, hard, through my skirt. "Had you somewhere in mind?"

He stepped back into the street and offered me an arm.

I did not take it, but we set off together in a companionable silence, and I feared no shadows as we passed through the cobbled streets.

A NOTE UPON: THE SARRE

The most adventurous Lady Traveller may desire to visit The Sarre, and here the authors of this guide must express reserve. Though The Sarre is a land of ancient ruins, myriad cultures, and great wealth, it is also the most disputed territory in Ceste. In recent history Seau, Kessan, and Arrent have stepped in to broker peace within its tremulous borders, but its governance remains unpredictable.

The Vigilant Lady Traveller must exercise all caution in this uncertain land.

FROM THE VIGILANT LADY TRAVELLER:
A GENTLEWOMAN'S GUIDE TO THE WORLD

CHAPTER 11

We shouldered through the press of a drinking establishment on the periphery of Old Harrow. I was familiar with the place, as the reader may be. Called The Three Trees, it is named for the ancient trees (the remnants of an imperial orchard) which battled for purchase in its narrow courtyard. Their rattling limbs and half-barren branches reached over the heads of those gathered outside as Harden and I passed through, they smoking and drinking without mind for the old fruit crushed beneath their boots.

That fruit filled the air with a sharp scent, just on the edge of rot, overriding even pipesmoke and beer. It gave way as we entered the main door and made our way to a corner table. The inside of The Three Trees, through some trickery of the proprietors, smells eternally of pine and rosemary and sparecrust (that is, the baked dish of bread, bacon, and buttery onions).

Harden sat with his back to one wall and I the other, each surveying the room from our own vantages. He saluted someone, presumably one of the other patrons—I could not see the fellow, or lady, whoever they were—and turned in towards me.

"Does Mr. Stoke know what you are?" he asked.

"No pleasantries or talk of the weather, then," I observed.

"Why waste time?"

I resisted the urge to clear my throat. I did sit back though, folding my hands in my lap and crossing my ankles beneath the table. We were far enough from the other patrons that I doubted the nuances of our conversation could be discerned, so I said, "No, he does not."

"You're sure of that?"

"Amply. But he knows what you are?"

"Aye, I assume so. Being a detective and all," he replied, cocking his head to one side.

"Are you inferring that he has discovered my secret?"

He shrugged expressively, like a stage performer determined to be seen by the back row. The expression turned into a grin as a girl of perhaps sixteen appeared with two mugs, which she deposited before us after giving the table a quick wipe with a cloth.

"Ale, unless the lady prefers otherwise?" she said, patting Harden on the shoulder with brief familiarity and casting me a genuine and unpossessive smile.

"Ale will suffice," I said, too distracted by her and Harden's mannerisms to smile back. "Thank you."

"Somethin' to eat?" She glanced from me to him.

"Not tonight, Lottie, love."

She smiled again, flicked her cloth at Harden in parting, and disappeared back into the tables.

"A bit young to be your sweetheart," I noted.

"My niece," Harden replied, a flicker of amusement in his eyes. "Jealous creature, you are."

I frowned over my ale at him, first in exasperation (only slightly feigned) and then in increasing distraction. "Lewis told you of our arrangement?" I said, repeating his admission from earlier.

He nodded and took a drink, now watching a nearby table. The occupants leaned close to one another conspiratorially, snickering over something in the newspaper. "Aye."

I hesitated, but my curiosity, my *need* to know what Lewis had said of me, made me press on. "What did he say, precisely?"

"Said it was a match made by *them*, with some strategic influence by your sister. He helped you escape and you flitted off for a few years God knows where. Then you met again by chance in Sarre Grand, at which time you commiserated over your mutual unhappiness and decided that leaving it all behind was the best choice, rather than trying to change anything for the better."

His words were obviously intended to jab, but I was too interested in Lewis to pursue that now. "And?"

"He turned to smuggling, as they pay him nix, and you came to Harrow and found Mr. Stoke," Harden finished.

"That is all?" I said, trying not to sound disappointed.

"You were expecting something more?"

It was my turn to shrug and take a drink. The ale was very good, dark and satisfying, and yet left a sick feeling in my stomach.

"No," I said, resigning myself once more. I conjured a smile and cast it across the table at Harden, silently forcing myself to consider the fine line of his jaw, the focus of his gaze, and the breadth of his shoulders. I would not moon over Lewis when another interested—and attractive—party sat across the table from me. I would *not*. "I simply need to know how much you have on me."

"A fair bit," he observed.

"Yes, and I am at the disadvantage," I admitted. I sat forward, set down my mug and tapped the pads of my fingers absently against its cool side. "How have you managed to evade *them*?"

His eyebrows rose. "You are bold, asking me that in public."

I gave him a flat look. "My past has already been aired, why not yours?"

"Your and Lewis's past, not yours, individually," he pointed out. "Not yet, anyhow."

"You first," I prodded.

"I was tested, as a child," he said after a moment. "Labelled an Affinate and left to my own devices. Turned out I was no Affinate."

"Oh?" I was startled. "They do not often make such mistakes."

He shook his head. "Was no mistake. I was promptly recruited into the Common Force."

My bewilderment must have been obvious.

"The Separatists," he said, lowering his voice. "The Guild Inquisitor had sympathies and was funnelling young people into the Separatists. So, I was protected."

I sat back, pondering. "I suppose I should not be surprised. There are those within with Rogue affiliations, like Lewis. Why not Separatists?"

He nodded and drank while I continued to muse.

"So you were taken by the cause at a young age," I surmised.

"Seven," he affirmed. "I left for a time though, I'll admit. My feet took to roaming, as the feet of the young are wont to do. The Force encouraged it, in truth. They want us to see the world, to see that not every country lives this way." He waved a vague hand at our surroundings, encompassing Harrow and the City States as a whole. I glimpsed something in his eyes then, something that reminded me of Pretoria, and perhaps even Madge. Drive. Burden. Conviction.

He carried on, "Lewis and I met in The Sarre, as you know, and we found ourselves a mutually beneficial business opportunity."

"Smuggling."

"Aye. Soldiers far from home have wants, and Baffin's army is laced tight enough to strangle. A Guild-loaned officer like Lewis has more freedom than most, more access. And I have the skills to see it all through."

I considered all this for a moment as the volume in the pub rose. Someone noteworthy had entered, apparently, and half the crowd seemed to want to greet them. I could not make the newcomer out.

Harden squinted across the room, too.

"Are you back for good now?" I asked once things had settled down.

He took another moment to return his focus to me. "Yes. We need all hands, with the situation as it is."

"Like the Zealot Queen Incarnadine framing you for bombings," I noted, citing the newspaper's tawdry title for the woman.

He nodded. That drive was still there in his expression, but darker, more fixed. "Aye. Along with Baffin quietly funding her."

I could not help a sharp intake of breath. There had been rumors, of course, that Baffin's perceived passivity towards the Zealots might be calculated. But to hear him claim Baffin was *funding* them? The repercussions were frightening and terrible.

"Why would he do that? Risk that?" I asked. "Allowing them to weed us out is one thing. Funding them is another."

"They are doing what he wishes he could." Harden shrugged. "Beating, tormenting, and murdering Entwined is a passion of his. But I believe it's more than that. Baffin is setting the stage."

"For what?"

"To save Arrent again. To foster anti-Entwined sentiment to the point where civil war will bloom, the Guild will be forced to act, and he has enough leverage to oust them."

"Baffin cannot oust the Guild," I asserted. "Their existence is a pillar of the armistice. It would mean far more than bombings and riots, it would be outright war."

"Precisely," Harden said. He started to go on, but I had more to say, and kept speaking.

"Nor would the Guild be foolish enough to risk a scrap of their power, not for Affinates and Rogues. You do not know them as I do. What proof do you have, of any of this?"

"That's above me," Harden said. He made a conciliatory gesture and went on, evidently changing tack, "Regardless, the situation in Harrow is worsening. We need Adepts. The Zealots may not have magic, but they have money, guns, and Baffin's blind eye. The police will not stop them. If we Separatists are routed? A few Affinates swinging from lampposts will be the good old days."

All at once, the ale tasted sour on my tongue. If I was honest, the grim reality he painted was not the only reason. It was the realization that his interest in me, as a person—as a woman—might be a ploy. That would leave me unwanted again, and it made me feel pitiful indeed.

"There is no hope for Harrow," I stated. "Your admission just reaffirms that."

Something harder entered his voice. "So you'll abandon your home without a care?"

"That is presumptuous." I lifted my nose, reminding myself passingly of Madge. "I do care. But this is not my home."

That seemed new information. "Where is, then?"

"Ummi?" My smile felt brittle. "As much as any place is. Home implies belonging, and I have never belonged to anywhere." I almost said more, needing him to see my pain and my reasoning, to understand why I needed to leave. I barely knew the man, but I could not stomach his judgement.

I was treading dangerously close to admitting who I was, too—the only fact that Lewis, it seemed, had neglected to share with his criminal compatriot. So I said no more.

I expected Harden to respond callously. Separatists were all the same, in that regard. They were blind for their cause and determined to erase the individuals within, to assimilate all into a single organism with a single goal.

(Even years later, I do not retract that statement. It has proved true time and again.)

But Harden let out a long breath and sat back, looking more thoughtful than anything else.

"I'm sorry," he said. He shook his head and considered his mug, which appeared to be empty. "I'm Harren, through and through. I forget not everyone loves this city as I do."

"It has its qualities," I assuaged. "There is a reason I chose to stay here, temporary though it is. Old Harrow is beautiful."

A smile touched the corner of his mouth. It revealed a dimple in his left cheek, startlingly boyish.

"I'll say no more on the Common Force," he said. "You know my mind and I know yours now. We'll let it be."

I nodded, grateful, and lifted my mug in a salute.

"You and Lewis must be close to leaving, though," he said.

I nodded again. "I believe so."

"Then you'd better have me while you can," Harden said,

waving down the serving girl again. He spoke so nonchalantly, so practically, it took me a moment to understand. "Limited opportunity, Miss Fleet."

I startled, very nearly offended, but the look he cast me out of the corner of his eye smothered the feeling before it could root. His grin was crooked and wry, that dimple on display again, and his posture easy, without threat. Any tension from our conversation lost its edge.

I found myself choking on a laugh, and was still smiling when the girl refilled our mugs. I was not blushing; the heat in my cheeks was certainly from the alcohol, and nothing else.

We spoke of lighter things then, and time began to slip past me. We fell into commentary on the other patrons, some of which Harden knew and could effectively gossip over. This carried us through another drink before I recalled my pocket watch and realized the lateness of the hour.

The heat in my cheeks faltered with a wash of cold reality.

Mr. Wake. Mr. Wake was waiting for me, and I was horrifically late.

I rose, concealing my haste. "I should go, Mr. Harden. Thank you for a diverting evening."

"I'll take you home," Harden said, picking up his jacket, which he had discarded over the back of his chair.

"That is not necessary," I chided, digging in my pocket for a few coins, which I cast on the table to pay for my drinks.

He frowned at the coins, then me. "Said something wrong, did I?"

I shook my head, more sincerely than I intended. My tongue, however, was quick to lie, "No, no. I really must be getting home. My... ah, cat, you see. I must let him in. The neighbor has been threatening to toss him off the roof if he howls at her window one more night."

"I'll walk you," he restated, his voice firm. "Where do you live?"

I relented, ostensibly to speed the matter along, but if I was frank with myself, I did not want to be alone. Not in the dark streets. And not with Wake lying in wait.

I pondered the latter as we set off and I directed Harden

over the bridge to New Harrow. I even parted my lips to tell Harden about Wake, to tell him everything, as the dark water swept below us and the wind tugged at my hair. His presence beside me was a comfort I had not known I needed, and yet his company had opened a well of loneliness that left me more vulnerable than ever.

My rational self, however, shook into wakefulness before we reached Mr. Stoke's office. I was tired, and lonely, and therefore subject to fleeting fits of emotion. It could mean nothing.

I stopped outside Mr. Stoke's office door.

"You live here?" Harden questioned, dubious.

"In the apartments above," I lied. "It is very convenient."

He made a noncommittal sound, but seemed to believe me. "Can I see you again? Tomorrow? Overmorrow?"

My heart had a traitorous little fit. "Both are rather soon."

"Take advantage of me while you can, Miss Fleet. As I said."

"That is not precisely what you said," I reminded him, but my gaze had strayed to his mouth. My nerves were fraught, imagining Wake on the other side of that door. Between my anxiety and my fatigue, I was unhinged—that is my excuse for what I did next.

I reached up and, putting a cool hand around the back of his head, pulled him down for a kiss. I made it a good kiss. I had little practical experience with such things, but I had studied my salacious novels quite devotedly, and the gentle press, pause and linger of the act felt quite natural. It was pleasant.

My calculated intentions, however, fled as soon as he kissed me back. His hands cupped my head in turn, a quick, hungry movement that pulled my chest flush to his and drew me right up onto my toes. He took my lower lip between his with a brush of tongue, then delivered softer, subtler kisses to the corner of my mouth, my upper lip, back to my lower.

I staggered a little as he released me. His hand dropped to my upper arm, steadying, and I blinked at him in a haze. My blood raced for an entirely new reason, and I found myself oddly tremulous, too hot and too close to him and yet not close enough. My imagination, such a helpful instrument, produced several vivid images of what we might do next, and it was all I could do not to reach for him again.

I had not thought of Lewis during that kiss. I was now, obviously, but only to reflect on his absence.

It was eminently freeing. Intoxicatingly freeing.

Harden broke me from my rambling thoughts to point at the door beside us. "I'll be here, eight o'clock."

"What?"

"Tomorrow night. I am taking you out," he stated, grinning broadly. There was something behind his eyes though, a rawness that had not been there before. Something hesitant. Something that was not sure how I would react to this little encounter, despite his bravado.

I composed myself, though my insides felt rather gelatinous, and my knees were not doing their part in stabilizing me.

"Very well," I consented.

He touched his hat and left, glancing back once as the sound of the door opening drifted down the street. He slowed, I noted from the corner of my eye, and watched discreetly until I closed the door and he was blocked from sight.

In the darkness on the other side, I threw the bolt and put my back to the door.

I had one moment, one breath in the dark, to shove aside my thoughts of Harden and the kiss and Lewis, and to ram steel into my knees.

"Mr. Wake?" I called. "I have arrived."

CHAPTER 12

Mr. Wake awaited me on the sofa in Mr. Stoke's office, elbows on his knees and one of Mr. Stoke's notebooks open in his hands.

"You are extremely late," the man commented, sitting back and crossing one leg over the other, notebook still in hand. "Who was the man escorting you, just now?"

"An admirer who I could not evade," I said, which was enough of the truth to be an effortless lie. "Do not worry, I made no mention of you lying in wait for me in the shadows."

He grunted and looked back at the notebook. "Of all the artifacts whose recovery Lord Stillwell might have entrusted to you, I find it curious that he gave Mr. Stoke the most valuable. Did they have a previous relationship?"

"I believe they knew one another from their military days," I replied, stopping in the doorway. "Lord Stillwell was an officer at the time, and Mr. Stoke owed him a debt."

Wake seemed to take me at my word. Overall his demeanor was eerily unoffensive despite my tardiness, the gun at his hip ignored.

I sat on the other side of the sofa. I noticed the notebook he had been reading was only half-full, many of its pages untouched and smooth. It was Mr. Stoke's latest.

"Where did you find that?" I demanded. "That was not here yesterday."

"I found it on Mr. Stoke," he informed me levelly. "I encountered him today. The meeting was brief. We scuffled, he refused to answer my questions, and did not appear to be in possession of the artifact. This did, however, fall from his pocket as he fled."

I was momentarily too stunned to speak. "You saw him? Where was this?"

"The museum island." Mr. Wake held out the notebook, surprising me further. "It seems he was in contact with a historian or some such thing, but their name is not mentioned. Do you know anything about that?"

Historian? Or Dr. Maddeson, the philologist?

"No," I stated.

"Read this as soon as you can and tell me what you think of it. Now, what have you learned since our last meeting?"

He laced his fingers over his knee as I slowly took the notebook. I was wary of a trap, but he retained his casual demeanor.

I discarded the notion of telling him about Dr. Maddeson. It was too valuable a lead. But I could hardly deny learning anything at all. I braced the notebook across my stomach and said, "I searched Mr. Stoke's house and determined that he did not flee entirely, at least not of his own accord. He left items behind of great sentimental value."

"There was no sign of the artifact?"

I shook my head. "Unfortunately not. Mr. Wake, if you saw him, I believe we may conclude he is simply in hiding. Likely from you. If you would cease your harassment, our mutual problem may go away."

"Ah, see, that is where my encounter with the detective becomes particularly interesting," Wake said. "He was running when our paths crossed, and seemed to consider me an unexpected inconvenience."

"He was running from someone else?"

"Yes." Wake's eyes were keen, searching my face as if he were waiting for something. A clue. A betrayal.

Well, he would learn nothing on this particular front, as I had nothing to share. "Did you not see who it was?"

Wake shook his head. "But your detective does not seem the sort to flee from common criminals. I lost him near the Old Citadel. Does he have friends or relatives in the area? Somewhere he might go?"

"He does not," I admitted, warming to the puzzle. Harden's mirror shop was close, but I was not about to say that. "I will go through his contacts. It would seem there is a third party involved in this affair, more dangerous than you. How disconcerting."

"Indeed," Wake agreed. "What else have you uncovered?"

Our conversation proceeded in a series of questions and cautious answers. I fetched Mr. Stoke's ledgers and address book, combing them for acquaintances in and around the citadel. This produced several names for Mr. Wake, which I presented as far more promising than I actually felt them to be. This seemed to satisfy him, however, and within half an hour, the man rose. I could only hope that I had not consigned those poor contacts of Mr. Stoke to violence.

"I will see you again, here, tomorrow night at the same time," he told me as he made for the door. "Do not be late."

CHAPTER 13

A Note to the Reader: Emeline and the Glass Coffin

She was Pretoria's first love. Her death was the hammer that broke the Guild's tenuous grasp on my sister, and turned her discontent into a bitter, driving force.

Her name was Emeline and she was, for five years in the Guild's hallowed halls, as good as a sister to me. Forcibly relinquished to the Guild by her Separatist parents at the late age of thirteen, she staunchly clung to her parents' views. Her willfulness and passion collided with Pretoria's natural inclination towards self-governance and petty insurrection, and together the two of them began to sow ever-increasing discord among the young mages at the Harren Guild Academy for the Instruction and Edification of Young Women.

The Guild paid little mind to love affairs like her and Pretoria's, so long as no unsanctioned children could be conceived and one still fulfilled marital obligations to the Guild. But rebellious ideals were another matter entirely. Young mages began to defect, their perceived poison to spread beyond the walls of the Women's Academy, and action was taken.

When I recall Emeline's face now, I remember it only in her final moments—submerged in water behind walls of glass, her auburn hair glistening like flame and her skirts of pale, sodden white adrift as she screamed and spasmed and drowned before a hall of mages.

That, dear reader, is the final punishment for a rebellious mage—the Glass Coffin.

CHAPTER 14

Present Day

I moved through the grounds of New Harrow's extensive university in the clean light of morning. A few hatted heads turned and whistles chased me across the campus towards the main building, where a shy young woman directed me to Dr. Maddeson's office on the second floor.

"Mr. Stoke sends his respects," I told the lean, brown-haired professor across his book-strewn desk. I had snared only a few hours of sleep, and the amount of coffee this lack had necessitated left me jittery. But I strove to remain composed. "I am his secretary, Ottilie Fleet."

"Tell him likewise, Miss Fleet." Dr. Maddeson's moustache, a long-tailed, drooping specimen, dipped further in discontent. His gaze flicked over me, searching for something. "You did not bring the artifact?"

Ah. Now there was a development.

"No, sir," I said, summoning one of the lies I had concocted throughout my largely sleepless night. Aside from the late hour of my return home, Hieronymus was feeling neglected, and had howled and batted my toes throughout the sparse hours in which I had found my bed. I had also been forced to scale the balcony again, which had fouled my already sour mood after meeting Wake.

"It was my understanding that Mr. Stoke had already

delivered it to you, and I was to retrieve it today," I lied.

"Well, well..." Dr. Maddeson said peevishly. "Would that were so. I anticipated your employer's visit yesterday, I even came into the office abominably early, but he did not appear. Did he tell you why?"

I swiftly added this to my mental logbook of events. "No, I had several days off and have not seen the detective."

"Well," Dr. Maddeson said again, his discontent deepening towards self-pity. "This is all very disappointing. It is one of the Landsdown Relics, you understand, and its examples of Old Sarren are impeccably preserved—both on the box and, likely, the object within. We have little of the language, so it has yet to be translated. That is my goal, Miss Fleet, my dream. To unlock Old Sarren."

His eyes drifted to the shelves of his office, and, following his gaze, I noted an extensive series of worn notebooks and bound sheaves of typewritten material. His research, I surmised.

"You are referring to the language on the box," I clarified. I intended to press more about Mr. Stoke, but the more information I could gather on the artifact, the higher my chances were of finding it—with or without my employer. "The wheel-like symbols?"

Maddeson's eyes lit. "You saw them?"

"Yes."

"But you do not know where the artifact is?"

"No, sir."

"Then... Is there any possibility you could transcribe the symbols, so that I might, at least, have a sense of them?" The hope in his voice was thin, as if he already accepted the futility of his request.

"I can," I admitted. "My memory is rather good, and I have a fair hand at drawing." One did not grow up with a sister as domineering as Madge without gleaning some of her skills.

Maddeson burst into movement, riffling together paper and pen and clearing off a chair for me to sit in at his desk. "Did you see the object within also?"

"No," I said, watching him flutter about. "What is it?"

"Would that I knew, that I knew! Though I suspect it to be made of Incarnate, whatever it may be, but of course, I cannot state with any certainty." He launched off into a ramble about his continued hopes of seeing the box, his expectations and minutiae of linguistics as I took the materials and went to work, pulling up my memories of the box and the warehouse.

I drew slowly but steadily. Dr. Maddeson finally slackened his rambling and hovered just behind me, close enough for his breath to rustle the strands of hair escaping my chignon.

"Sir," I said. "Might I have a cup of tea?"

"Pardon? Oh. Oh, of course," the man fumbled. The gusting of his breath withdrew and I relaxed as he left the room.

I glanced at the shelf with the manuscripts and notebooks, already halfway out of my seat, but footsteps in the hallway plunked me directly back in my chair. I attended to my sketching until they passed by, then finally rose and pulled out the first manuscript.

The Arasi of Old Sarre: The Vanished Peoples and the Proposed Origins of the Entwined.

I reread the typewritten title. What did The Sarre have to do with the origins of the Entwined? No one knew where the Entwined had come from, but it was widely accepted that we had developed, as a people, far distant from humanity.

Footsteps sounded again, this time two sets in concert. I darted back to my chair and was dutifully sketching when a young man appeared with tea. Dr. Maddeson came in behind him and shooed him back out the door as soon as the tea service was placed.

"Oh," Dr. Maddeson crooned as he saw the symbols I had completed so far. "This is superb, Miss Fleet. You are doing an incredible service to me and the university, though I do still need to see the artifact itself, as I said."

"Many times," I murmured.

"Pardon me?"

"Oh, I was simply agreeing."

"When is Mr. Stoke back in his office?"

"Next week," I said, still sketching and grateful for the

excuse not to look at the professor. I pushed the sketches I had finished closer to him. "Have you any idea what these mean?"

"Let me see... All this waiting has been very frustrating, you know. I have been waiting on this for some time."

"Yes, I am aware."

He continued with an anxious, preening demeanor, "There is a fire under my feet, you see. My research is funded by Grand General Baffin himself."

I stilled my pen. "Why would the Grand General have interest in the artifact?"

"Not the artifact—at least, not until I told him of it, after Mr. Stoke reached out. Now he is quite interested. But because this is the language of the ancient Entwined," the professor said with the air of one delivering a great revelation. "The Arasi, the oldest known civilization in The Sarre, *were* the ancient Entwined. Or so I propose. Deciphering the Arasi language is the key to learning the true origins of the Entwined—their creation."

Creation. My mind caught on that word, but the professor prattled on.

"That history is recorded upon the Landsdown Stele. You likely have not heard of it—I will elaborate. The Stele is the pride of the Landsdown Trove, and is the longest Old Arasi text we possess. It is, however, not intact. To all appearances, some sections were intentionally removed. By whom? Why? To hide its secrets? To erase the Entwined's history? To utilize its precious stone? Perhaps all of them, though the latter would be a most heinous crime. Several missing pieces of the Stele *were* at the original dig site, but have since, yes, disappeared. I believe there to be ten such pieces, with the Stele itself constituting the eleventh."

"You believe one of them is in the box with these symbols?" I clarified.

Maddeson nodded emphatically. "It is a puzzle box, Miss Fleet!"

"Ah, I did notice that."

"Very astute."

"Thank you. Where is the Stele itself?"

"It is rarely in one place for long," Maddeson said. "Shared between the great museums of the Continent, for its own safe keeping. It presents a tempting target to thieves, as you can imagine."

The world shrank away from me just then, leaving Dr. Maddeson's voice echoing into the silence of my skull.

A tempting target to thieves. Thieves, like Pretoria. I had begun to believe her assertions of innocence, back at the museum, but now...

"I see. Fascinating," I finally found the words to say. "However, what do you mean by 'creation' of the Entwined?"

Dr. Maddeson was truly alight now. "The Entwined look human, bleed and breathe and procreate as humans. Because they *are*. The Entwined were made, Miss Fleet. They are no more than humans granted great magical ability through artificial means. That is what the Stele will tell us, once wholly translated. The suggestion is already there, I believe, but with the writing incomplete—"

"What means?" I interrupted, baffled and not a little offended. "By what means were the Entwined *made*?"

"A question I can only answer once I decipher Old Arasi and thus the Stele, once it is whole," Dr. Maddeson finished, riffling through my symbols and seemingly unaware of the vitriol in my voice. "This is the end to strife in Harrow, Miss Fleet. My research will bring harmony and understanding. Peace, Miss Fleet, is within reach."

That all sounded grossly optimistic. Instead of feeling hope at his words, all I felt was a rush of pity and a spike of apprehension. In an ideal world, the revelation of common origins might forge kinship between peoples, but this was no ideal world. There were so many layers of hatred and conflict, so many wrongs done on either side.

More than that, the peril of such an idea could not be exaggerated. If humans believed there was a way for them to become Entwined, the carved box and whatever relic was inside it was worth far, far more than a stack of banknotes.

It was a secret to kill for.

Where *was* Mr. Stoke?

I was, I realized, beginning to feel ill. "May I see those papers again?"

Dr. Maddeson relinquished the symbols, then cried out as I tore the pages down the middle.

"I have remembered incorrectly," I stated, tearing the papers again and shoving the pieces into my teacup. They immediately soaked. "It was arrogant of me to believe I could recall them clearly. Now that I know the importance of them, I would be remiss to submit these to you."

Dr. Maddeson looked as though he had choked on his tongue, or perhaps wished to strangle me. But he forced a nod. "Perhaps you are correct. When can I see the artifact itself, then?"

"I will bring it by as soon as I speak to Mr. Stoke," I promised.

It was almost the truth.

CHAPTER 15

I had never considered myself a particularly selfless person. By most standards I had a pampered childhood, despite the absence of my father, the eventual detachment of my mother, and separation from my sisters. The Guild Academy, where I had spent over a decade, was my greatest and longest trial. Yet it had taught me self-sufficiency and transformed me into an admirable mage, as well as equipping me with an endless repertoire of useful skills—skills I had relied upon since my escape.

I was used to thinking, primarily, of myself. I had to. For in a world where I was both hated and feared, where my parents could not protect me and the Guild sought to rule me, I was the only one who would—aside from Pretoria and Madge, in their sporadic and flawed ways.

So it was that as I sat in a back pew in the Almany Cathedral with my head tilted back, holding my hat in place with one hand and staring at the endless opulence of the gilded ceiling, the feeling I endured was both unfamiliar and unwelcome.

Obligation.

Grand General Baffin was funding research into the supposed creation of Entwined. I thought the notion absurd, the highest form of wishful thinking on behalf of humanity and Harrow's Entwined-hating leader. But Dr. Maddeson had been passionate, and that passion left a hollow of doubt in my chest.

Add to that Harden's assertions that Baffin was funding the Zealots and propelling Harrow towards civil war, and a grim picture was being painted before me.

Finding the artifact was about far more than saving myself, claiming my reward and escaping Harrow. It was about ensuring that my enemies did not come into possession of potentially dangerous information.

Such responsibility made me squirm. I wanted nothing to do with it. I wanted a ship, and the horizon. I also wanted Lewis, when I was not kissing Harden, but all that was ridiculous and unnecessary.

I closed my eyes and let out a long breath. Mr. Stoke had contacted Dr. Maddeson about the language on the box, but whether he had understood the professor's course of research was unclear. The detective had always been neutral in the conflict between humans and Entwined, which was part of what had drawn me to him. I could not imagine him supporting research that could cause more conflict, or being foolish enough to share Dr. Maddeson's idealism.

For what might have been the first time, I allowed myself to truly, deeply, miss Lewis. The fortnight of ocean between us suddenly felt untenable, absurd, when I needed him here and now. We were friends and allies. I should be able to turn to him and—after I had spent the last two years saving to buy us a new life—he should act.

I needed his help. *Someone's* help. Or rather, I wanted someone to take this responsibility from me.

With that little flight of self-understanding, my resolve hardened. No. I had to make my own choice, choose my own path. And that choice? It had already been made, long before these complications arose.

Find the artifact and Mr. Stoke. Claim Stillwell's reward. Meet up with Lewis. Carve a new life.

In all likelihood, Maddeson's research would come to naught, anyway. I decided that. I decreed it.

It was not my responsibility.

I rose. I straightened my skirts and sash and adjusted my hat. I tucked away the last of my guilt and swept out of the cathedral without a backward glance.

Newly restored and courageous as I was, the discovery that policemen awaited me at my apartments was a rather heavy blow.

No sooner had I unlocked the front door of the building than my landlady's prim tones summoned me through the door of her private sitting room at the foot of the stairs.

Suppressing a weary retort, I pulled off my gloves. "Yes, Mrs. Temberley?"

I froze in place as two men stood, one in the customary uniform and helmet of a patrolman and the other in a bowler hat and suit.

"Detective Sergeant Supford," the man in the bowler hat informed me. "And this is Constable Blakely. We are here to ask you a few questions, Miss Fleet, about the location of your employer, Mr. Uriah Stoke. Please, have a seat. Mrs. Temberley has been kind enough to permit us the use of the room. Privately."

Mrs. Temberley, who had been watching my startled expression with the demeanor of a satisfied cat from beneath her frilled cap, caught herself.

"Oh, yes. Yes, I see. Do call if you need anything," she said with faux civility, and left.

Slowly, I sat on the edge of a stiff-backed chair while the constable took up position next to the door and the detective sat across from me on the sofa.

"Miss Fleet," the detective began. "When was the last time you spoke with your employer? You should know, he is an old associate of mine. We were stationed together at Heddon Street, before his retirement."

"I see." The constable's glare was a physical force on the side of my face, and I felt gooseflesh prickle across my skin.

"I saw him two... three days ago?"

"Mrs. Temberley has informed us you were out quite late the night before that. Where were you?"

"Mrs. Temberley does so struggle to mind her own business. It is an affliction, as I understand it."

There was a twitch around Detective Supford's eyes, but it was gone before I could decide if it was amusement or irritation. "Please answer the question."

"Late nights are a requirement of my position, sir. Mr. Stoke required me at a private meeting. I take notes and such."

The man watched my face, alert for any lie. "Who was the meeting with, and what did it concern?"

"I apologize," I said, rather than replying. "But what is this about? Is everything well with Mr. Stoke?"

Detective Supford's expression betrayed nothing. "Do you know where your employer is?"

"On holiday," I said, grateful for an easy deflection. "He did not intend to return for a week or so. He instructed me to take the time off and he would reach out when he came back."

At the door, the constable made a disbelieving sound and glowered harder.

"Where?" Supford asked.

"He did not share that with me."

Detective Supford sat forward, resting his elbows on his knees and clasping his hands together. "Did you make the travel arrangements, as his secretary?"

I shook my head. "He only informed me the day before. It struck me as a personal matter—no, I have no details."

"Were you aware that your employer's office has been ransacked?"

I had the presence of mind to feign startlement. "No! I— Oh no. Why? Who would do such a thing?"

"Those are questions we hoped you could answer." Supford's demeanor shifted then, from general inquiry to a grim conviction. "As you were seen entering and exiting the office several times in the last two days."

I resisted the urge to scrub my face in despair. I shifted the movement into a casual adjustment of my hat, discreetly loosening the hatpin. The weight of Mr. Stoke's pearl-handled revolver was heavy in my pocket.

It did not occur to me to wonder, just then, if they had observed Mr. Wake at Mr. Stoke's office as well.

"There is also the matter of this." Supford pulled a familiar envelope from a pocket inside his coat and set it down on the coffee table between us.

Lewis's and my savings, carefully stowed over the past two years, puffed the envelope wide. A small fortune, and nearly every penny we had.

"You searched my rooms!" I accused. "You had no right!"

"We had every right." A second reach into his pocket, and the man produced a typewritten warrant, then a picture. My picture of my sisters and I, a prized possession which I had stashed with my money. "Miss Ottilie Rushforth, Rogue Eventide Adept."

I was rendered speechless.

That moment was my undoing. Detective Supford sat back, his air one of satisfaction and conviction. At the door, the constable widened his stance and twitched his baton.

"Why would you say that?" I managed.

"This"—he pointed to Madge, in the picture—"is Margaret Rushforth, recently arrived in Harrow. It is the constabulary's business to know every Guild representative currently in this city—for their protection, you understand."

I managed not to snort, but only just.

"The Rushforths, as you well know, are infamous," the detective went on. "Your ambassador mother. Her string of powerful husbands. Your sister Pretoria and her tragic death. And this"—he indicated me in the photograph—"is you. I could not be certain until I saw you myself, but now I have no doubt."

"That is hardly me," I said. "She is years younger than I, far thinner and her hair is too dark. Our jaw lines are different. And if I were found dead in a swimming costume that gaudy, I would come back to life just to burn it."

Supford was not amused. "The photograph is obviously dated. The fact that you have aged is not a defense."

"I am not Ottilia Rushforth."

The detective raised his voice, his patience beginning to fray. "No, you are *Ottilie* Rushforth, and if you have any dignity, you will cease to play the fool. You are a Rogue Entwined, unchecked, uncontrolled. You are in possession of a great deal of money, in cash, while your employer's safe is empty, his offices rife with the signs of violence, and he has vanished."

Rage threatened to blind me, and my senses narrowed. The increasing thud of my heart. Closed room. The constable's baton.

Unchecked. Uncontrolled. He did not know the meaning of those words.

"The money is my wages—I neither trust nor require banks," I began, speaking with deathly calm. "I purchased the picture at the novelty market in Honeywell because I thought it entertaining and reminded me of my own sisters, who I have not seen in some time, which depresses me. Yes, I did know Mr. Stoke's offices had been searched, but I am being blackmailed by a rather thuggish employee of Lord Stillwell, who contracted Mr. Stoke to track down a certain artifact, which went missing along with Mr. Stoke. Did you not see him at the office, too? This thug threatened to kill me if I contacted the police, so for the last two days I have been searching for him and the artifact quite desperately, in fear for my life. I am simply a secretary, sir, a secretary who does not trust banks because I will not allow my hard-earned wages to pad the pockets of indolent well-to-dos. I am a victim of horrible circumstance, and I am certainly no Entwined."

Silence followed my rant. The constable muttered something under his breath and the detective raised a quelling hand.

Briefly, I thought I may have won my case. My mind raced ahead, planning my next steps. I would pack a hasty bag, find Hieronymus—damn, I had forgotten to buy a travelling basket, I would need to do that, too. We would flee and hide before the frustratingly astute Supford found enough evidence to arrest me.

That ship, however, had apparently left harbor some time ago.

"Miss Ottilie Rushforth." Detective Supford rose to his feet. "We will continue this discussion at the precinct. You are under arrest for suspected involvement in the disappearance of Uriah Stoke. You are charged with larceny and living as an Unregistered Entwined. I am placing you under arrest."

A Note Upon: Silvers

Silvers are the most common Entwined of the Moon, but that should not lead The Vigilant Lady Traveller to complacency. They are widely known to be predatory, predisposed to violence, and possessed of unnatural strength. Powerful Adepts also wield the power of Leeching, in which, through physical contact, they drain the energy of their victim to heal and strengthen themselves.

Beware, gentle ladies, silver threads beneath the moon.

From The Vigilant Lady Traveller:
A Gentlewoman's Guide to the World

CHAPTER 16

I kept my chin high as I stepped out of the police wagon in front of the station. My cheeks still felt cool with shock, but the short ride had given me time to compose myself.

People in the street stared—curious, fascinated, accusatory—as I raised my bound hands to adjust my hat, tilting my head at a dignified angle to hide my features.

More stares beset me as I entered the station proper, passing through a waiting room full of petitioners. A clerk handed the constable, Blakely, a sheaf of papers which he began to fill out, conversing with her quietly as Detective Supford and I passed into a hallway.

I expected further interrogation. I had prepared for it. But instead I was divested of my possessions, including my hat (which I found rather unnecessary). Then I was deposited in an isolated cell, hidden in the back of the station, and left to stew for an unmarked stretch of time.

At last I was fetched by a new constable, his hands noticeably covered with leather gloves to prevent our skin from touching as he took my arm.

"Very pleased to meet you," I said when he failed to introduce himself. I looked pointedly at the pin on his chest, which read *J. Hopgood*. "You may call me Ottilie. May I call you Jack? Jacapo? Jebediah? Jethro."

I saw the corner of his mouth twitch. "Constable Hopgood will do."

"I feel we are quite past that, given how friendly you are being with my upper arm. Did you know that in Ummi, a lady's arms are considered as salacious as her thighs?"

His grip spasmed but remained in place. "Please, do not talk."

"I talk when I am frightened. Jacapo?"

"This way," he ordered, and set off at a brisk walk.

We passed through a gate and into a hallway, then through an area with a long counter and several offices, all of which seemed abnormally quiet compared to the waiting room and the streets outside. All the walls were wood-panelled, sparsely decorated, and the entire place smelled of cigars, hair wax, and cologne.

These were overpowered by a whiff of something stark and corrosive as we mounted a set of stairs. At the top another hallway stretched, and my guard rapped knuckles on a closed door.

"Come in."

The door opened and the scent I had picked up tripled. Formaldehyde. Decomposition.

Death.

Detective Supford stood on one side of a table. The room was a crude thing, barely an improvement upon my cell with its single window—open, for the smell—creaking floorboards and limewashed walls. But my gaze did not linger on the room, or even on the detective. Instead, they fell on the sheet-draped cadaver on the table.

Dread, thick and sickly and poisonous, coiled through my belly.

"Who is that?" My voice emerged surprisingly steady, girded by a flash of hot, nervous anger. If Supford thought he could play with me, unbalance me by putting me in a room with a corpse, he was wrong.

In answer, Supford pulled back the top of the sheet.

The world went mute. No clatter and chatter from the street. No heartbeat in my chest. No breath through my lips.

Trapped in that soundless realm, I stood in the doorway with my hands shackled, fingers limp, face slack.

A man's discolored, sunken face gaped up at the ceiling. Tweed jacket. Dark hair, just starting to grey. A mutilated, shattered jaw.

The silent world collapsed inwards and sound rushed back, assaulting my ears like a nest of disgruntled wasps. Before any true comprehension could reach my brain, my knees gave out.

Constable Hopgood caught me. I staggered and tried to find my feet, but I could barely breathe, let alone stand.

Supford watched me, his impassive expression softening just a fraction. When he spoke again, it was more of a statement than a question. "You did not know."

"No," I managed. "No, I did not."

Supford stood there for another thoughtful moment, before he came to a decision and began to re-cover Mr. Stoke's face.

"No!" I snapped, stepping out of Hopgood's supportive grip. He did not stop me. "Let me see him. It cannot be him. It *cannot*. I must see."

Supford nodded and I, with limbs that were not my own, crossed the floor.

My employer was nearly unrecognizable. His face was blackened and battered, one cheek caved in and his jaw broken. Bruising rose about his throat and across his shoulders, signs of a struggle that he had failed to win.

Nausea assailed me, but I managed to say, "It looks as though he was cudgelled to death. How can we be sure this is him?"

"You do not believe it is?" Supford asked. He nodded to Hopgood. "Constable Hopgood and I both knew Stoke, back in the day. We are certain it is him."

I glanced at Hopgood. "You may be right, but..." Clearing my throat, I studied the corpse with an attempt at clinical detachment, but it was no easy thing. "When was he found?"

"This morning, around seven o'clock. He had not been dead long."

"I see..." I took a deep breath to gather myself, but only took in more of the stench. "The clothes are his. His height, weight... What did you find in his pockets?"

"He had these on him." Supford picked up a box from a side table and held it out. "Do you notice anything unusual?"

It did not occur to me until later that, with that question, I had begun to fade from the realm of suspect to victim—at least regarding Mr. Stoke's probable demise.

My spark of hope died as I saw the contents. In the box lay Mr. Stoke's pocket watch, a billfold, cigarette tin, a book of matches, scrap receipts from his usual shops, and a familiar pen. The sight of them filled me with immeasurable sadness, and all at once, I could not bear to look at the body anymore.

With gentle hands, I pulled the sheet over Mr. Stoke's face, careful to hold the chain of my manacles out of the way. Then I clasped my hands before my skirts and turned to Supford. "Where did you find him?"

"At the Mithos," the detective replied, citing one of Old Harrow's middle-class hotels, some three blocks away. "In a room booked under an assumed name."

"Was there anything else with him? In the room?"

"No. Should there have been?"

I made an uncertain expression. "He disappeared with an artifact, a box marked with circular symbols, the one I spoke of before. We were hired to retrieve it for Lord Stillwell. It is likely the reason he was— It is valuable enough to kill for, in any case."

Supford shook his head. "There was nothing of the kind."

"Perhaps his killer took it," I observed. "Will you speak to Stillwell on the matter?"

"In due course," Supford said. "But I must warn you, Miss Rushforth. You are not yet above all suspicion."

A moment of quiet settled over the room.

"Pardon me, sir, but can she not... look?" Hopgood asked the other man. "As an Eventide Adept. To see the killer."

The notion nauseated me. "No."

Hopgood looked perplexed.

"I mean..." I gathered myself, setting one hand on the

table beside Mr. Stoke. My gloved fingertip brushed the sheet. Somehow that small touch finally broke through the desert of my shock, and my eyes began to moisten. "I may not be able to see anything important. Deceased humans and Entwined become inanimate objects upon their death, all memories prior to that are erased. Sentient, self-aware life is a magic all its own, and when it departs it takes more than animation. Death corrodes the memory of life. Once a corpse is cold, I can see nothing before its death."

Supford nodded. "I understand. Would you be willing to look, regardless?"

The urge to flee the room overwhelmed me. It was becoming increasingly hard to breathe, let alone think. But I nodded.

Supford closed the window, and dimmed the lights, leaving us in an approximation of twilight.

I mustered my strength and brushed one finger across the body's one intact, swollen eye.

I saw Supford and the constable. I saw a medical examiner with a narrow face and sad eyes. An alleyway, and a cudgel.

Crack. Crack. Crack.

I jerked my hand away and described, as quickly and passionlessly as I could, what I had seen.

"Could you see more at twilight?" Supford inquired.

"Perhaps, but unlikely. The body is recent enough that I have already seen its entire history," I deflected, increasingly desperate to leave the room.

"Are you willing to try again, regardless?"

I could not bring myself to speak, so I gave a listless nod instead.

"Very well." Supford accepted this. He glanced at his watch, and seemed frustrated by what he saw there. "Early tomorrow morning, then. I've an appointment tonight."

I nodded again.

"Miss Rushforth," Supford began, and for the first time in two years, I turned to my true name. "I beg several more questions of you before I leave. Can you tell me what you think of this? I must reveal the body again, I apologize. Prepare yourself."

I retreated a step and the detective pulled back a section of the cloth to reveal Mr. Stoke's unmoving chest. There, just beneath his heart, was a bruise so dark it looked like a piece of night carved from the sky. A bruise in the shape of a handprint, fingers slightly crooked to leave tight, scar-like lines of nails.

"This, as near as we can determine, is what killed him," the detective said. "The damage to his head was done postmortem, as you confirmed, and all his other injuries are unlikely to have caused his death. As to this... bruise, we assume it is sorcerous. The work of a Silver, perhaps, though I have never seen, nor heard, of their Leeching being used to the point of death."

"Neither have I," I admitted. My mind leapt to Harden, but despite his criminal affiliations, I could not imagine him doing something like this. That did not mean he was above suspicion, though, or that he might share some insight into the higher abilities of his kin.

With a jolt, I remembered my intended outing with the Silver that very night, and felt a dash of disappointment. At least languishing in prison was a valid reason for standing him up.

There were more questions from there, about the artifact, its recovery, Mr. Stoke and myself. We took our leave of the body and briefly retired to the detective's office, where I answered his queries as best I could without admitting to any crimes, namely smuggling the artifact into Harrow, and tried to quell the storm of questions in the back of my own mind.

At length, Supford said, "I believe we are finished, Miss Rushforth. However, I should warn you. I have notified the Guild of your arrest. I had no choice. Not only is it procedure, but it was only a matter of time until they learned the truth. Your landlady did not strike me as the kind to keep quiet, nor shy away from listening at a keyhole."

"No," I agreed. I should have felt more fear, I supposed, more desperation, but I had begun to numb. "Is the Guild sending someone to retrieve me?"

"They may try. But I will not relinquish you easily. If you are a suspect in a murder, you are mine and will not leave this station." Supford, to my surprise, spoke the words with surprising gentleness.

I met his eyes, wary of a trap. I knew, in theory, that not every power in this city despised my kind as much as Baffin, and Supford had been an acquaintance of the moderate Mr. Stoke. But what were the chances that he was truly sympathetic to my plight?

There was sincerity in his eyes, however, just awkward enough to lend it legitimacy.

I gave a small, grateful nod.

Mr. Wake, at least, could not reach me in a cell.

I paced my cell as darkness fell, sending twilight creeping through my window to awaken my threads. I unbuttoned my collar and trailed my fingers over my skin, feeling the threads like gilding.

My hand stilled as footsteps approached and a key turned in the lock.

A woman entered my cell, her masses of blonde curls pinned up around a square face. She wore no hat and her fine, waist-length jacket partially concealed the intricately embroidered bodice of what could only be an opera gown. Her throat was bare, as was a fair portion of her chest.

"Ottilie," she said.

"Madge," I replied. I caught sight of a man behind her in the hallway; the same one who had been on her arm by the river. His salt-and-pepper hair was perfectly parted and his eyes, though aloof, were not as cold as Madge's. "Is this your husband? I assumed he would be younger, given the sum of your progeny. Perhaps what he lacks in vigor he makes up for in industry?"

The man was half-concealed by the shadows, but I still saw his posture shift and his jaw flex. Good. My barb had landed.

Madge's icy-blue eyes travelled across my frame. "He is my second husband, Everard Moran."

"The first had served his purpose?"

"He was assigned to another woman." However Madge felt about that, she did not let it show. It was entirely possible, given the icy condition of her heart, that she truly did not care.

"Why?"

"Your sister has proven herself too valuable for the likes of him," Madge's husband replied. His voice was surprisingly warm, rumbling in a pleasant, masculine way. His gaze, now firmly upon me, was intent. I felt knowledge in that gaze. It was a familiar thing, the way so many elder, elevated Entwined considered the young.

Knowledge of me. Knowledge of my past. Certainty of my future.

It stoked a fire of resentment in my chest.

"Margaret, may we proceed?" he asked my sister.

Madge nodded and swivelled her midwinter gaze back to me. "We are securing your release. The constabulary is protesting, but they will be overruled."

"I see. Shall I prepare myself for a Glass Coffin?"

Madge's chin rose slightly, her gaze becoming even more imperious. "No sister of mine will die beneath the glass."

"Emeline did."

"She was not my sister."

"She might as well have been."

"Margaret," the older man, Moran, spoke up again. "I will make the arrangements, unless you require me?"

"I have matters in hand," Madge said dismissively.

The man turned on his heel and left without another word. With his every step, my dread compounded. Supford had promised to keep the Guild from taking me, but neither Madge nor her new husband seemed even slightly concerned.

Madge waited until the gate at the end of the hall clanged before she turned back on me. "What were you thinking?"

"Pardon? You will have to be more specific."

"Associating with Pretoria," she hissed. Only that drop in her voice and the barest hunch of her shoulders hinted at any emotion. "She's been seen in the city, Ottilie. I know you to be malleable, but I never thought you would be so foolish as to continue associating with her."

The need to defend myself stirred. As entrenched as Madge was in the Guild, as different as we were, she was still my eldest sister.

"I am neither malleable nor foolish, and I am not associating with Pretoria," I stated. "Despite her efforts. She came to attempt to persuade me to her cause, as you are right now."

"Her cause? The cause of theft and villainy?"

I shut my mouth, but my expression was likely answer enough.

Madge raised her chin. "Ottilie. The Grand General is manipulating the Zealots, and is intent on destroying the Entwined, even if he must tear this city apart to do it. He will turn everyone, from grandmothers to schoolchildren, against us."

Harden had said the same thing. My skin prickled, gooseflesh brushing across my upper arms.

"You know it for a fact?" I asked. "You have evidence?"

Madge nodded grimly. "You are in danger, Ottilie, and too valuable to lose to this wretched city. Come to the Guild willingly, and you will want for nothing. You may have your choice of husbands. I know you care for Lewis and he has waited for your return, but there are better men."

"A gilded cage is still a cage," I said quietly.

"You know nothing of cages," my sister replied, the impassiveness of her tone more chilling than any malice. "We will take you back to Golden House tonight, regardless of what you desire. So let me help you. You know what will happen if you continue to resist the Guild."

Golden House. The Guild's headquarters within Harrow.

I said through gritted teeth, "Forced pregnancy, stolen children, a Glass Coffin. Yes, I am aware. But I am unclear what your help is worth. When have you ever tried to help *me*, truly?"

"That is Pretoria talking, not you." Madge stepped closer, the fine beadwork on her gown glittering, white and cream backed by the palest, powdery violet. She was a winter dawn, still cast in shadows of night. "After seeing what the Zealots are doing to this city, can you not understand why the Guild matters? How being a Guild mage would benefit you? I offer you a life free of fear. A life where you will need never hide your face, your threads, or your name. You can be Ottilie Rushforth; you can step into a position of power."

"What Entwined can kill," I asked, voice still low, "with the touch of a hand?"

Madge's eyes flashed, caged and perplexed, but before she could reply, the gate clanged and several sets of footsteps came towards us.

The constable I had met earlier, Hopgood, looked at me with grim, apologetic eyes as he unlocked the door and stepped aside.

Madge and her husband stood side by side in the passage now. The door of my cell was open, but my only path forward was into my sister's pale, cold, outstretched hand.

"Come, dear sister," Madge said. "You are safe, now."

A Note Upon: The Entwined of the Sun

The Entwined of the Sun fall into the following classes of mage: Gold (Glim), Copper, and Bronze. These are the most devious and misleading classes of Entwined, leaning towards proficiency in the arts, exuding charm and charisma that may lead the most Vigilant Lady astray.

From The Vigilant Lady Traveller:
A Gentlewoman's Guide to the World

CHAPTER 17

A Note to the Reader:
In Which I Take Flight

I escaped the Guild on a humid summer night, seven months after Lewis's and my engagement. He was the instrument of my freedom, for in his company I was permitted to leave the Guild's fortress at Kesterlee and indulge in a supposedly romantic evening at the theater in Harrow city. This, I later understood, was part of Pretoria's grand scheme for my liberation.

I use the words 'escape' and 'liberation'—let the reader not be misled. I was entirely unaware of the events that would unfold that night. As such, kidnapping is a more precise term.

Lewis did not seem himself that night. We had rarely seen one another since we were engaged, though we both lived at Kesterlee. The fortress is something of a miniature kingdom, a small town in which several hundred mages lodged and worked, waited upon by human and Affinate servants. But we had our occupations, and Lewis was frequently travelling.

At that point he served as a Bronze Scribe for the Mage Regal—the Guild's chief council member in residence. I assisted in the Guild's extensive archives, as Eventide mages often do, with the end goal of becoming an Archivist. These placements enabled us to be, generally, closer together in the interim between engagement and marriage, which the Guild considered profitable.

I am straying from the point, however. On to my kidnapping/liberation.

Lewis was not himself that night. He sat in silence across from me as our carriage cut across the mist-strewn hills and twilight settled in. The trees and earth and rock were still hot from the heat of the day, but the breeze off the distant sea was cool.

Unfortunately, we received little of it. The carriage itself was stuffy and smelled of old perfume. I leaned forward to open the little window and the twilight spilled across my throat, exposed collarbones, and a rather generous—and intentional—expanse of bosom. My threads ignited, twining across my skin in a pleasant prickling.

I felt his eyes on me. I sat back and met his gaze with a half-smile. "Are you well?"

I had hoped to catch admiration in his eyes, but his focus was on my threads, and was sadly clinical. He raised his attention to my face. "I am, only distracted. My apologies. How are you, Ottilie?"

"Well enough," I said. "Where were you and the Mage Regal, these last few weeks? Can you say?"

"Harrow." Lewis settled back into his bench a little, though his posture was still immaculate. He looked very fine in his dress uniform, with its Guild bars. "I was approached by Major Barristan about a new position, abroad."

I could not conceal my unhappy surprise. "Abroad? Abroad where? Why would he ask you that now?"

"He was unclear, but it would be some years away. Time enough for my current duties." He smiled a little to soften the practicality of that description, which obviously included me, our pending marriage, and expected attempts at cultivating magelings.

I was grateful I did not blush. We spoke often enough on the topic.

"Is it a position you would enjoy?"

He nodded. "I would. Very much. It would involve a great deal of travel. I would see the world, and be out from under the Guild's thumb."

Lewis, despite his connections to the Rogue Pretoria, rarely spoke of the Guild with any negativity. From him, this phrasing was tantamount to revolt.

I was happy to hear it. My adverse feelings towards the Guild were strong, but there were times I feared Lewis was too comfortable at Kesterlee.

"Is this a position I could accompany you to?" I asked. "If I am not with child. If we... reach that juncture."

Something different entered his expression. I might have called it pity, or concern, but Lewis was not an easy man to read.

We both jostled in our seats as the carriage went over a bump in the road. There was a crack, and a shouted curse from our driver.

Lewis, rather than look startled, let out a long breath.

The carriage stopped, and dread crept up my spine.

"Lewis?" I asked lowly.

He cleared his throat, opened his mouth to say something, then seemed to give up. "I was not opposed to our future, if that was within Guild walls," he said, instead. "We would have made a good go of things, I am sure. I hope we will meet again someday, Ottilie. Do not fear for me."

I gaped at him. "What?"

The carriage door opened. A rifle mouth appeared and levelled at Lewis, accompanied by an unfamiliar voice. "Out!"

Lewis gave me one last look, then complied. I stared at the empty doorway and the slice of misty forest night for an instant, then started to go after him.

Another figure climbed up into the carriage and sat across from me. In trousers, loose jacket, and a low cap, Pretoria's lean frame might have passed for a man from a distance, but up close there was no true disguise.

My sister tore off a false moustache with theatrical gusto and tossed it out the window. The carriage door closed as shouts and gunshots took over outside, and the carriage rattled back into movement.

"They will make a good show," she promised me, beaming. "Lewis will be under no suspicion. Hello, dear sister."

"You are taking me from the Guild," I surmised.

"I am. I promised to, eventually. Why, had you given up on me?"

Perhaps I had. I felt oddly dull at the realization. "You did, but I did not... I did not ask you to do this. Not now. I am not sure I am ready."

I am not ready to part with Lewis.

"You did not have to ask me," Pretoria replied with belligerent affection. "And we are never truly ready for the great leaps in life, we must simply close our eyes and take them. Tillie, I did not expect you to fling yourself on me in thanks, but you seem almost displeased."

"Is Lewis not coming?"

Evidently, that was not the question she expected. She furrowed her brows at me, then her brown eyes rounded in realization. "Oh dear. No, love, he is not. He did not... You two did not discuss this? He decided to stay."

I pinned my lips closed. A great wave of emotion, churning and complex, crashed over me, and I found myself unable to speak. The carriage rattled on and on, and Pretoria watched me with an elder sibling's insight, concern, and benevolent condescension.

"I did not expect it to happen like this," I said by way of explanation. I let out a heated breath. "I'm unsure what I want, just now."

"Then it is good I have decided for you," she stated with a shake of her head. "They have their claws in you, darling, but I shall pry them out."

I did not know what to say to this, still numbed with too much feeling, so I moved on. I sat a little straighter, pushed the final image of Lewis from my mind, and folded my hands in my lap, mirroring my sister across the carriage.

"Very well," I said. "Where are we going?"

A Note Upon: Golden Entwined

Golden Entwined, more commonly known as Glims, possess golden threads and uncanny abilities in the realms of art, whether that be painting, sculpting, or even the composition of music. The beauty of their works cannot be denied, however neither can their dangers. For to be painted, sculpted, or otherwise have one's likeness captured by a Glim is to be robbed of a piece of one's self—an emotion, a memory, a fraction of soul. To listen to their music is to expose oneself to their influence and seduction, as one must be cautious of any written word penned by a Bronze.

There is danger in great beauty, especially in regards to a Golden Entwined.

From The Vigilant Lady Traveller:
A Gentlewoman's Guide to the World

CHAPTER 18

Present Day

Golden House was tucked between embassies of various nations, in the shadow of Baffin's glittering, jagged palace in New Harrow. Officially, however, it did not exist. It was on no maps and bore no sign, as stipulated by the Guild's temperamental concord with Baffin.

The house was not gold, at least not in terms of glittering ore or evident extravagance. The copper roof of fish-scale tiles had just begun to green with age and the building was cut off from the road by a tall iron fence, ornate and austere. Elements of New Harren architecture decorated its façade to a limited degree, enough to mark it, to sully the legacy of the Entwined, but not to lend any real beauty.

The grim effect was softened by moonflower ivy—a tactful and symbolic measure on behalf of the Guild gardeners, as moonflowers were an ancient symbol of the Entwined. The delicate, round white flowers bloomed in the autumn night, resilient to the cold, and lending a thin, sweet scent to the air. The scent was all memory—memory of the academy where I had spent so much of my youth, and of Kesterlee, where I had labored in the Guild Archives and begun to think of Lewis as more than an ally.

The guards at the gate—no doubt Silver Adepts—were mirrored on the opposite side of the street by a pair of Baffin's soldiers on permanent assignment. The Entwined guards opened the gate before Madge alighted from the carriage, and bowed as she and I took the short walk to the front stairs.

I did not bolt, however much I might have wanted to. Even without the watching Silver guards and their rifles, there was the looming threat of Madge at my side and Mr. Moran at my shoulder.

I knew I was caught. But that did not mean I could not escape, in due course.

Servants (Affinates of various affiliations) met us in the entryway. They took Madge's cloak and parasol and Mr. Moran's outer jacket, and vanished again at a wave of Madge's hand. They left us in the clock-ticking quiet of a sleeping house.

Where the façade of Golden House might not be noteworthy, the interior very much was. Out of view of Baffin's watching eyes, the Guild's full wealth was on display. The floors were delicately arranged parquet that resembled twining threads, glossy and dark and interspersed with lavish carpets. The walls were a veritable museum of treasures, displayed with calculated precision.

I had little doubt that the rooms beyond would be even more lavish. But every door was closed. To the left, to the right, down a short hallway, and up the long sweep of the staircase. Closed doors. Shuttered and curtained windows.

No way out.

Madge exchanged a quiet word with her husband, then led me up the stairs alone. We encountered several more servants, waistcoated or aproned. Every one turned to face the wall as we approached, doing their best to transform into inanimate objects, and did not move again until we were out of sight.

"A lively reception," I muttered. "Are there many mages present?"

"A great number," Madge said. "Come to deal with Baffin's increasing antagonism. But they are either out or abed at this hour, as we soon will be. Here. These will be your chambers."

She opened a door and turned the valve for the gaslamps. Their golden light swelled to reveal a comfortably appointed room, with thick carpets that begged for bare toes and a large bed with heavy drapes drawn back. The walls were a deep plum wallpaper printed with obscure gold motifs.

There were no windows.

Madge returned to the doorway. "This will be locked. There are no servants' doors or stairs in this room, so it will do no good to search for them. A Silver will be set on guard."

I registered each barrier and threat she listed, but held them at arm's length. After the shock of my arrest, of seeing Mr. Stoke's corpse and finally falling into the hands of the Guild, I was inured to further intimidation.

"Does it not say a great deal about the Guild," I observed, "that you have such rooms at the ready?"

Madge ignored me. "You cannot escape, and Pretoria certainly cannot reach you here. I urge you to reflect on your situation tonight, little sister, and make your peace with it. It is for the best."

I might have been inured to fear, but not to anger. It smoldered high in my throat at her words, her tone, her presumption. I wanted to snap at her that I was no child, that I was a grown woman with my own mind and a future that was not for her to conduct.

But she would not care. Already she was leaving, with a gentle, "I will see you in the morning."

She closed the door, leaving me in a beeswax and lavender-scented stillness, as the gaslamps flickered.

The bed was supremely comfortable. I resented this as I lay there the next morning, cushioned in quiet and shadows. The radiator hissed softly and somewhere beyond the walls, a light female voice laughed.

I tried to hold my mind still, suspended in that solitude, with my cares at a distance. It lasted only moments before I thought of Mr. Stoke, laid out upon the table with his face beaten in and a blackened mark over his heart. Lying as I did now, back flat, hands at my sides.

I sat up sharply. The bed creaked, the blankets rustled, and the door opened.

The mechanisms of the gaslamps clicked with a slow swell of orange light as Mr. Moran stepped in and closed the door.

I was out of bed in an instant. I was still mostly clothed, having slept in my underthings and a robe which I had found in the room, but I felt immediately exposed under his open, critical scrutiny. I felt at once measured and judged.

"What do you want?" I demanded.

"You asked Madge what Entwined can kill with the touch of a hand," he stated, unruffled by my intensity. "Why? What do you mean by that?"

I resisted the urge to wrap my robe tighter, holding his gaze. Did he truly not know? Had Supford not disclosed that detail of his investigation?

If so, I might have erred in voicing the question to Madge. But I had voiced it, and here I was closed in with a powerful Guild mage of unknown but undoubtedly significant power. I did not have much more to lose.

Might as well prod the bear.

"My friend was murdered. There was a mark over his heart, in the shape of a hand." I advanced a step towards him, showing him—and myself—that I was not afraid. "Supford suspected a powerful Silver had done it, but I have never heard of their Leeching being used to such an extent. Are you a Silver, Mr. Moran? It would surprise me, the Guild sullying my sister's fine blood with your common kind, even if you had such an ability."

I looked him up and down, appraising him as he had me. He remained in place, just inside the closed door. There was calculation in his face rather than offense, and a thread of suspicion.

I again felt the knowledge in his gaze, a sense that he knew far more about me, about my past, present, and future, than he had any right to.

"I am not," he replied. "I am Starlit, as your sister Pretoria is."

That took me aback, derailing my line of inquiry. Starlight

Entwined were as uncommon as Eventides like me. Now their pairing made more sense. It also increased my concern, as it meant that if Pretoria came to rescue me, there was someone here who could see through her magic.

Someone who could, very likely, stop her.

"How have I not met you before?" I asked compulsively. "Your accent is not Harren, but certainly Arrentian. Where have you been hiding?"

He held my gaze for one last moment, then said, "Your sister awaits you in the River Room," and left without another word.

In the ensuing quiet, I forced three slow breaths into my lungs, then tied my hair in a cursory knot atop my head and opened the door.

Mr. Moran was long gone, but a soldier watched me from across the hall. For the blink of an eye, I could almost have mistaken him for Lewis in his green and grey and stiff collar, but of course, this was not him.

"Take me to my sister," I said.

Madge was situated at an easel as I entered. My attempt at rudeness by wearing the robe was mitigated by the fact that she too had not dressed. But rather than look like a cat freshly shaken out of a bag, as I did, she looked disarming and gentled, with a silk and lace night gown barely covered by a heavily embroidered robe and her hair braided over one shoulder.

The soldier closed the door, but his footsteps did not depart.

I caught the flash of my own reflection in a mirror as I crossed the room. Madge was painting a self-portrait with its aid, poised with her brush in a pool of morning light. There were few details to the portrait yet, all broad strokes and suggestions of shapes, but it was already striking.

"Still indulging in bad habits, I see," I commented. There was a tray of coffee, toast, cheeses, and meats nearby, and I poured myself a cup of the dark liquid. "What tedious emotion are you killing today? Maternal affection? Common decency? Or is it a memory?"

"Nightmares," she said mildly.

I paused over my cup. Steam tickled my nose, thick with the scent of coffee. "Nightmares of what?"

She turned her steady gaze to me, and the piercing blue of her eyes looked more soulless than usual. But her threads, oh, her threads. Golden and lovely, they twined her throat and down her shoulders, spilled up over her jaw and crept out from her hair, across her temples. Her pale eyelashes were full of light, unlined and unaltered by cosmetics, and just barely pinked by lack of sleep.

"I no longer remember," she said, adding a shadow to her portrait. "It is already gone."

There was a stretch of quiet, interrupted only by the passage of her brush. I cleared my throat. "Your husband came to visit me. He questioned me on the manner of Mr. Stoke's death. I suspect he knows who may have done it. Do you?"

"Mr. Moran and I keep our work separate, as much as we may," she replied, focused on her portrait. "It is more congenial to the marital state."

"A marital state which the Guild hopes to produce more Starlight Entwined."

"Yes. Mother's bloodline produced Pretoria. With Moran, I stand a good chance of doing so as well."

I swallowed a knot of revulsion, not only at the thought of my sister and Moran's endeavors in conception, but at her impassivity to it all.

"What is his work?" I asked, redirecting.

"Influence," she replied. "For instance, today he and several others are meeting the Grand General to discuss his intention of ousting the Guild from Harrow, followed by the systematic expulsion and eradication of our kind from the entirety of Arrent."

She spoke this mildly, but each word was pointed.

"He cannot oust the Guild completely," I replied. "Madge, if you know something about Mr. Stoke's death, if a Guild mage was involved—"

"Why would they be?" she asked coolly. "And Baffin *can* evict us, if Incarnadine and the Zealots have turned the entirety of the city against us. I outlined this for you last night.

If he is successful, Baffin will be the hero once more, saving a desperate Harrow from the poison of the Entwined. Bring me coffee?"

I looked from her to the tray, to the ornate pot. Deciding against petty refusal, I poured her a cup and brought it to the small table beside her easel.

"Mr. Moran will return from his meeting in the next few hours," she said, sipping the coffee and giving me a passing, soulless smile of thanks. "I will inquire about your murderous mark and possible culprits, as a sign of my affection for you."

Affection. The word felt like a wound.

"But why would someone want to murder your employer?" she went on. "Who did he cross?"

It seemed Supford *had* kept his cards close to his chest, and not informed the Guild of the artifact and Lord Stillwell.

That was all very good. I hardly needed the Guild catching wind of the artifact and further muddying the waters.

The thought was a brief one, but it resonated through me, digging in and making space for itself between grief for Mr. Stoke and fear for myself.

I quietened. The Guild certainly would have a vested interest in the artifact and in stopping Baffin's research, and perhaps, in that, I had found a way to assuage the whisper of guilt inside me. A way to shirk that pesky weight of responsibility.

Of course, a selfish part of me affirmed, *this is not about heroics and the greater good for you, is it? It's about money. That ship. The horizon.*

Mr. Stoke was dead, as painful as that was. But if I found the artifact, I could still deliver it to Stillwell. I could still get paid and be rid of Wake. If I kept Mr. Stoke's portion of the fee for myself, Lewis and I might still be able to afford our new identities and lives—if only just.

Then I could alert the Guild to the dangers of the artifact. They would claim it from Stillwell and stop Baffin, all while I sailed away and... forgot. Forgot Mr. Stoke and the murderous mark. Forgot Harrow.

It was a good plan, if I did not look at it too closely,

and ignored the complex tangle of my emotions. And an intrusive memory of kissing Harden in a darkened doorway.

I realized the room was very quiet and Madge was studying me.

"You have gotten yourself into trouble," she observed, brush poised.

"You found me in prison," I replied, reflecting her own icy exterior back to her.

"Why, *were* you the cause of his death?" She asked the question so calmly, so easily—as if this were plausible and perhaps even a little expected.

"No." I recoiled.

"Hm," she murmured. She slowly took another sip of her coffee, cleaned her brush in a teacup of water, and tapped it out on the leg of her easel before mixing a new shade. She glanced at her reflection in the mirror and went back to work. "Well, whatever you are hiding, I'm sure it will come to light. If it is relevant. You, however, may ask me whatever you wish. I will hide nothing from you."

I suppressed a snort and sat down in a chair of my own. I forced myself to sit back, presenting a posture of ease and relaxation that I did not feel. I had more questions of course, about Silvers and possible avenues of escape, but suspected that even skirting such topics would not get me far.

So I turned my focus to Madge. To the woman. To my sister.

"How are your children?"

"Well."

"How many are there now?"

"Five," she replied. "Willhelm, the eldest, has proved himself to have an exceptional mind. Minerva, my second, is diligent in her studies but distractable. She is too active. Her threads twine towards painting, as mine, but she lacks the patience. I have suggested she be applied to sculpting, so she might work with her hands until maturity calms her."

I forgot to drink my coffee, watching Madge over the rim. She spoke of her children with pride, but there was a distance to it. She had always been cold, but now she struck me almost as a caricature of herself. Of who she had once been.

I flicked a glance at the painting.

"Ophelia and Imogen, my third and fourth, have presented Glim threads, naturally, but are too young to do much of note. Their nannies say, however, that they are both observant creatures, which is promising."

"You have not seen this yourself?"

"I have been elsewhere."

"Ah. Where is the fifth?"

"With Ophelia and Imogen. The infant was born this summer and has yet to show threads, but between my blood and Everard's, I've little doubt she will be noteworthy. A Starlight."

I blinked from my sister's face to her stomach, and back to her face. "You've left her already?"

"The situation in Harrow is too serious for maternal indulgences," Madge replied. "Her wetnurse is exemplary, what other use is there in my presence?"

I found I had nothing to say to that, because the answer was too vast, too intimate. My chest ached and my head filled with the recollection of how my mother had wept at Madge's departure, all those years ago. How stricken she had been at Pretoria's. And how, by mine, she had simply watched from the window, dull-eyed and distant.

Madge continued to paint.

"What is her name?"

"Who?"

"Your baby."

"Oh. Venecia."

I thought of the tiny child, this niece who would live out her days with only marginal connection to the woman who bore her, and felt my heart rupture anew. I could almost feel her in my arms, small and helpless, and resolved once more that I would not give the Guild the chance to do to me what they had to my mother—and to Madge.

"When was the last time you saw our mother?" I asked, attempting to hold my own emotions in check.

Madge's brows contracted, ever so slightly, in thought. Or consternation. "I do not recall."

"You painted it away," I accused.

She shrugged. "Perhaps."

We fell silent, after that. I set my coffee aside, and simply watched my sister finish her painting. She sat back as her threads quietened, smiling with professional satisfaction at the portrait before her.

It was exquisite, incomparably lifelike but still signature, edged with Madge's soft, haloed style. She had captured herself perfectly, every illuminated strand of hair and the fall of every shadow. The only thing that differed from life were her eyes.

The eyes of the portrait were emotive, full of lament, and a lingering ghost of fear.

Nightmares, Madge had said. What did she fear, in the dark of the night? Whatever it was, it was trapped within oil, pigment, and canvas now, and there it would remain until circumstance—time, intention, or accident—destroyed the painting.

"Now," Madge said, turning to me. "Is there anything you would like me to paint away?"

"No," I snapped.

She looked startled by my response. "You sound as if I offered to torture you."

"You do not paint Pretoria and I," I stated. "You promised Mother that. You promised us."

From Madge's expression, she had disremembered that. "Ah. Yes. Well." She glanced down at herself as if she had also forgotten her state of dress. "Time to prepare for the day. Shall I do your hair?"

I consented to dress in borrowed clothing and arrange my own hair, if only to distract from Madge's terrible suggestion and arm myself with several more layers of fabric. I now regretted my refusal to dress earlier. I felt exposed in a way I should not have before my own flesh and blood as I donned Madge's plainest ensemble, a pale blue skirt with a shirtwaist of exceptional quality and a matching jacket.

It was a strange prison, this lovely room with the quiet company of my soulless sister, but it was a prison indeed.

I had just finished pinning my hair around a form when Mr. Moran entered. As he had with my chamber, he did not knock, but simply appeared.

This time, however, he did not close the door at his back.

"Everard," Madge greeted him.

"Margaret. We must speak privately." He gave me a pointed look and nodded to the hallway. "You will be escorted back to your room, Miss Rushforth."

Madge paused, but whatever she wanted to say, she chose not to do so in front of me.

My gaze drifted back to Madge's portrait, then to my sister herself. I nodded slowly, murmured a lackluster farewell, and left the room.

As I was escorted back to my chamber, I turned over Madge's offer. My sister had painted away so much of herself. I almost envied that, just then. I wished I could forget Mr. Stoke and his horrific, butchered face. I wished I could give away the unrequited affection I harbored for Lewis, and perhaps even my attraction to Harden. I wished I could evict the thread of responsibility that tied me to the artifact and Baffin's research.

Still, I would not submit to Madge's brush, not willingly. Yet I understood that willingness might no longer matter. A childhood promise not to paint me, not to manipulate me in that way, might no longer hold now that I was back in the Guild's grasp and Madge had so... changed.

I would not be the first malcontented mage to find their rebelliousness culled by a Glim's brush. The method was imperfect, but it struck me now that Madge's portrait itself was a statement: a lovely, beautiful warning.

At what point would her offer turn to a threat?

I saw Mr. Stoke's face in a flash of grief and guilt, and closed my eyes for half a breath.

I had to stay focused. Find the artifact. Claim the reward. Meet Lewis.

Escape.

CHAPTER 19

Madge came to me sometime later. There were no clocks, and no windows to see the sun by, but I felt the passage of time in the emptiness of my stomach.

"Come with me," she said, and led me downstairs with a Silver mage at our heels. She said no more, and try as I might I could not read any clues from the perfect lines of her posture and her lovely, caged face.

Down the stairs. Across the foyer. I felt a shock of trepidation, then a shudder of confused hope as a servant opened the door and we swept outside.

That hope surged as I saw a carriage waiting at the gate. The city was calm in the dusky half light and my threads openly twined, creeping above my collar and over my jaw and temples.

"I am sending you to Kesterlee," Madge said, gesturing me towards the carriage. "Matters in Harrow are growing increasingly unpredictable, and there is no need for you to remain. These mages will ensure your safety on the road."

I noted several Silver mages standing beside the carriage in fine but practical travelling clothes. They would present a challenge, but I could not have hoped for less.

Kesterlee was a long journey, a day and a night. We would need to stop to rest, to at least change the horses.

There would be a chance to escape. Or to be rescued.

But Madge had to know that. So why was she taking this risk? Was it truly to keep me safe, or simply to have me out of the way?

I eyed her. "Why are you doing this?"

She looked down her nose at me, white lashes thick around her blue eyes. "Pardon me?"

"What has changed?" I asked.

She glanced from me to the waiting mages. That was her only movement, other than a twitch of her hand. Her hand that bore her wedding ring.

It might mean nothing, but I remembered how Moran had looked at me that morning—the interest, the appraisal—and instinct whispered a fresh warning in my ear.

"Be safe and well." Madge produced a smile. It was a strange, unhealthy thing, a studied turn of lips, like a puppet. "I am glad to have you back, Ottilie."

I could not force a smile in return, no matter how hard I tried. So I simply stepped up into the carriage. "Goodbye, Madge."

"Goodbye, Tillie."

I sat back in the coach, letting the shadows inside hide my face and calm my threads. One of my handlers climbed in across from me, the door clicked shut, and the carriage began to move.

I did not look back at Madge, or wave goodbye. I could not. The shutters on the carriage windows were closed.

I allowed a span of time to pass as I corralled my thoughts and worries. It was easier, now that I was on my own again, away from Madge and the Golden House. Whatever had spurred the sudden change of plans, I was away from it. I had eaten, slept, and washed, and the heels on my boots were hard enough to crack a skull.

It was time to escape.

We trundled away from Golden House. I noted each jostle and turn, marked our speed, and bided my time.

My escort, meanwhile, adjusted the tight fabric of his trousers across muscular thighs, sucked his teeth, and settled back with spread knees, pistol glinting under one arm. He was perhaps forty, with short hair neatly parted in the usual style.

He met my gaze with a squint. "Do not do it."

"Pardon me?" I asked, feigning affront.

"Make an attempt for my pistol," he said. "I am a Silver. I will subdue you."

I held out an ungloved hand. "Can you do it anyway? It seems unconsciousness would be preferable to your company."

He scowled, reached into his pocket, and produced a pipe. He lit it with the click of a lighter, momentarily filling the carriage with a wavering warm, orange light. Then he blew a long stream of smoke into my face.

I screwed up my nose and fought not to cough. I reached to open the window.

He lifted a foot, of all things, and planted it over the latch. He continued to survey me from this lounging position, puffing and waiting. The smoke thickened.

I leaned back, eyebrows high. "You are no gentleman."

"Mr. Moran doesn't like gentlemen," my escort said. "Too many scruples for his line of work."

"I see." I watched him. "What is his line of work?"

"Wouldn't you like to know," he leered.

I considered pressing the topic, but escape felt more relevant at that point. My internal clock was ticking. "What is your name?"

"Howell."

"Well, Mr. Howell, I wish I could say I am sorry, but I find I am not."

His gaze narrowed.

"You should have been better informed before taking this assignment," I said, and, rocking back on the seat, kicked him with both booted heels. Between his legs.

He curled up like a squished spider, limbs coiling, head bowing. His pipe dropped. He hardly made a sound, just a long, thin wheeze.

I lunged across the carriage, snatching up his falling pipe by the bit. Reaching around him, I grabbed his pistol. Naturally, he tried to stop me. It was a valiant effort, considering how direct my kick had been. I did not allow him to touch my skin—my neck, my face. I flicked the burning ash into his eyes and stuffed the bowl of the pipe into his mouth. He spasmed, wailing and choking breathlessly.

The carriage door was locked from the outside, unsurprisingly. But the window was less secure. I smashed the shutters open with an elbow.

So it came to pass that as the carriage trundled through the darkened streets of Harrow, I squeezed out the window and fell flat onto my back on the cobblestones.

I had no time to be winded. In a flash, I saw the carriage wheels trundling right towards my temples. I rolled.

Another figure landed next to me, bellowing for the carriage to stop—a second mage, apparently having been riding with the driver—while a third leapt off the back of the contraption. She landed practically on top of me, only to stumble backwards as the horn of a motor car blared.

I took half a second to check my surroundings. We were still in New Harrow, heading west. The last of the sun had descended over a skyline of roofs, chimneys, and smoke ahead of us, while to the east the Grand General's crystalline palace glittered on its hill, overlooking all. It looked bloodied and bruised, in the last of the setting sun. A knife covered with gore.

The blare of a horn snapped me back to myself. I located my feet just as the mage who had been with the carriage driver made a grab for my arm.

His hand did not land. I danced aside and shot him in the knee, turned, and did the same to the second mage, the one who had been on the back of the carriage. I blinked rapidly then—a quick snap of eyelashes as I processed what I had done. Brutal. Efficient.

Just as the Guild had taught me to be.

I threw the pistol aside with a curse and bolted into the evening crowd.

A NOTE UPON: AFFINATES

Entwined Affinates, while they possess no willful magic, still keep the tendencies of their class and with them, the dangers. A Silver Affinate might enjoy notable physical strength. A Starlight Affinate's innate sense of time may result in an admirable punctuality, but also acute awareness of their surroundings. A Copper Affinate may be particularly disarming, charismatic, and charming— and manipulative.

Do not be taken in, dear lady.

FROM THE VIGILANT LADY TRAVELLER:
A GENTLEWOMAN'S GUIDE TO THE WORLD

CHAPTER 20

My first destination was Old Harrow, with its warren-like streets and convenient shadows. I approached Pointer's Bridge, my steps swift and my gaze vigilant.

Just as I reached the entrance to the bridge, I saw a carriage clatter up. The driver had barely reined in the nervous horses before my escort, Howell, stepped out onto the sidewalk. His movements were slow but deadly with rage and intent. The light of a streetlamp washed over him as his gaze swivelled, through some preternatural sense, right to me.

"Silvers," I cursed under my breath, and bolted onto the bridge.

More carriages passed, wheels clattering, hooves flashing. Prettily dressed couples strode arm in arm. A motor car coughed exhaust into the breeze, gusting it right into my face.

Footsteps pounded at my back. I wove past a startled couple and hurtled over the crest of the bridge.

A horde of merry makers blocked my path. I diverted into the street.

A tram bell rang frantically. I looked up into the vehicle's glaring, orange lamps, and lunged back towards the sidewalk.

An arm laced around my waist.

My mind was still blinded by the streetcar, but my body knew what to do. I turned into the movement, grabbing my attacker's wrist and driving my shoulder right into his stomach. I charged, propelling him backwards into the bridge railing with a vengeful cry of exertion.

For half a second, we struggled against the rail. He was stronger, not simply because he was a large man but because of his innate Silver strength, and it took only that half second for him to spin us around, making to pin me against the rail instead, stomach first.

I let him. It was a risk—if he had found bare skin and Leeched me just then, it would all have been over. But I was dressed for the weather, every bit of skin covered, and he had only brute strength.

Strength which I turned against him. Surprise flashed through his eyes at my sudden lack of resistance, then all I saw of him was a blur of clothing as I took his weight by one arm, hinged forward and, in one great and glorious effort, hurled him over the railing and into the river.

I straightened, panting, swaying. My hat was askew and partially over my eyes, accompanied by a swoop of unpinned hair.

Belatedly, I heard the satisfying *splash* of Howell hitting the river. I cracked a breathless laugh.

"I say," a staring bystander said, gaping at me around his prodigious moustache. He had a bicycle beside him. "That was remarkable."

"Thank you," I panted. Shouts came from up the bridge now. Staring pedestrians parted with alacrity as two more Guild thugs stormed into sight.

Below, in the river, a furious bellow marked Howell's position.

I pushed my hat and hair out of my eyes and made for the moustached bystander. He recoiled as I gathered up my skirts, stuffed them into my sash, and mounted his bicycle without a word.

"Thank you," I puffed again, tearing my hat away. I bit the hatpin—now my only weapon—between my teeth and handed him the hat. "Reparations. Sell it," I explained around the pin, and escaped into the warren of Old Harrow.

I took a winding and perplexing route into Old Harrow, spent a good quarter hour stashed under a bridge watching for pursuers, then made my way to the hotel where Pretoria had taken up residence: Hotel Cherron. It was in the center of Old Harrow, its lintels and corners decorated with ethereal, windblown statues and its windows glistening with the light of gaslamps.

I hid my bicycle around the corner, shook out my skirts, then spun my windblown hair up and fixed it with the hatpin as I approached the doors. The valets looked at me oddly as I passed, but I was dressed well enough that they offered no protest, despite my flushed cheeks and lack of a hat.

I surveyed the lobby. It was, perhaps, too much to hope that Pretoria would be there at that very moment, in the splendid dining room to one side, or reclining on the many chairs situated between potted trees and orderly carts of luggage. Still, my heart sank a little at the unfamiliarity of the faces all around.

I was exhausted. My nerves were raw. I was also not entirely at peace with my coming here, but between the police, the Guild, and Mr. Wake, I doubted home or Mr. Stoke's office would provide any respite.

Besides, Pretoria had offered her help to find the artifact. It was about time I accepted.

I strode up to the woman at the counter and cited the false name Pretoria had given me at the museum. "Please inform Victoria Russel I am here."

A few moments later, I stood before a lavishly carved door on the hotel's top floor. The bellboy who had accompanied me knocked, then stepped aside with a bow.

There was a moment of quiet beyond the door, then a brush of wood—an eye at the keyhole, I sensed. I gave the little glass orb a pointed look, brow arched, trying to hide my weariness.

The door opened and Pretoria stood before me in a skirt and an exceptionally ruffled blouse.

"Stop staring at my bosom," she scolded me.

The bellboy went scarlet and promptly dismissed himself.

"That blouse is... voluminous," I observed. "Trying to make up for something?"

Pretoria grabbed me by the arm and tugged me into the room. "I searched the entire city for you," she said, locking the door and delivering me an accusing look. "Until I heard the newsboys shouting. You're in the damned papers, Tillie. '*Rogue Adept arrested for murder of Harren War Hero*'."

I paled, more at the reminder of Mr. Stoke than the distortion of the truth.

"*Then*," Pretoria went on. "I go to break you out of prison and find you taken by the Guild. *Then* I go to Golden House, and find you had already been shipped north!"

"I escaped at that juncture," I said, gesturing at myself and my obvious presence in the room. I furrowed my brows, looking from her to the room itself. There were a jacket and hat on the large bed, set out next to a fine little revolver and a parasol with an oddly shaped handle. There was masculine clothing, too: a tweed waistcoat and jacket cast over the opposite side of the bed, along with a fashionable walking stick and bowler hat.

I heard muffled movement and a splash, and noted a closed door. There was another person here, in the washroom.

My nerves jangled.

"Who is that? Your husband, or a paramour?" I asked, but the inquiry was factual, without judgement or vitriol. I couldn't summon either.

"My husband." Pretoria rubbed at her neck, her façade of irritability falling away as she took me in. A haunted quality entered her eyes and, for all her bravery, wit, and gusto, I saw the harried woman beneath. The fretful sister. "Ottilie... I am so sorry. Your Mr. Stoke. Your arrest. Madge..."

I stood poised, so still I began to tremble. Memories of Mr. Stoke assailed me once more, interspersed with flickers of Madge's face, painting in golden light. Mr. Moran, standing between me and a closed door. Howell, leering across the carriage. Mr. Wake, waiting in the darkness of Stoke's office.

On sudden, overwhelmed impulse, I closed the distance between us and embraced my sister.

There was a certain stiffness to the gesture, an unfamiliarity that faded as she let out a long breath next to my ear and clasped her hands behind my back. She set her forehead on my shoulder and for a lengthy while, we did not speak.

"I escaped," I reassured her, voice muffled. "Madge could not keep me. They could not."

"Of course they could not," she said, but she sounded as though she were reassuring herself.

"But it was horrible," I confessed. "She is horrible. She is... There is so little of her left, Pretoria."

She held me tighter and I battled within myself, summoning and casting aside a dozen things I might have said.

"I deponticated one of their thugs," I offered finally, permitting myself a brush of smugness at the memory. "Right off Pointer's Bridge."

"Of course you did," she said, gave me one last squeeze, and stepped back. She flicked a few stray hairs from her face, took my cheeks in her hands, and kissed my forehead.

Something very painful happened inside my chest. I was saved from her seeing whatever pathetic facial expression accompanied that feeling as she glanced at the bed full of weapons and clothing. "I suppose I won't be needing these. So long as you are sure you were not followed?"

"I am sure."

"Good, then shall I order dinner?"

"Yes." I nodded emphatically. "Then, we need to talk."

She eyed me at that, but nodded. "Perry!"

The washroom door opened and a young man appeared. His mop of black hair was damp and the towel about his hips cursory, flashing a good deal of thigh. His eyes were long, pointing to partial Ondi heritage, and his pale skin was smooth, unmarked and unbearded. He was tall, too, with an athletic physique. He was, in short, precisely Pretoria's type, as far as men went.

But, in the predictability of his appearance, he was also not what I anticipated. Pretoria had lovers. Pretoria had intimate friends. But Pretoria had never expressed an interest in marriage, let alone to a presumably Entwined man. That union was precisely what the Guild would have wanted, and for that reason, it was suspicious to the highest degree.

"Oh," Perry said in mild startlement. "Who are you?"

"Ottilie," I replied. "Your sister-in-law."

He looked suddenly self-conscious and glanced down, ensuring his towel was closed. It was not. "I see. A moment?"

He vanished back into the bathroom and Pretoria pointed me towards a seating area near the tall windows. "Make yourself comfortable. I will order us some dinner, then we shall conspire."

I settled myself in a comfortable chair and stared out at the sleeping city. Meanwhile, Pretoria summoned a maid to order dinner, then vanished into the bathroom to converse quietly with Perry.

I watched a paperboy on a street corner, hawking the last of his newsheets.

"Grand General Baffin summons Cabinet to emergency meeting! *Harrow Herald* speculates!" The voice was muffled through the glass. "Baffin calls emergency meeting in wake of Separatist bombing! Sorcerers return to Unified Council!"

"Quite the state this city is falling into," Pretoria said, sitting down across from me. Perry came too, his hair neatly parted and combed and his tall frame clad in trousers, shirt, and suspenders. "Are you ready to let me sweep you away now?"

"Not quite," I replied, sitting back and looking between the two of them. "First, I need your help."

I outlined the situation for my sister in broad strokes. Mr. Stoke had been killed, presumably by a very powerful Silver mage. Mr. Moran, I suspected, knew something of it. Madge was even more soulless than we anticipated. I was still hunted, presumably, by Lord Stillwell's thug, Wake, and of course the Guild. I could well imagine a bedraggled Howell stalking the streets as we spoke.

"It sounds as though we ought to leave immediately," Perry surmised.

We were eating now, feasting off an excessive array of hors d'oeuvres which Pretoria considered a meal. The food was a temporary distraction from my increasing fatigue, and I poured myself a coffee to stave off unconsciousness.

"No," I said. "I intend to find the artifact first. Stillwell offered a great deal of money for its return, and I need those funds to replace my savings, which the police confiscated. I also would very much like to know who killed Mr. Stoke. But I understand that may be impossible."

"It may. But, Tillie, I have funds," Pretoria said. "Let me take care of you. I can break into the station, too."

That was an idea for a later time, but I still needed Stillwell's money to buy my future.

"He offered five thousand Harren marks," I stated, flint-eyed.

Pretoria and Perry both went still. After a heartbeat of processing this information, they glanced from one another, and back to me.

"Where should we begin our search?" Pretoria asked.

And just like that, I had two accomplices. Accomplices I intended to leave behind, but accomplices, nonetheless.

I did not let myself think of Pretoria's embrace, and how warm, how like *home* it had felt.

"Our first line of inquiry is thus," I summarized. "We must interview Lord Stillwell, who contracted Mr. Stoke to find the artifact to begin with. He may have more information, particularly on other parties who might be after the artifact. He also has the power and finances to, perhaps, hire a Rogue mage like the one who attacked... killed Mr. Stoke. Perry, what class are you?"

"Copper Affinate," Perry replied without inflection.

I could not suppress a startled glance between the two of them. "You... are not an Adept?"

"Try not to look so astonished." Perry conjured a winsome smile. "I won your sister despite my inadequacies."

"I am sure you are more than capable," I reassured, though in truth, I was unsettled. Here, I suspected I had found Pretoria's motivation, the blush of rebellion that had taken this man from lover to spouse.

An Adept entering into an official relationship with an

Affinate was, in some ways, more appalling to the Guild than if she had taken on a human. He was the most useless of our kind, the weakest. He was their shame and their failure.

So she had married him.

I looked between the two of them, particularly the soft-eyed way Perry beheld my sister, and hoped I was wrong.

"Lord Stillwell," Pretoria redirected us. "Do we know where he is?"

"The Stillwell ancestral home is out in Bellundin," I said. "A full day away by train."

"The trains are not running," Perry said, crossing one ankle over the opposite knee and leaning back. "Nor are the ships."

I stared. "Baffin has shut them down?"

"In fear of Separatist bombings, ostensibly," Pretoria said. "The roads are still open."

"Yes, but let us consider Stillwell's position," Perry cautioned, gathering the pair of us with a gesture. There was a spark of arrogance in him then that I did not precisely like. "After losing Sarre Grand to the Seaussen and the rebels, he is battling to regain his power and influence. Baffin has called a meeting of the Council of Lords—this will give him ample opportunity to do so."

"He will be in Harrow," I concluded, remembering the newsboy's shout earlier. "And he will be in the thick of things. But he does not have a house in town, unless he has rented one. Or perhaps he is at one of the upper hotels?"

"He should not be hard to find," Perry said. "Allow me to do so. I can begin this evening—everyone who is anyone will be about. There is no chance of him recognizing me, and I may be able to learn something without showing our hand. And, forgive me, Ottilie, but you look exhausted."

I rubbed at my forehead. "You are not wrong."

"Then rest, and after we can go together. In disguise," Pretoria suggested.

I considered her dubiously. "Last time I allowed you to 'disguise' me, I could not remove my moustache for a week."

"I have found a better glue, dear."

I returned my attention to Perry, who watched our exchange with patient expectation. It crossed my mind that I was granting him a great deal of trust after a very short acquaintance, but he seemed competent. And if Pretoria trusted him to pursue my best interests—and a great deal of money—I had to, too.

"All right. Perry, please see if you can learn where he is staying," I said. "And we can visit him together under cover of darkness, once I am capable of standing again."

"Is that the entirety of our plan?" Pretoria asked. "There is nothing else you wish to tell us?"

I thought of Dr. Maddeson. I ought to at least check in on the philologist—given his obsession with the artifact and its connection to Baffin, he might have learned something new.

But that would bring Pretoria close to his research and its possible value, and I was not sure I wanted to expose my sister to such an interesting quandary just yet.

Not until I was wholly sure I could trust her.

"First, I fear I must sleep," I admitted. "But then... ah, I must retrieve my cat."

CHAPTER 21

Hieronymus was not my only reason for returning to my apartments. I had to retrieve my possessions, both of monetary and sentimental value. I felt the urge to explain this to Pretoria as we traversed the circumference of Old Harrow the next morning, buffeted by a frigid autumn wind off the river. Boats swept by, carriages and motor cars trundled past, chased by the pinging of an impatient streetcar. Fallen leaves from the boulevard trees scudded ahead, rasping and whispering on the stones.

Pretoria pulled my arm through hers, both clad in warm, fine wool—hers a rich burgundy that beautifully complemented her brown skin, and mine a borrowed coat of pale yellow with a stiff, embroidered collar in the Lorvan style with a high waist.

We made a rather fetching pair and attracted more than a few lingering glances from passersby, save for the occasional moments when Pretoria skewed time to dissuade anyone from following us.

It was late morning, and my eyes were still swollen from exhaustion. Despite Pretoria's magic and vigilance, I kept a weather eye for Howell, and Wake, and anyone and everyone else who might be looking for me.

"Ottilie," Pretoria said, herself bright-eyed and energetic. "You needn't explain yourself. Though... a pet? Perhaps it is best you let the creature loose. Surely there are enough rodents in Harrow to feed one more stray."

I tried not to be offended. "Ronny is entirely lacking in independence," I said. "And he was a gift from Mr. Stoke."

"Ah." Pretoria nodded soberly, patted my arm, and said nothing more.

She skewed time as we approached my home, free hand floating at her hip as we passed through the open iron gates and into the courtyard. The rustle of the wisteria and the twining of the neighbor's cello distorted into a perplexing swirl of sound, harmonious and hair-raising all at once.

It quietened as we slipped through the front door, up the stairs and down the hall to my apartment. We narrowly missed one of the other tenants, marked by a closing door, and Mrs. Temberley was nowhere in sight.

The door was locked, the handle hung with the crest of the constabulary and a warning not to enter, which we naturally ignored.

"Hieronymus?" I called softly into the quiet, stuffy room.

There was no answering yowl, no rustle of cloth or thump of tiny, padded feet. The cat was not here, which both worried and consoled me. At least he hadn't become locked in the small space.

I surveyed my former home with a knot in my throat. My rooms were rarely tidy, but at that moment everything was a disaster. The police had spared no consideration for my possessions, nor even Mrs. Temberley's furniture. The upending of the latter might have satisfied me under other circumstances, but the sight of my haven in shambles was enough to make my eyes burn.

Pretoria followed my gaze in sober silence, then picked her way across the main room. She glanced into the closet-like kitchen and the tiny water closet (which probably *was* a repurposed closet) and then stationed herself by the balcony doors.

"Open those, please," I said, gathering myself. "With any luck Ronny will wander back before we leave."

She nodded and I went to work. I retrieved several carpet

bags and packed them, waging an inner battle between the need for efficiency and the desire to give Hieronymus more time. I noticed Pretoria eyeing my possessions as I went, feeling her quiet judgement at their quantity and nature, but she offered no criticism.

Finally, with three laden bags beside the door, I came to stand next to Pretoria, surveying the balcony. There was still no sign of the cat.

"We can return another time," Pretoria offered.

"Just one more minute."

She opened her mouth to protest, but silenced as I took her hand and squeezed it. Her fingers were soft and just slightly cool. They reflexively tightened around mine.

A minute, then two passed as the cello twined. Laughter and the clink of porcelain came every so often, chased by a baby's contented coos. It was idyllic, despite the chill—a moment of peace and stillness amid the upheaval that defined my life.

"I am sorry," Pretoria said. By unspoken agreement we released one another's hands and turned, leaving the balcony door open, and took up my bags. "I can see you were comfortable here."

"When the landlady did not lock me out." I forced a smile and glanced out into the hallway.

A shadow and a creak made me pause. I shot Pretoria a meaningful glance and stepped away from the door, wishing yet again I still possessed Mr. Stoke's revolver.

Pretoria advanced on the door with one hand raised, palm open, fingers relaxed. She stuck her head out into the hallway, paused for a moment, and then waved me on. "Just one of your neighbors. They went into an apartment."

I accepted this with a nod. I sent one last longing look at the open balcony door, the slice of cool light across worn floorboards and scattered bedding, and walked out.

When we returned to the hotel, Perry was still gone. I contemplated trying to slip away to go see Dr. Maddeson, but the weekend had arrived. There would be no classes at the university to ensure Maddeson was there, and I had no idea where he lived. Breaking into the administration office or some such place to find his address would be unwise in my condition. I had no time or energy for fool's errands.

So, I spent my time in regaining strength. I ate a great deal, took a long bath, and nap.

I felt refreshed and restless by the time darkness fell and the city took on its nightly patterns of lamplight and shadow. My threads twined as, from the hotel window, I parted the curtain to watch the Opera House spill the melodious cacophony of a rising orchestra into the street. Men and women filed inside arm in arm, laughing and chattering and simpering, heedless of the looming conflict all across the city. Their world glittered and glistened, and brimmed with music. Mine was hushed now, with the curtains drawn.

Melancholy weighed upon me. Its roots were not simply Mr. Stoke's demise, the Guild, our plans, or Hieronymus's absence, though those were heavy enough.

Mr. Howell and the Guild would still be searching for me. Wake, too, was still in play. Perhaps he had heard of my arrest, perhaps not. Perhaps if he had, he would eventually unravel who and what I was, and learn of my escape. Either way, he was likely hunting me in earnest.

Furthermore, Perry still had not reappeared from his mission to Stillwell. Pretoria lay on the bed on her side, propped on a stack of pillows, and perused a newspaper while pretending not to worry.

"He seems a capable man," I said at length. Darkness had fully settled now, and my threads had gone dormant in the room's cautious gaslight. "Try not to fret."

"Fret?" Pretoria waved her newspaper dismissively. "I will fret tomorrow. For the moment, I am peevish. Look."

She pointed to a headline, which read in bold, capital letters, *'GUILD AGENTS PLUCK MURDER SUSPECT FROM PRISON – THE HARROW HERALD SPECULATES.'*

"Does the *Herald* ever do anything other than speculate?" I muttered. "Mr. Wake will certainly know I am not in prison now."

"A common thug is the least of our concerns." Pretoria folded the paper with a snap and sat up. "We are wasting a perfectly good night, so I shall no longer wait. Shall we hunt down Lord Stillwell ourselves? Perhaps we will find my errant husband along the way."

I eyed her for a moment, attempting to gauge just how deep her denial was. Her expression was simply one of disgruntled determination.

"Yes," I decided, advancing on the wardrobe and opening its doors to reveal Pretoria's and Perry's array of garments.

I selected a sleek, heavily beaded copper and teal evening gown. "I know just where to begin."

A Note Upon: Seau, the Kessan, and the Continent Proper

The authors of this guide recognize that the Proper, as one may call the continent south of Arrent, is very likely the destination of The Vigilant Lady Traveller, and will therefore spend the body of this work extolling its wonders and unveiling its dangers. It is storied, diverse, and cultured.

However, notable areas of concern include, beyond the most sensible vigilance over one's person and possessions, that of the station of Entwined. Various Guilds exist across the continent to contain the Entwined, but despite official stances and laws, the extent of their control is inconsistent.

The Vigilant Lady Traveller must be attentive to these variations as she crosses the borders of the Proper.

From The Vigilant Lady Traveller:
A Gentlewoman's Guide to the World

CHAPTER 22

The Opera House stewards paid Pretoria and I no mind as we merged with the crowd at intermission. We passed through wafts of pipe and cigarette smoke, snagged tall glasses of a vaguely green sparkling wine, and faced one another.

Pretoria clinked her glass against mine, the rich, deep blue of her gown shimmering beneath a layer of gossamer and a fur wrap—twin to my own—which, conveniently, concealed her throat. She looked lovely, as always, but thanks to the tactful application of cosmetics, not quite herself.

The same was true of me. The differences were subtle, but persuasive. I doubted Lord Stillwell would recognize either of us in passing, given the passage of time and the bustle of the crowd.

"To the hunt," she murmured, and I felt a quiet thrill. I might disagree with much of my sister's choices in life, but there was an addictive quality to moments like these—when we were united, resolute, competent.

Together, I felt, there was little we could not do.

"The hunt," I agreed, raising my glass and sipping. The wine was sweet, tasting distantly of fennel and anise and ginger. I immediately glanced back to the refreshment table, wishing I had taken two for myself. Coffee may have been the better choice, given my fatigue, but my nerves were taut.

Pretoria sipped at her glass, raised her brows in approval, and sashayed away.

I went in the opposite direction, meandering through the laughter and chatter. Bedecked though I was, I still drew little attention in such a crowd. There were gowns finer, faces lovelier, but drawing attention was not my purpose.

I surreptitiously studied the older men in the room, searching for Lord Stillwell or, at least, another council lord. I was discreet, but several returned my gaze, some with curiosity, others disregard, and one with invitation. None of them were my quarry.

I left the reception hall and passed through two grand, square-columned doors into the opera hall proper. Ladies and gentlemen intermingled among the rows of red velvet chairs under the gaslights, and I tugged my wrap a little higher.

A burst of male laughter drew my eyes upwards. I turned, looking towards the central gallery.

Once, Empress Alessandra had occupied that gilded box, encircled by her sons and daughters and consorts. Now, General Baffin lounged in her throne-like chair, surrounded by drifts of cigar-smoke and a dozen officials.

My glance was brief, but it was long enough. His gaze snagged on me, casual and assessing, and my stomach dropped. Would he, somehow, recognize what I was?

Relief and unease made my blood light as he looked away. I moved out of the balcony's line of sight, debating whether to check in with Pretoria, when the occupants of another box caught my eye.

Madge and several other Guild Adepts, all familiar to some degree, sat in a box nearly as fine as the Grand General's. Several Guild soldiers, uniformed and armed with sabers and pistols, stood to attention at the gallery's curtained door.

Evidently my escape had not impacted Madge's social calendar. My icy sister was here, and I was one glance away from being seen.

Fortuitously, I felt a presence at my back. I turned, one hand already reaching out to drag Pretoria to safety.

Mr. Wake's arm slipped around my waist. He leaned down to murmur in my ear in a façade of intimacy, "Come with me quietly."

"I would rather not."

"You missed our meeting."

"I am following a lead."

His grip tightened, hard enough to make me flinch. The orchestra began to play a tremulous melody, instrument after instrument joining in to a rising chorus. Intermission was over, and within moments Mr. Wake and I were surrounded by merry patrons hurrying back to their seats.

I jerked in his grip, but the confusion had failed to distract him. He prodded me against the tide and into the mouth of a staircase.

Wake led me around the bottom of the stairs to the upper boxes and downwards instead. The light shifted, shadows taking over. My threads prickled, though not enough to show, I hoped.

I brushed at that power. Memories swept over me, transferred by the painful grasp of his hands. I glimpsed his recent passage through the crowd, his watching the window of Pretoria's hotel room from the shadows across the street, and following the pair of us back from my apartments. Seeing us leave again, and enter the Opera House.

"Clearly my disguise was not as good as I hoped," I observed.

Mr. Wake snorted and pushed me against the wall. I kept my shawl tight.

"You are Entwined?" he asked, still grasping my arm. "I saw the papers. Ottilie Rushforth, alias Fleet, was arrested for murdering her employer. A prison cell to the opera in two days?"

"Guild privileges. You are very brave, accosting me in sight of their box," I said coolly.

Wake's grip twitched. "No one would notice us in that crowd, not even a Silver."

"You are adorably naive."

He ignored me, continuing, "Besides, you are not a Guild mage, you are a Rogue, and I have done you a favor by whisking you away. Your handler is looking for you. You can thank me by telling me where the fuck the artifact is."

"I see we have resorted to foul language now," I commented, buying my scrambling mind precious seconds. Given how he had followed Pretoria and I from my apartments, he must have mistaken her for my Guild handler.

He moved closer, crowding me into the wall.

I frowned up at him. "Brute intimidation? Really."

"Enough. Fleet. Rushforth. You, allegedly, killed Mr. Stoke. Oh, and I spoke to the professor. I know the artifact is connected to the Entwined, so it's no stretch to realize you would have an interest in it. Perhaps *that* is why you are in an opera house instead of a Glass Coffin. Have you given it to the Guild? Buying forgiveness for your reprobate ways?"

The chill that prickled down my exposed arms had nothing to do with the cool wallpaper, with its patterns of waves and birds on the wing. I felt myself on a precipice, a point of decision that might save or condemn me.

As Pretoria had said, a thug like Wake was the least of our concerns, even if he had proved himself capable of following us. But he was also the most efficient route to Lord Stillwell, and potentially, finding out where Perry had gone.

It was time to take another chance.

"I want to speak to Stillwell. In person," I said flatly. "Then I will tell you where I hid the artifact."

He stared me down for a long moment, clearly debating whether to believe me. "You did take it?"

"Of course I took it," I scoffed, as if my supposed crime was the most natural thing in the world. "But I have not handed it over to the Guild, not before I have proper assurances, which are being negotiated."

"At the opera?"

"Why not at the opera?"

"Fucking Guild," he said, disgusted. His grip slipped down to my hand where he grasped my fingers—rough, and slightly sweaty. "Follow me."

We emerged from the stairwell to find the performance back underway. On the stage, a woman sang in Kessan, reminding the watchers of her woes and setting the tone for the second act. I could not resist glancing towards the Guild balcony. Only Madge's face was distinguishable, her bold features set in a slice of gaslight.

A steward quietly opened the doors for us. The music hushed as its sturdy, carved wooden face closed once more and Wake and I proceeded across the lobby hand in hand. My palms were sweating, and I resisted the urge to pull away.

I looked for Pretoria among the tidying stewards and spattering of patrons, but did not see her.

A few people lingered outside the doors as we exited onto the street, mostly a group of young men. I kept my face down in the play of light and shadow, forced my gaze ahead, keeping pace into the night.

CHAPTER 23

Our hansom passed through the heights of New Harrow, a lattice of meticulously patterned streets below the palace hill. The roads were broad, built for motor cars with walks for pedestrians and room for intermittent trees. The latter were a burnished plum, the first of their fallen leaves scattered across broad paving stones. The houses were adorned with bold, square columns and geometric patterns to their pale bricks, along rooflines, mantels, and lintels. Electric streetlanterns shone bright, not a single one in disrepair.

As we exited, a troop of drunken young well-to-dos clattered by, surrounding one fellow on horseback, bedecked as a god of the sea. One grabbed my hands and spun me around, heading for an inebriated kiss—he was rank with the smell of wine—but before I could deliver him a well-deserved knee to the groin, Mr. Wake grabbed him by the back of the neck and thrust him on up the street. The fellow flailed, just managed to keep his feet, and threw an obscene gesture back at Wake.

Wake returned it twofold.

I cleared my throat, patting a few stray hairs back into line. "If you are finished?"

Wake ignored me and pulled me onwards, not towards one of the grand houses, but into an alleyway behind them.

As the miscreants trooped off in pursuit of debauchery we strode into the darkness, away from the light.

We travelled a great deal further than I expected, and by the time Wake knocked at a back door, I was thoroughly turned about.

"Lord Stillwell has rented a town home?" I observed.

Wake nodded. The door opened. He exchanged quiet words with a bleary-looking scullery maid, then led me through the innards of Lord Stillwell's manor until, through a cramped servants' stair, we emerged into a dark study.

"We will wait here," Wake said, turning on a desk lamp. For an instant, I might have sworn there was something strange about the way the light chased the shadows from his face. But my eyes were burning with fatigue, and I discarded the notion.

I moved further into the room, scanning the walls. There was a large painting in an unexpectedly lavish golden frame—the rest of the space was spare, with clean lines, no clutter, and not a book out of line.

The painting depicted the open green of the South Quarter, with the river in the background and the Old Citadel burning on the horizon. Armies of humans and Entwined clashed in a romanticized motif of flashing sabers, lines of pluming rifles, and a carpet of the dead and dying.

In the center of it all, a rendition of the young General Baffin held Queen Alessandra by her long black hair and looked at the stormy sky, as if in thanks, or in prayer. In his other hand he held his sword, the very one I had seen at the museum. The sword that had beheaded the last Entwined Empress.

Unease stirred in my belly. Stillwell, despite his station, had never struck me as a particularly passionate participant in the rivalry between humans and Entwined. He had flirted outrageously with my mother, back in the day, and even if he had not been an ally, he certainly had not been a devout foe.

I cast the rest of the office a second, more lingering look. Stillwell was obsessed with antiquities, but everything in this room, aside from the painting, was notably modern.

Slowly, I looked at Mr. Wake. He had situated himself in

a comfortable chair and, as our eyes met, he cocked the pistol in his hand.

"This is not Stillwell's house," I determined.

"No." He grinned and, with that expression, the thug I had known vanished. The smile was mindless in its malice, the smile of a madman on the gallows, and it sent a chill down my spine. "Sit down. The Grand General will be home soon."

I charged him. The gun went off and I twisted, barely evading the path of the bullet before I seized his wrist in one hand and slammed his elbow with the other.

I heard, and felt, the joint crack. A shock of victory shot through me.

It died as quickly as it came. I looked down at where my hand still clutched his exposed wrist, where our skin connected, and saw my fingers had gone grey.

"You're Entwined." The words stuttered from my lips as all my strength, all my energy, fled my body. Leeching. A Silver's Leeching. With it went my shock, and any wonderment I might have had at the alliance of a mage with General Baffin.

Wake only grunted in reply, prying off my locked fingers and shaking out his supposedly broken arm. Another crack and it refitted itself, leaving Wake whole and uninjured.

I, however, could not move. My blood was too slow, my vision blurred. The amount of energy—my stolen energy—required to heal a break was not small, and this, dear reader, is my excuse for what happened next.

I fainted, quite dramatically, onto the floor of Grand General Baffin's study.

I awoke with a start and a shriek; my mind still embedded in the moment before I collapsed. But I was drowning now, drowning in the taste of oak, smoke, and spirits. It burned in my eyes and nose and sent me into a fit of coughing.

"A waste of good whiskey," a male voice muttered.

I swiped at my eyes and discovered my hands had been bound in front of me. I stared at them, my breathing ragged, my eyes blurry and burning, then registered the men standing over me.

Grand General Baffin was dressed in his opera garb, though he had shed his coat and hat. He stood with an empty bottle in hand, the last few drops pattering onto the rug beside my ear.

"General," I managed. Despite the raspiness of my voice, I sounded unruffled. I might have been proud of myself on any other occasion. But just then I could feel no victory, no confidence, and certainly no hope.

No, Mr. Wake did not work for Lord Stillwell. I had been deceived and had bargained myself right into the hands of my kin's greatest enemy. Worse, I had convinced Wake I knew where the artifact was.

Yet Wake himself was Entwined. A Silver, given his Leeching abilities. A Silver working for General Baffin.

Mr. Stoke's dead face flashed through my mind, his shattered jaw and the clawed, deadly bruise. Then I recalled the mad smile on Wake's face, and a chill raced over my skin.

I knew it was him. He had killed Mr. Stoke. I knew it like I knew my mother's face and the swift, graceful characters of Lewis's writing.

But if I was right, Mr. Wake was the most powerful Silver I had ever encountered, had ever even *heard* of. How had the Guild misplaced him?

Mr. Moran's steady stare sifted up in the back of my memory.

You asked Madge what Entwined can kill with the touch of a hand. Why?

My blood began to race.

"Miss Rushforth." Baffin tilted his head to one side as he considered me, then prodded me with a foot, none too gently. "Get up."

I fumbled to do so, coaxing my drained muscles into a semblance of life. I made it to my knees, then staggered to my feet as Baffin watched, unimpressed. Wake took up vigil by the window, most of his attention turned to the world below.

"I have had a long day," Baffin said. Behind him, I could see the portrait of his younger self, holding Empress Alessandra by the hair as he prepared to kill her. "I am impatient, and tired, and will brook no deceptions. Tell me where the artifact is. Mr. Wake will fetch it. If your word has proved true, I will not kill you. If you lie, I will see you tormented in every way I know, and only after you are wholly broken, I will open your throat from ear to ear."

I had no quip this time.

Time. If I could buy time, maybe Pretoria could track me down. But with Perry still in the wind, her attention would be divided. And what if the Guild had spotted her last night? Perhaps she was as much a captive as I.

A dozen lies spun through my mind, but none of them would buy me enough opportunity to regain my strength and forge my own escape.

Then, it struck me.

"Emrys Harden. The smuggler," I said. Guilt, fear, warning battered at me, so forceful I could barely wall it out. I had to be rational. If anyone could handle Wake, it would be another Silver. It was the Separatists. Even given my suspicions about the level of Wake's power, Harden was smart. And, I assured myself, there was a chance Wake wouldn't even find him.

"He is a friend," I said, aware of the irony of that word as I set a killer on his trail. "I left the artifact in his care. Tell him I sent you, and he will comply."

"Where does he live?"

"I do not know."

"You do not know where your friend lives?"

"He is a criminal, sir, he does not keep visiting hours."

Baffin came closer, looming over me and taking in every bit of my expression. I stared back, not bothering to hide my growing fear. It was a stomach-turning, maddening pressure, aggressive and unstoppable.

Abruptly, Baffin looked at Wake. "Put her back to sleep, stow her away and go find this Harden."

"Stow me away? What does that mean?" I shot a look between the two of them and instinctively raised my hands to ward off Wake. "Honestly, I am very tired, if you would just show me to a guest room, I will not bother trying to escape."

Wake took my wrist.

I awoke for the second time to screaming muscles and a pounding of blood in my skull. I tried to turn my head, discovered I could not, and pushed outwards.

I met resistance on all sides. I struggled and made a frustrated cry, only to deafen myself.

I was in a closet. No, that was not right, gravity pulled in the wrong direction. I was in a box. My mind jumped to the chest in Baffin's office, beneath the painting.

"Baffin, you bastard!" I shrieked.

There was no answer.

I pressed my hands, still bound at the wrists, up against the lid. It did not budge.

I drew a breath, as deep as my contorted body, my opera gown and the limited air would permit, and reached out with my power. Memories began to come to me from the wood of the chest, memories of lingering dark and occasional tumults of light. I was not the first person to suffer this confinement.

The terror and screams and sobbing of those previous occupants went straight to my heart. I slammed on the end of the chest again and again with my feet, determined to at least make a nuisance of myself. I had recovered some of my strength (I tried not to think of how long I must have been unconscious to accomplish that) and if I could just force them to open the lid...

Voices entered the room. I kicked all the louder, cursing Baffin with every profanity in my multilingual vocabulary, but was rewarded only with a chuckle and, judging by the movement of chairs, indifference.

I pressed the palms of my hands to my eyes and forced myself to breathe, raking in my own stale air again and again.

As my nerves quietened, the voices of those outside became clearer.

"...bombing in Old Harrow, and there are rumors they will begin to target the bridges." The voice was a woman's, practical and deep.

"Have soldiers stationed at each one and set patrols along

the riverbanks," Baffin's reply came. "Bring all suspected Separatists in and reopen the Old Citadel cells. That will send a message."

I thought of Harden in a sickening flash. He and the Separatists had enough on their plates, and I had sent Wake after him?

In that moment, I despised myself.

Baffin went on, "Offer leniency for any information that proves helpful. And discreetly place some of our Affinates among them, to keep their ears to the ground. Notify Thera immediately."

"Very good, sir." There was a moment of quiet, then, in a lower voice, "If you kill the Rushforth woman, there will be more conflict. The Guild will not stand for it, even if she is Rogue."

Kill me? Why would Baffin kill me? I was his last living connection to the artifact, and until that artifact was in his hands—which would not happen, as Harden did not have it— he was not stupid enough to dispose of me. Was he?

I listened in growing, horrified bewilderment.

"No," was Baffin's calm reply. "No, they will not, but my hands will be clean. Reach out to Incarnadine and make the necessary arrangements."

The Zealot Queen Incarnadine. I realized I was not breathing and forced myself to inhale and exhale.

"Sir," Baffin's companion tempered her voice, but I caught the tension in it. "Given the Zealots' recent escalations, might it not be time to cut ties? If your accord were to come to light now, especially in this matter, the damage may be irreversible."

I expected Baffin to cut the woman off, to rebuke her, but he did not.

"Soon," he replied, calm and factual. "My moment of action must be precise, and for the moment, Incarnadine is still useful. Give her the Rushforth woman."

A Note Upon: Bronze

Bronze Entwined possess the power of the written word, with the ability not only to convey visceral images and experiences with those words, but to implant memories, thoughts, and beliefs in the minds of their readers. They are chillingly useful in the efficacy of propaganda and various forms of entrapment, but also in illicit, mind-altering novels. The latter, dear reader, are never as harmless as they may seem.

Bronze-written materials are found across the world and are virtually indistinguishable from natural, powerless handwritten scripts, upon first glance. But in this, we find their greatest limitation. Bronze writing must be inked by hand, by a mage. Copies possess no power, nor do typewritten texts.

Thus The Vigilant Lady Traveller may avoid Bronze lures and entanglements by selecting typewritten materials such as this humble guide.

From The Vigilant Lady Traveller:
A Gentlewoman's Guide to the World

CHAPTER 24

After the voices of Baffin and the woman faded, I used my captivity to contemplate the depths of my misfortune. I was quite pitiable, I decided, locked in a box and at the mercy of my people's greatest enemy. All my plans, all my determination—they could not break me out. Lewis was a world away, I had selfishly exposed Harden to danger, and the artifact? Perhaps it was wholly lost.

And now it seemed Baffin would use my death at the hands of the Zealot Queen Incarnadine as a tipping point in Harrow's conflict, forcing the Guild to act and giving himself an excuse to move against them.

But why would he give me up before I had led him to the artifact? I conjured and discarded a dozen scenarios, but ended up with two possibilities. Either he deeply believed I'd given the box to Harden, in which case my skills at lying were to be commended, or he had found it elsewhere.

In the end, his reasoning did not matter. I needed to escape the trunk and get back on course, but I would have to wait until the lid opened again. I could only hope that Harden had overpowered Wake, and the Silver hands that found me would help me, rather than Leech away what little strength I had.

An indeterminate length of time passed before the lid of

the trunk lifted. Unfortunately my escape plans were thwarted by the fact that I was asleep when it happened, having slipped into blissful unconsciousness where cramped muscles, gnawing hunger, and impending murder could not torment me.

The next thing I knew, I was being carried over someone's shoulder, as tenderly as a sack of barley. I could barely breathe, due to a shoulder in my gut and a bag tied over my head.

I was tossed unceremoniously into the back of a carriage or wagon. No one spoke, but after a clattering journey I was hauled out again. I sensed us descending stairs, felt a waft of damp cold, then a wash of warmth.

I was deposited in a chair. Light and a matted tangle of hair blinded me as the bag was hauled off, and I faced my intended killer.

I pushed my hair away with bound hands and squinted.

The infamous face of Incarnadine peered back. She bent over before me, hands on her knees as she examined me in turn. Her eyes were an uncanny green, green as southern waters under a warm sun. Her hair was a simple brown, pulled up under a bowler hat. She wore a practical walking ensemble in a slightly faded plum, the jacket currently unbuttoned to show a plain blouse. She was, according to the papers, around forty-five, but looked younger—a gift of her soft, round cheeks.

I met her gaze until the moment stretched too long. Discomfited, I leaned back in the chair and glanced at the other occupants of the room.

There were half a dozen. I recognized one from the papers, a Zealot lieutenant known as Mr. Graves. I had taken the name for popular nonsense but now that I saw him in person, with his pale skin, heavy shadows under his eyes, and thickly muscled upper body, I found it apt.

"Rushforth," Incarnadine muttered, straightening. "He wants me to kill a Rushforth. Not that I am opposed, but I do tire of our Grand General pretending I am his lapdog."

"You could *not* kill me," I suggested. I found I felt particularly brazen, in a numb, harried sort of way that made my blood light and my wits shallow. "Are these hangings and such not overdone? Whipping a dead horse, as it were.

The masses are desensitized. My suggestion would be not to involve death, though I understand if you feel a casual beating might be necessary. I make a fine ransom. And do you know what money buys? Guns! Explosives. Better hideouts." At the last, I looked meaningfully around the room, which was a bare cellar that stank of floodwaters.

"No, I want to kill you," Incarnadine replied, her voice so calm and cool even Madge might have shivered. She continued to take me in, seeming particularly unimpressed by my rumpled gown. "It's not often I have one of your kind in reach."

"My kind? I hate the Guild as much as you do."

"I very much doubt that."

"I'm a Rogue. I am trying to stay away from them."

"You are the worst of your kind," she replied. I had struck a nerve and found myself regretting that under the intensity of her glare. "You, assured of your value, the value of your power and your blood. Your *worth*. And yet you run and hide, withholding that power."

"You sound like a Separatist," I said.

She smiled, her eyes lightening a fraction. "I was one, for a time. But they consider themselves above a powerless human, even if I was born onto the same blood they were."

I paused. "Pardon me?"

"I was born to Guild parents," Incarnadine stated. Her people looked on, unsurprised. This was no secret, it seemed, within her underworld. "But I have no power. A failed experiment of their monstrous breeding regime. So, I know you. I know your kind. I know your family. We are two sides of the same coin, you and I. You, born with power, I, without. You, elevated, I, cast aside. But at least I have done something with my life instead of hiding."

"Bombing civilians is truly something to aspire to," I snapped. My skipping, agitated mind slowed with these revelations, the complexities of the situation mounting.

The head of the Zealots was not simply the figurehead of ignorant discontents. She had lived inside the Guild. She was informed, intentional, and her crusade was personal.

I could already feel a noose around my neck.

"We do not bomb civilians," Incarnadine replied sternly. "Separatists do."

"I thought we were being honest with one another."

"We were, and it was cathartic," Incarnadine said, letting out a short breath. "You will be the most noteworthy Entwined I've ever killed."

"I am honored," I said, but wavered. My bravado was failing—I had to get it back. Rallying, I lifted my chin and asked, "How am I to be murdered?"

"Do you really want to know?"

"I have considerable stakes in the venture."

Incarnadine tilted her head slightly to one side. "You are one of those, I see. All jest and bravado, until the noose is around your throat."

Her words elicited a rise of terror, momentarily overwhelming. But my expression did not waver.

There was a knock at the cellar door. One of Incarnadine's lackeys opened it and exchanged a word, then closed the door again and handed a note to Incarnadine.

She stepped away from me and read the missive. She turned partially away, but I caught a flicker of irritation in her eyes. The light from the lamp cut across her face and throat. She would have made an imperious mage, if that throat had not been devoid of threads.

A greater sense of dread came upon me. But up through that mire swam one clear thought. One possibility of, if not salvation, perhaps division, and reprieve.

"Baffin intends to betray you," I said. "When you are at the end of your usefulness."

Incarnadine glanced from me to the note again. She lifted it between two fingers, apparently unbothered by my revelation. "He wants you hung before dawn."

"I overheard him say—"

"I am well aware of my position with the Grand General, but he would do better to be aware of his position with me," Incarnadine replied. She caught Graves's eye and nodded.

I found myself being hoisted from the chair. My terror

broke. I fought back, kicking and shouting, and was hurled into a wall for my trouble.

Thankfully, I may spare the reader further coverage of my indignities, for at this point my story takes a far more important turn. One that involves a certain Guild soldier and the shadow that crossed the high, narrow window.

Glass shattered. There was an explosion, a cloud of choking smoke, and the crash of a door. Screams began, and gunfire. I kept to the floor as the initial barrage of shots flew, then staggered upright and bolted for the door.

Smoke wafted across my path. I was forced to divert, narrowly avoided a club to the head, and thudded into someone.

Dark blond hair. Shocked, relieved eyes. Large hands, pulling me closer, then pushing me onwards, up a slippery set of mossy stairs and into the cold of a Dockside afternoon.

My attention tore, divided between the fact that Lewis was charging up the stairs at my back and Madge was waiting calmly beside a carriage just down the street. Her husband stood at her side, one hand raised and making absent movements in the air in a mannerism I recognized from Pretoria. Protecting them inside a skew of time.

"Not you!" I burst out in frustration.

Madge frowned, an emotion I could not read flicking through her. This transitioned into a shout of rebuke as someone tackled us from the side. I heard Lewis's voice, too—so familiar and so outlandish, so out of place—as I was dragged away in a sudden mob of shouting, riotous strangers.

"Go!" another voice shouted in my ear. Mr. Harden. I stumbled, not from shock—there was too much to be shocked about now—but from the cramped state of my legs and my impractical clothing. "Run! What's wrong with you?"

Someone jostled into me and I nearly fell. Harden caught me, not at all gallantly—it was more of a flailing snatch. Still this saved me from knocking myself senseless on the rail of the riverside balustrade.

"Curse it," I heard Harden mutter. Then I was in the air, a shoulder slammed into my stomach again, and I found my face in the small of his back.

I would have protested if there were any air in my lungs, not to mention the rush of blood to my head. I was close to passing out when Harden set me on my feet, leaning me against a wall like an umbrella before he staggered back, pushing sweaty hair from his eyes.

"What's wrong with you?" He panted. His words might be callous, but his gaze was anything but. "What've they done to you?"

"Nothing, no," I dismissed. My head ached and I knew my face must be red as a cherry from all the blood pounding in my skull. My hair was in my eyes, annoying and tickling and stiff with sweat. "I was locked in a trunk in the Grand General's study for the night, that is all."

An outraged "What?" burst from him.

He asked me something else, but my mind was slurring away, back through the streets. Lewis. Was there any possibility he had been a figment of my imagination, a result of chaos and dehydration and stress and longing? He could not truly be here, *with Madge*.

"Why was Lewis with her?" I felt myself ask.

Harden still panted, fingers buried exasperatedly in his hair. Then a whistle came from the next street over, evidently some kind of signal, for he straightened. He fumbled for a knife and quickly slit my bindings, kicking them into a gutter, then offered me an open hand.

"Let's get somewhere safe, then we can talk," he said, his voice firm and kind.

I cleared my throat, blinked unexpected moisture from my eyes, and let him lead me away.

CHAPTER 25

A Note to the Reader: Regarding Reunions

Pretoria and I arrived in The Sarre on a picturesque summer's day. We descended the gangplank in our voluminous Sarren trousers, pale cotton shirtwaists and snug vests, sunhelmets in place and laced boots echoing on the white-washed boards.

I had seen much of the world by this point, including other warm southern nations, but the sprawl of Sarre Grand lit a fire in my chest. Copper roofs sparkled in the sun against a flawless blue sky. The breeze off the ocean was cool, the black stone of the quay warm. Steamships and sailing vessels of all sizes packed the waters right up to the port's three massive bridges, one spanning each of the three rivers which emptied here into the sea.

The city was built not only on the banks of the rivers, but on the bridges themselves. I do not call them 'massive' without reason. Each was three times the length of our steamship, with colossal pillars sunk into the riverbed. Buildings of up to four stories clustered atop them, marvellously painted shutters and strings of laundry peppering the black stone with color.

The bridges were a marvel of ancient engineering—or so the animated academics who had entertained Pretoria and I over breakfast had proclaimed.

Our trunks waited on the docks, quickly taken up

by porters at Pretoria's direction and borne along as we approached the iron rails which guarded the berth from the crowds. Locals, clad in various combinations of tunics, trousers, skirts, and loose, off-shoulder shawls, offered new arrivals hotels and carriages and horses and tours, along with a dizzying array of wares and foods. Foreigners, ranging from bewildered to jovial to scowling at the chaos, bottlenecked at the dock's open gates.

A woman fought her way through this throng and waved to us. She wore a long local tunic over trousers similar to ours, and her brown hair was wound into a dishevelled bun. Her cheeks were high and full of color—color which deepened fractionally as she took Pretoria's hands and kissed her cheek.

"Welcome," she said, a little breathless. She looked from Pretoria to me and added, "Adelaide Kerrie, though I am sure you know that already."

"I do." I smiled in greeting. "Tori has told me next to nothing of you and your compatriots."

Pretoria tucked Adelaide's arm through hers. "Ottilie does not like to know the details of our club's activities. She will spend her time reading and staring at dusty relics, I imagine."

"Club." Adelaide repeated the word with a half-grin. She added in a low voice, nearly lost in the bedlam, "A rather timid way of describing the hope of the Entwined?"

That was where my patience for the meeting waned. I cleared my throat, nodding to the waiting porters, and we proceeded through the gate.

A private carriage carried us to Adelaide's residence, which proved to be atop one of the bridges, with dark, frothy water of the southmost river rushing below. The steady passage of that water hummed through the stones and scented the air with a sweet cleanliness, despite the closeness of the city.

Adelaide was not the only one in residence—a dozen people greeted us between the street and the stairs, the parlor and the room we had been assigned. This was the nature of our travels, and, indeed, that of most of the other 'guests.' Adelaide's home, perhaps I need not say, was a safehouse for Rogue Entwined.

I still did not classify myself as Rogue, at least not in the sense that Pretoria and Adelaide did. We were all hiding from the Harren Guild, or the Guilds of other more stringent nations, but theirs was an active roguishness, and mine was distinctly passive.

So over the next several weeks, while Pretoria, Adelaide, and an assemblage of their unruly brethren set about some scheme of theft or subterfuge, I explored Sarre Grand and read in the quiet of our room. I visited the city's vast museums—under the close and corrupted supervision of the Seaussen, though this was before the invasion proper—and joined tours outside the city to ancient sites. These consisted of ruined temple complexes and lofty, crumbling fortresses.

It was at one of these sites where I, quite by chance, saw him.

Lewis Illing stood in the shade of a fortress wall, speaking with another officer. His pale khaki uniform was well-maintained but his boots were covered with dust. His pith helmet was under one arm and there was perspiration on his brow while, with his free hand, he passed a flask to his companion. Both wore Guild pips on their high collars.

Every thought in my head evaporated, along with any claim I had ever made that I had not, in fact, fallen for Lewis Illing.

A cluster of Lusterless soldiers passed between the Guild officers and me, followed by the cough and roar of a canvas-clad truck.

When the truck had passed only one figure remained. Lewis watched me with a startled furrow in his brow, and the flask forgotten in his hand.

A fragment of sense returned to me and I nodded, stiffly, towards the shelter of a stand of trees. Then I set off, endeavoring to put one foot in front of the other with dignity and grace.

I stumbled on a rock. A nearby gentleman in a boater hat and a blindingly white linen suit happily caught me, his hands lingering and his smile too wide.

"Whoa there, now," he said. "Why, you are far too pretty to be here alone, miss."

I 'accidentally' stepped on his foot. He let me go, more in consternation than pain.

"She is not alone," Lewis's familiar voice said. His arm came through mine and he touched the brim of his helmet—now returned to his head—at the man in the linen suit.

The touch of Lewis's muscular arm did nothing to subdue the conflict inside me. Increasingly flustered and irritated with myself, I was grateful for the shade under the trees as we moved on.

"What are you doing here?" I asked him in a low voice.

"What has Pretoria dragged you into now?" he asked at the same time.

He had let go of me and stepped a pace away, facing me under the shade of the leaves. A sea breeze rustled over our heads.

I shrugged in answer to his question.

He frowned, and answered mine. "Officially, I am on loan to the Harren Settlement Office, via the Guild's agreement with the General Army." His pale eyes searched my face, quietly assessing and concerned. "Unofficially, I am guarding stuffy tombs and securing antiquities for the Guild."

The simplicity with which he confessed this no-doubt confidential truth made me raise my brows.

"How adventurous," I observed. "What does the Guild want with Sarren antiquities?"

Lewis shrugged. The gesture was so casual, so common, it made our unexpected meeting feel all the more surreal. "Wealth and prestige, same as anyone else. Do you truly not know why Pretoria is here?"

"I did not ask," I said with the barest, humorless smile. "I am sure you are aware of a Rogue element in the city."

"I am," he admitted. He glanced out from under the trees, checking our surroundings. "I am expected back at the dig, soon. We should meet again."

"Yes! Yes. Tonight?" I said, perhaps a bit quickly. The way he had spoken sounded too vague—I wanted to secure a meeting. "The fountains before the temple, in the city center."

He hesitated, looking as if he were about to decline. Then

to my relief, he said, "I will be there, but it may be very late."

"Very well. I will bring a book." I smiled at him and, finally, he smiled back. That smile threatened to disassemble me all over again. It was warm and sweet and a little distracted, leaving me longing for more of his focus, more of his attention. For his admiration.

I disliked myself for it. I was young and naive enough to be besotted, yet old and aware enough to recognize the folly of that condition.

He touched his helmet. "I will see you tonight, Ottilie," he said, and left me.

For the sake of the present narrative I will pause at this juncture, but let me assure you, dear reader—this is a tale to which I will swiftly return.

CHAPTER 26

Present Day

There had been a change in the city since Wake lured me through Baffin's door. I noted it in a disengaged way, absorbing a series of subtleties that, together, cast the impressions and rhythm of city life into a tenser, more ominous light.

There were fewer pedestrians on the streets, and fewer smiles on the faces of those I did see. No governesses walked children home down the riverbanks in bows and lace. There were soldiers at the feet of the bridges, and though the traffic slowed in their presence, there was no honking, no shouting. The liveliest scene we glimpsed was a crowd at a corner around a collection of newsboys, who were doing a roaring trade despite the later hour.

Harden glanced at the boys and the stacks of papers in their carts, but we did not stop.

The scent of rotting fruit drifted to me as we slipped in the back door of The Three Trees. Harden beckoned me down a side passage then a stair into the cellar, where multiple voices sounded.

I blinked. The cellars were round-topped and extensive, larger than the establishment itself. They were also full of people—bustling people, running people, wounded people, talking people. A girl darted past with no less than six rifles burdening her arms and an old man deftly stitched a gash on the face of a crying, younger man, who despite his tears stood straight-backed under the light of an oil lamp. The lamp ignited the scar-like threads of a Gaslamp Entwined—a relatively new breed, as far as my kinfolk went, and the result of two centuries of selective breeding by the Guild.

There were tables laden with supplies, rows of well-lived-in bunks, and even rows of drying laundry off in a corner. An old woman perched near these lines, a pair of woven bassinettes at her side—complete with one visible, chubby infant foot—and a pile of mending at her feet.

"Oh, I see," I said tonelessly, standing amid the bustle. "This is a Separatist hideaway."

Harden nudged me forward with a gentle hand on my back, passing me off to a matronly older woman. "Can you look after her, Maggie? I think she's in shock. I've got to—"

"Go." The woman Maggie waved him off and bundled me away. "Come, dove, what's your name?"

"Ottilie," I said. I craned to look back at Harden, but he had his back to me, speaking urgently with several other people.

I submitted myself to Maggie's ministrations, which extended to wrapping me in a blanket and depositing me on a bunk with a cup of tea.

The tea grew cold as I watched the chaos. I glimpsed Harden several more times, but always in passing. He caught my gaze, here in concern, there in distraction.

His attention, or lack of, felt distant and unremarkable. All I could think of was Lewis, and the pall of the subdued city above lingered over me like a fog. I remembered Lewis bundling me out of the cellar—saving me, ostensibly, to deliver me right into the hands of Madge. What was he even doing in Harrow?

Harden had to know something more. Eventually I rose to find him, setting my blanket aside. As I did, I noticed a table nearby. It was scattered with random items, including a number of pamphlets.

I picked up the closest and surveyed its bold lettering. *'CITIZENS OF HARROW RISE: A CALL TO ARMS'* shouted out from the page, along with a depiction of an

Entwined man—shirtless and covered with threads—strangling a fainting human woman.

I tossed the paper back down in disgust. It landed next to another pamphlet, which declared in similar fashion, '*ACT NOW OR WAIT FOR THIS*,' followed by a sketch of Entwined conquerors in the double-breasted, low-collared uniforms of the Old Empire treading screaming humans, including children, underfoot.

I took in the entirety of the table. There were half a dozen different pamphlets, all Zealot propaganda, represented here. All looked virtually new, right off the press. One was tucked between the pages of today's newspaper.

I remembered the crowds around the newsboys, and clenched my teeth.

Baffin had to know about this. Perhaps, he had even initiated it, in some underhanded way.

Like my death by Zealot.

"Who the hell are you?" A voice snapped me from my reverie as a large frame loomed over me.

I was not in the frame of mind to be threatened, but I was also exhausted. I raised fighting fists only to find one wrist grabbed by a large man, built and dressed like a longshoreman. He crowded me back towards the bunks.

"Harden brought me," I said, jerking in his grasp, then forcing myself to relax a margin. This was one of Harden's comrades. This was a mistake, and I had no patience or energy for a confrontation, let alone the repercussions.

I flicked a glance around, looking for the motherly Maggie, but she was absent.

The man squeezed my wrist, making my fingers shudder into claws and my anger spark. "Never heard of the bloke. Get over here, you fucking spy—"

The pain of his hold broke through my reservations. I executed a crude but nonetheless effective twist and snap which left my attacker staggering backwards with a dislocated elbow—past the stunned Harden.

"Right," Harden said, stepping between the two of us and ushering me aside as Maggie reappeared to take charge of the now howling man. "That was Jasper. He is a bull-headed bastard and deserved that. Mag?"

"Got him," Maggie said, prodding the half-crumpled Jasper back. Around us people stared, but activity continued.

Over by the laundry, the old woman absently rocked one of the bassinettes with a foot as the baby began to fuss.

Harden led me back to the bunks. I sank back down, feeling utterly drained.

"I've no desire to be dramatic," I muttered to Harden. "But this is all rather much. Did you see those pamphlets?"

He gave a halfway nod. "We've been discussing them. They're not the first, of course, but the city will be papered with this latest run by tonight. The Zealots have escalated."

"I would have been the main feature," I groaned, burying my face in my hands. Then, beset by sudden memory, I looked up again. "She was a Separatist. She told me, Incarnadine did. Did you know?"

Harden glanced across the room as if looking for someone, his expression inscrutable. "That's... interesting."

"Did you know?" I repeated.

"*I* didn't," he said with emphasis. "But I am not the head of this operation."

That raised the question of just what role he did play in the Separatists, besides smuggling, but there were too many other things on my mind to chase it just then.

"What about Lewis? Did you know he is in Harrow, with the Guild?"

Harden shook his head. "No. But he could've caught us, and he didn't, so take that as you will. He let us go—met my eyes and all."

I stared at Harden without really seeing him. "So, he may not have sold me out. Perhaps he just arrived, and was intercepted. I didn't see him at Golden House."

"Could be." Harden shrugged. His expression shifted at my mention of Golden House, but he stayed on topic. "I'll find him and sort this out."

I refocused on the Separatist, rallying now that I had a purpose in sight. "I should do it."

"No, right now you need to tell me everything," he corrected. "I received your message, but it was vague."

I frowned at him. "What message?"

"The mage who tried to Leech the life from me," Harden said. "Called himself Wake and demanded I hand over that box you and Stoke brought in."

I clapped my hands over my mouth. "Oh, no. Harden, I'm so sorry—"

"As I said, I got your message," he cut in. He looked at me hard, not unkindly, but as if I were the piece of a puzzle that refused to click into place. "Good thing I didn't believe he'd actually release you once he had the box."

It was my turn to stare. "What?"

"I gave him the box, in exchange for your being let loose," Harden clarified.

I shot to my feet. "Pardon me?"

Harden's brows rose high. "What am I missing here?"

I pressed a hand over my eyes, trying and failing to think. I heard him start to ask another question, and threw up my other hand to silence him. "Just... Just stop. Wait. You had the box?"

He nodded. "Mr. Stoke gave it to me for safekeeping."

Slowly, I sat back down. Mr. Stoke *had* fled with the artifact. He *had* left me to face Mr. Wake alone, even after Mr. Wake attacked him and ransacked the office.

He had abandoned me.

The hurt of that met with the reality of Mr. Stoke's death in a blinding wave of emotion. I was unseated, unmoored, lost to the maelstrom. There were excuses in that tumult, frail hopes and explanations that tried and failed to soften the blow.

"I sent Mr. Wake to you because I hoped you might be a match for him. He is a Silver, too," I heard myself explaining, though I neglected to note just how powerful I suspected Wake was. I was trying to excuse my actions, not dig my grave deeper. "I was in desperation for my life and... I am sorry. I did not know you had the box. When did Mr. Stoke give it to you?"

"I'm flattered you thought me his match." Harden was still watching me, but with more concern now. "Mr. Stoke left it at the mirror shop, hidden behind the counter. I found it soon after our last meeting. I didn't see Stoke, so I can't rightly say when he left it."

"Was there a note?"

Harden nodded. "No explanation, though. Just asked me to hold the thing, and I would be well compensated."

"Yet when Mr. Wake showed up, you handed it right over?" I clarified.

"Of course I did. Stoke is dead, that was all over the papers. And you had vanished. Why not trade some old wooden box for your life? Didn't turn out quite so simple, but I found you in time."

I opened my mouth to ask something further, but no words presented themselves. Instead, I lost myself in my own head for a long, long moment.

I came out of my fugue when Harden took my hand. He peeled it off my chest, where I had unconsciously clamped an arm across my ribs, as if trying to hold myself together.

He folded my hand between both of his, warm and comforting.

"Ottilie, it's time you tell me everything," he said.

I drank in his touch. It was an anchor I wanted to cling to desperately. It was a direct path to my innermost fears and I had never been more grateful for a gesture.

Perhaps it made me short-sighted. Perhaps it proved me fickle, even when Lewis's shadow loomed. But Harden's expression was one of patience and a protective kind of trepidation, and his grasp was firm.

"The day after you gave us the box, Mr. Stoke sent me home early," I told him. "He informed me he would take a holiday, and would not need me for some time. But he would leave my pay from Stillwell in the safe.

"The next morning I came to retrieve it, but Mr. Wake was there. He said he was Stillwell's man, and that Mr. Stoke had failed to deliver the artifact and vanished. He demanded that I help him find Mr. Stoke. So I started looking. That night we crossed paths? That's what I was doing, out so late."

Thoughts passed behind Harden's eyes but he did not interrupt.

"I had no idea Mr. Stoke took the artifact with him," I said, numb. "I thought someone else had and we were both under threat because of them."

"Stoke didn't strike me as that kind of man," Harden murmured. He watched something transpire across the room, half-focused. "To off with the artifact and leave you high and dry."

"Nor I," I admitted. "But there are... other factors."

He returned his attention to me. "Like Wake *not* being Stillwell's man? Some shock I had, when I trailed him right to Baffin's own house."

The flow of my honesty slowed then, and I searched myself. Just how much could I disclose? How much did I trust Harden?

I was not sure of the answer, despite the way his touch calmed and steadied me.

So I did not tell him of Pretoria or my time at Golden House. Instead, I focused on my time with Baffin, recounting the trunk and the conversation I had overheard between Baffin and his aide, of allowing the Zealots to kill me in order to provoke the Guild.

"Baffin succeeded, in that," I concluded. "The Guild did intervene."

Harden nodded, noncommittal and distracted. "A box," he muttered. "He put you in a fucking box."

"I was not the first." I recalled all the memories I had pulled off the wood. "Not by far."

"How do you know that?"

I realized, nearly too late, that I had yet to confess what class of Entwined I was to Harden.

"Scratch marks," I said with a soulless smile. "On the inside."

His hands tightened on mine but, thankfully, he did not linger on the topic. No, he moved on to something far worse.

"How did you escape from the Guild?" He raised his eyebrows at my wince. "It's in the papers, Ottilie. There are rumors, too, about who you are."

I had forgotten about that. I pulled away from him. I hated

to lose his touch, but just then, I needed the space. I leaned against the opposite bunk post, taking a moment to order my thoughts. But there were too many voices in the Separatists' den, too much happening, too many lies crying out from the table of propaganda in the corner of my eye.

"Who am I, then?" I asked, bracing myself.

"Ottilie Rushforth."

I felt something inside me give way. "Do they know?" I asked, nodding to the Separatists all around.

Harden watched me for another breath, then appeared to come to a decision. "Yes."

"Then am I a prisoner?"

His expression was wan. "What use would you be as a prisoner?"

"You might force me to fight with you. There are only twelve Eventide Entwined in Arrent. A hundred the world over."

"Yes, yes, you're very special. But you're also useless, unless you're willing to cooperate."

"Then you will not try to convince me to fight with you?"

"I already did. You said no, and I said I'd speak no more of it. I keep my word."

I met his gaze, gratitude and respect loosening my chest and allowing me to breathe a little easier. They were a balm, but they could do little against three, undeniable truths.

First, I was unmasked. The papers knew Ottilie Fleet had been rescued from prison by the Guild, and rumors that I was a Rushforth were swiftly turning to fact.

Second, Grand General Baffin had the artifact. His hopes of learning how to transform human into Entwined could now be pursued, with Dr. Maddeson's enthusiastic support.

Third, Lewis was in Harrow.

My worries began to... not peel away, but to dampen, to grow more distant. My plans were threatening to disassemble, as was the city itself. The waters were so muddied I felt I could no longer see through them, save for the fact that, once more, I faced a choice.

I could walk away. I could run to Pretoria—wherever she was now—and allow her to save me.

Or I could keep fighting, keep reaching for the future I wanted.

Perhaps if I reframed the recent, terrible developments, they would not seem quite so bad? I now knew where the artifact was. Lewis was here, not in The Sarre. If he could be extricated from the Guild's clutches, we could flee *together* as soon as the artifact was turned in and Stillwell's bounty paid. Given the secrecy of Baffin's plans, there was a chance Stillwell, semi-disgraced after his failure to hold The Sarre, remained ignorant of it all, and still simply wanted his artifact back. If not, perhaps I could find another buyer. Pretoria certainly could, if I was willing to let her in.

My plans were still in motion, and with them, Lewis, Pretoria and Perry, Dr. Maddeson and Lord Stillwell. It was time to rejoin them on the game board.

I looked at Harden. "How do you feel about helping me rescue Lewis from the Guild?"

CHAPTER 27

Harden did not look as surprised as I expected. "I have already considered it."

"Then you will?"

He glanced at his people. "Yesterday, I would have. Today, the Zealots almost killed a Rushforth, the Guild is mobilized, and there are soldiers on the streets. I have obligations, Ottilie."

This blindsided me—which likely said a great deal about the extent of my self-absorption.

"Stay here, hide here," he suggested. "You'll be safe until things settle down. Then, yes, I will help you rescue Lewis. I'll help you get out of Harrow, too."

That wouldn't be much use without funds, but I did not say that. I was grateful for the offer and still might need to accept it.

"Mayfair!" someone shouted, affirming Harden's words.

Harden stood up, looking at me apologetically. "Consider it? I'll be back."

"Sure. Go on." I watched him hasten away, closing further in upon myself with each step he took.

I could not go after Lewis alone, even if I was sure he had not betrayed me. The Guild was simply too powerful. Pretoria might be able to do it, but convincing her would be no easy task.

My thoughts churned off from there, and I will spare the reader the extent of my ramblings. Suffice it to say that by the end, I had found a course of action that put me back on my feet.

Retrieving the artifact from Baffin was a daunting and highly improbable prospect. But if I moved quickly, I might not have to.

I took a shawl of a nearby chair and wrapped it about my shoulders, silently promising to return it someday. Then I looked for Harden, to say goodbye. But I could not find him.

I crossed a street, down which I glimpsed smoke in the northern sky, above the slated and tiled roofs, decorous gables, and a slowly turning weathervane. A cluster of soldiers moved from door to door of the shops along the way, ushering owners inside and checking locks. Several glanced at me, disheveled in my shawl and opera gown, but only to shout, "The city is in lockdown! Off the streets, order of the Grand General!"

"On my way!" I shouted back as I ducked into another alleyway.

Twists and turns passed me by. I was cold, but my skin prickled with anxious sweat. At one point I crossed a broad, echoing and empty market hall where the dispossessed clustered in dirty corners, conferring and eyeing me as I passed.

"Not safe out there, lass!" a man called, his voice quavering with age and worry.

I only touched my forehead and shouldered open a stiff outer door.

I made it a dozen feet down the next street before gunshots cracked. I threw myself under a cart. Someone called an order to stand down. Another gunshot cracked. Glass shattered.

On my belly, I watched soldiers sprint past. I did not see whoever they pursued, but judging by a smattering of whoops and howls, the perpetrators were enjoying the chase.

Zealots, I surmised. *Or looters*. Baffin was truly despicable, using Incarnadine and her crusade to tear the city apart and justify his own vendetta. Trying to use *me*.

The latter may not have come to fruition, but it clung to me. It made what I intended to do next all the sweeter.

The streets around the Hotel Cherron were thick with police and soldiers, coordinating and ordering locals about. I kept my head down and ducked into the alleyway where I had, not two days ago, stashed my stolen bicycle after throwing Guild Mage Howell off Pointer's Bridge.

The contraption was gone, perhaps taken by another pair of needy hands. But the spot was deserted, and safe to catch my breath.

It took longer than was helpful. I had gotten so little sleep over the last few days, and next to no solid meals. I braced my hands on my knees in the shadow of the wall and stilled a wave of dizziness.

I needed rest. But first I needed to find Pretoria.

I eyed the front door of the hotel. Harassed-looking bellboys stood beside the doors as guards, but no one came in or out. I doubted my sister was still here, but even if she was not, she would have left a note. Or...

"Finally," Pretoria said. She stepped seemingly from nowhere with a haze of skewed time, and gave me a fixed, low-chinned look. "You have ruined that gown. Where were you?"

I smiled a compulsive, relieved, and guilty smile. "I knew you would find me."

"That is not an answer, dear."

I took her in, head to foot. She was dressed in a simple walking ensemble, parasol in hand, and appeared none the worse for wear.

"The Guild did not spot you?" I asked. "Or did a Silver mage call at the hotel?"

She frowned. "Mage? No, though the bellboy warned me someone had been watching the premises, and I secured a new den. The Guild, the opera—that was a near thing. I was recognized by a mage and detained momentarily, but made my escape. Too late to find you, however. Where did you go?"

I closed the space between us and slipped my arm through hers. "I will tell you everything, once we are somewhere safe."

We did not speak again until the door of Pretoria's new safehouse was closed.

The place was in the worst part of Old Harrow, right beside the docks and stinking of fish and river. The room had faded wallpaper and threadbare rugs, but it was quiet, and the room itself smelled of freshly laundered sheets.

Perry glanced from his station at the cracked window and gave me a tense greeting. Beyond, the docks spread out to the flow of the river, and one could see a narrow view of the street and front door.

"You live," I observed.

"As do you," he returned. "We've been worried."

"Ottilie?" My sister's worried tones drew my attention back to her. "What happened?"

I had prepared for this moment during my walk, but still, I took a moment to reply. What had *not* happened to me, in the last six days? I had been abducted and arrested, threatened and attacked, glimpsed my erstwhile fiancé, kissed a Separatist, thrown a Guild mage off a bridge, and lost my cat.

I had suffered the upending of my entire life and future.

"I want to trust you," I said to Pretoria. My eyes burned, but otherwise, I was composed. "I want to tell you everything. But first, I need some assurances. Perry, do you mind giving my sister and I the room?"

Perry glanced at Pretoria. I could not read the look they exchanged but he touched her arm and left, as requested. The door clicked, and my sister and I were alone.

Pretoria sat on the opposite bed with a soft creak. The moment stretched long and I sensed her struggling to find something to say. I, too, found myself reluctant to begin.

Finally, she spoke. Her voice was stripped of pomp and bravado, so much so she might have been another person entirely. "You do not have to trust me, or tell me anything. Other than what you would like me to do."

I weighed this. It was quite the gesture on her part, and I sensed it was genuine. But it was not enough.

"I require you to swear you will not take me out of Harrow against my will," I replied. The words came from somewhere deep inside of me, whole and full. "Swear to me you will not manipulate me or corral me into going anywhere with you. Swear to me that you will leave me to do as I please, as soon as I tell you to. Swear to me that you will accept that my choices are my own."

"Ottilie—" She cut herself off, clearly swallowing offense at my words. Then, slowly, she nodded and said with sincerity, validated and verified by the pain and frustration in her eyes, "All right. I swear."

Those two words had such weight to them. They hung in the room until I could bear them no longer.

"Now," I said, erasing them with my voice. "There is a great deal more to the artifact than I initially understood. Grand General Baffin believes it is the key to learning how to turn humans into Entwined, and he now has it in his possession."

Whatever Pretoria had anticipated me saying, this was not it. Her eyes grew wide. But she did not interrupt.

"However, there is a chance it is not properly *in his possession*, as it were, at this moment. He has been funding the research of a professor at the university, a philologist, and I believe he will take the artifact to him for translation."

"Or bring the professor to the artifact," Pretoria pointed out. Her expression grew keen, a challenge-hungry edge that I recognized well.

"That may be," I conceded. "And if it is, we will have to adjust. But we must start somewhere. If I was Dr. Maddeson and I had just been handed the artifact—and I had a choice in the matter—I would be in my office, with my books and research."

"Then we go to the university," Pretoria surmised. "But if Baffin wants the artifact, will Lord Stillwell still pay for it? Perry?"

There was a moment of quiet, then the door slowly opened and Perry stepped back into the room. There was not a scrap of shame on his face at being caught eavesdropping, just a winsome Copper's smile.

"Lord Stillwell was still very much in want of the artifact when I spoke with him yesterday," the man said. "He did mention that someone had come to him, making inquiries about it and offering to purchase it from him, but he seemed to consider the matter innocent enough. He also told me that his valet had gone missing. It seems he sent him to meet with Mr. Stoke, the night of the bombing."

"Mr. Wake likely killed him, so he could impersonate him," I surmised. I felt a flicker of regret for the faceless stranger, but the chill I felt when I thought of Wake was stronger. "Even if Stillwell is not willing to pay, could you find another buyer?"

"One who would not yield to Baffin?" Pretoria mused. "Certainly."

Reassured, I nearly smiled. "Good. Then let us proceed."

From there, we began to lay out plans. I did not, however, speak of Lewis or the following phases of my plan—to rescue him and flee to Ilandrume. I did not tell my sister that, once the dust from all this had settled, I would take every penny of the reward and leave her behind. I would leave her as I had intended to leave Mr. Stoke. I would turn my back on her, her love and her meddling, and walk away.

A second time.

CHAPTER 28

A Note to the Reader: Regarding Plans Made While Inebriated

Lewis did indeed meet me that night in Sarre Grand, before the twin spires and heavily carved edifice of the central temple. He was very late—midnight was close and I had just been evicted from the patio of the café where I had been waiting for the past four hours, a shawl over my head to conceal any stray threads.

"Deepest apologies," he said, stopping before me. He seemed flustered, for once, and unsure of how to greet me. There was even a moment when I thought he would try to shake my hand. He settled on turning and placing a hand on my back, guiding me away from the closing café. "Let us find somewhere to sit."

I allowed him to lead me to a bench by the courtyard's central fountain. It had eight chambers, seven surrounding the smaller, central pool, like a flower, and was heavily tiled in the style of the last great southern empire, the Telgette.

We were not the only people about. I felt a swell of pride at how Lewis and I must appear—a proper couple, just like the others scattered around the fountain or wandering through the square.

"Are you well?" I asked as we sat. "You do not seem like yourself."

He gave a tired laugh. "There was an attempted robbery

at one of the sites whose security I am responsible for. It happened last night, but I only learned of it this evening—the site is some distance away."

"You were blamed?"

"Naturally," he said with a weary laugh.

"Ridiculous," I pronounced. I reached into the satchel at my hip and produced a bottle of wine, which I proceeded to uncork with an ornate penknife. I had had hours to contemplate this meeting—I knew my role by heart. "This will help."

He took the bottle and turned the label towards the light of the oil lanterns suspended over the square. "A Phinatine? Where did you find this?"

I smiled. "I may have smuggled it in. It is still your favorite?"

"Yes. But you do not appreciate it, as I recall," Lewis noted, looking from the bottle to me.

"I developed a taste for it, on your recommendation," I said.

Lewis made a considering sound and glanced around. "We've no glasses."

Of course, Lewis was not the type to drink straight from a bottle. As he spoke, I unwrapped two glasses and set them on the bench between us. I was thoroughly satisfied with myself, and made no effort to hide it.

Lewis grinned. It was a genuine expression, a shedding of a weight, and it lingered in the glimmering of his eyes as he expertly poured for us, set the bottle aside, and passed me my glass.

"To unexpected reunions," he said, and we drank.

We drank the entire bottle, actually. Phinatine wine is known for its remarkably high alcohol content, and on an empty stomach, the distinguished substance was nearly toxic.

"This is unacceptable," Lewis declared as I blinked broadly and squinted at him. "We must have dinner."

"It's nearly three in the morning."

"Tourists never sleep. With me, Rushforth."

Arm in arm, we made for the docks and the lavish tourist hotels. There we had a fine dinner in the sparkling, slightly blurry light of chandeliers. Lewis was as relaxed as I had ever seen him, and I was warmed through by his company and the steady stream of his conversation as he told me of digs and relics and ruins. My heart sang.

It was not until we had sobered somewhat and retired to the balcony of the hotel, overlooking the water and its forest of picturesque boats, that his mood darkened.

"I should have listened to Pretoria," he said quietly.

I paused over the thick, spiced coffee. "Pardon me?"

"When we secreted you away from... that place," he said, evidently unwilling to name the Guild in the quiet of the balcony. We were alone save for several older gentlemen at their cigars, but sound did travel. "She tried to convince me to accompany you."

I recalled that night clearly, though just then my head was beginning to ache from drink, and fatigue crept over me. I took a sip of the coffee. "You still can."

He shook his head. "I will not be a Rogue, rootless, forced to move from place to place to stay free. It has occurred to me to go to Ilandrume and claim asylum, but asylum is not free, nor is the new name and identity I would need to get there and live in true freedom."

"What do you mean?" I stared at him. "Asylum?"

"Ilandrume is offering asylum to Entwined—quietly, so as not to ruffle too many feathers, but word has reached me. Officially, they are doing it as an act of charity. Unofficially, it comes at a price. But Entwined and Non-Entwined reside in remarkable peace there, or so I have heard."

"I knew nothing of this," I said. I felt oddly gutted by the realization. There was no way Pretoria had not known something so momentous, even if it was not being publicized. "Pretoria must have kept it from me."

"Pretoria loves you deeply," Lewis said. "She will always do what she believes is best for you."

"Even if that is deceiving me."

"Withholding the truth is not deceiving, precisely."

"Semantics."

We fell into silence. Perhaps it was the lingering effects of the drink that led me to what I said next. Perhaps it was my unrequited and ill-advised affection for the handsome young man across from me. Perhaps it was that strange, surreal quality that comes from the warm darkness of summer nights.

But I said, "I would go with you."

He surveyed me, a note of hesitation in his eyes.

"Not as your fiancée—though that is a façade which we would need to maintain for the journey, perhaps. What I mean to say is, I would go to Ilandrume."

"You are unhappy with Pretoria?"

"I am no Rogue." I shook my head. "Well, I am, in the broadest sense—I am outside the Guild, and I am not a Separatist, so I am a Rogue. But... I am rambling. I do not want to spend my life flitting about, deprived of any honest means of supporting myself, forced to theft and villainy. This is Pretoria's world. The Guild is Madge's. I would like the chance to find my own."

Lewis watched me with searching eyes. "Do you mean that?"

"I do," I said.

There was a long, long stretch of silence.

"We would need money," Lewis said, with a tone of reminder. "I only have limited and somewhat... unsavory means of gathering funds."

I raised a questioning brow.

"Smuggling," he admitted lowly. "Baffin's Army is a strict affair and as a Guild officer I have connections."

"I see," I said with a sage nod. I was ill at ease with that, but I had no desire to question Lewis. "I could take a position somewhere. Perhaps as a governess, or librarian, or secretary."

A smile brushed his lips at these suggestions, and I might have seen a flicker of affection in his eyes. I might have imagined it, too.

"Pretoria would not encourage that," he pointed out.

"I would have to leave her to do it," I acknowledged. "I think... It pains me, but it is time. I cannot live my life clinging to her skirts."

"Where would you go, though?" he asked.

I stared out at the water for a span, thinking. "The place where the Guild would least expect. Back to Harrow."

CHAPTER 29

Present Day

Shadows of quavering branches danced around my feet as I plodded through damp grass and leaves in a fresh, if borrowed, shirtwaist, skirt and coat. The twilight tasted like snow, riding a night wind that bit my cheeks and pried under my scarf as I led Pretoria and Perry through the university gardens.

The city was silent, now—the silence of indrawn breaths and coming storms, of a hunter taking aim. A strict military curfew had been placed and soldiers patrolled the streets, the tromp of their boots and the occasional fist on a door the only sounds.

No one heard our footsteps, not in the streets, nor now, in the soft, damp grass of the green and its blanket of leaves.

"Please hurry," Pretoria complained, clutching her scarf about her throat with one hand. The other hovered, concealing us in a bubble of skewed time. "The cold gives me such a headache."

A few lights peeked out from windowpanes and curtains as we approached Maddeson's building, but there was no one to question us when Perry swung the front door open. The building was, to all appearances, empty, and my hope waned. But if Maddeson was not here, we would look elsewhere before conceding that Baffin had already found him. His home. The museum island.

Pretoria kept her sorcery flowing as we passed by study parlors and closed office doors.

Even if we had not had Pretoria's magic to conceal us, we did not look out of place on the university grounds. We were all styled as students, Pretoria and I in skirts, shirtwaists, vests, and trim jackets, and Perry in a tweed suit with a satchel at one hip. The satchel, rather than containing books, held the bullets, binoculars, lockpicks, and various other tools of his and Pretoria's trade. I had a satchel as well, though mine was empty in anticipation of the artifact.

"This is it." I pointed to Maddeson's door. Light seeped beneath the barrier and I grinned in satisfaction. "He is here."

Perry took the lead, resting his fingers on the handle and meeting his wife's gaze. "Ready?"

"Ready," she affirmed.

Perry swung the door inwards. Electric light poured around Pretoria's skirts as she strode into the room, skewing time afresh with an effortless crook of the wrist. I followed next, hands ungloved.

The office looked the same as the last time I had stood here; the shelves packed with books, oddities, and treasures strewn about and the carpet beneath our careless boots depicting a fine Eleshi motif.

But it was not Dr. Maddeson at the desk.

"I assume you are not the professor," Pretoria said, sounding more than a little disappointed. She dropped her hands and the room sunk back into the proper flow of time.

A gangly young man shot to his feet. His chair toppled and his pen rolled, trailing ink across the paper he had been scrawling. He noticed the pen at the same time as me and lunged forward, snatching it up before it could stain an open book.

"Who—" the young man asked, clutching the pen like a talisman. I recognized him as the one who had brought me tea, on my last visit. "Who are you?"

Pretoria crossed the room slowly. "Someone who is very disappointed to find you instead of Dr. Maddeson."

Behind us, Perry pulled a pistol from the back of his trousers and rested it pointedly against his thigh.

"I am his research assistant!" The young man reared back into a bookcase, his eyes now flicking between the three of us. His gaze focused on me as I approached the shelves beside him. "I know you. You're that secretary! Oi—do not touch that!"

"Where is Maddeson's research on the Entwined?" I demanded, pointing to the newly empty shelves where his notes had been. I looked from him to the rest of the room, but though there were stacks of books and papers in numerous locations, none of them seemed right.

My stomach sank. The answer seemed clear, though I needed confirmation before I accepted it. Baffin had already been here, and he had taken both Maddeson and his research.

"Where is the professor?" I asked.

The boy seemed, at this point, to forget his tongue.

Pretoria sighed, straightening and pulling one of her hatpins free. It proved to be a fine dagger, which left an equally delicate sheath in her hat with its twin.

Pretoria tossed the blade casually into the air and froze it in a skew of time between her and the assistant. "Hear me, young man. You find yourself in the company of the very finest mages in Harrow. All Adepts, the lot of us. You can see for yourself what I am. The mousy one, she is an Eventide. And that handsome fellow there with the gun? Well, I shall let you learn for yourself what he is."

"Where is Maddeson?" I repeated. "And his research?"

"Mr. Maddeson went to the museum! The Grand!" the young man rattled out. "With a police detective. Said he needed to identify an artifact of some kind."

I stilled. "A police detective?"

"Yes!"

"Detective Supford?" I tried, bewildered though I was.

"That's him." The assistant lit up, as if I had thrown him a lifeline.

"What artifact was he required to identify?" I pressed.

"A Landsdown Trove artifact," the young man said. "Of Incarnate stone."

The gears of my brain shuddered, ground, and began to turn. In chasing the carved box, I had lost sight of the fact that the treasure was not simply the box itself—but its contents.

Could it be that Baffin had the empty box, and the police had somehow found its separate contents?

I laughed. I had to. There was no other response to the strain and absurdity of the situation.

The assistant looked even more perturbed by my laugh.

"What about the professor's research," Pretoria prodded. The knife glittered. "Did the police take all that?"

"No, someone came to collect it, not half an hour ago, from the Grand General, I believe. The unrest, and all. Our sponsor: he expressed concerns about the university's security." At this he stared at Pretoria's knife again, the aptness of his words clearly not lost to him. "And so he had it moved. I do not know where. They do not tell me things."

"Did this someone from the Grand General also ask where Dr. Maddeson was?" I asked.

The assistant nodded.

"And you told them."

Another nod.

"Damn." I met Pretoria's gaze. "We need to move quickly."

Pretoria reclaimed her knife and waved it at the assistant. "Get your coat, dear. You are coming with us."

We stepped back out into the cool of the night to the sound of distant gunshots, somewhere out in the city. We were a grim but determined procession, hastening through starlight and shadow, back through the university grounds and to a side gate.

Pretoria's threads began to twine in the starlight. They were gentle, pale things, and seemed to pulse with distant light. She lifted her chin with a satisfied sigh and shook out her shoulders, settling into the increase of power.

When the change in the night came, it was subtle. A whisper and a breath. Pretoria must have felt it too, for her magic faltered for an instant, and then—soldiers.

Six of them stepped from the night. Perry raised his pistol in the same instant as Pretoria threw us into a new skew of time.

One soldier stepped right through it, levelling a rifle right at her face. Pips glistened on the soldier's collar, above which she wore the same threads as Pretoria. Another Starlight.

Maddeson's assistant made a strangled sound and raised his arms high over his head.

"Lay down your weapons," the other Starlight mage demanded.

I barely heard her, because my eyes had landed on the soldier directly before me, his blond hair darkened by the shadows, and his eyes inscrutable hollows beneath the brim of his cap.

Lewis.

I cannot say what possessed me. It was, I think, a momentary madness brought on by recent events, coupled with our need for haste, and an instinctual, desperate need to know whether my erstwhile fiancé, looking at me down the barrel of a rifle, was truly my enemy.

I grasped the barrel of the rifle and pulled it straight out of his hands. He reacted a fraction too late, hands tightening, body lunging. I had already sidestepped. I used his own momentum to throw him into one of his comrades and stepped back with the rifle to my own shoulder.

"What are you doing here?" I demanded.

He opened his mouth to reply. Then his eyes flicked right.

Pretoria had vanished. The soldier next to Lewis dropped like a stone, his legs kicked out from under him, and chaos broke loose. Perry hurled himself behind the nearest tree. Several soldiers leapt to intervene. The rest cried out in alarm, moving under the Starlit soldier's instruction to find Pretoria.

For that scattered moment, at least, they left Lewis and I to our own devices.

I stared at him down the barrel of his rifle. I almost repeated my earlier question, but there was no time for explanations.

"Do you require rescue?" I asked.

He faltered in something between startlement and a desperate laugh. Both were gone in a flash, replaced by a raised hand and a warning, "Patterson, wait—"

I twisted, bringing the rifle to bear just in time as a hand seized the back of my neck.

A thread of my energy evaporated, and my vision blurred. A Silver.

"Leave her!" Lewis shouted.

The hand departed. The contact had been brief enough that my energy returned in a rush, and I took immediate advantage of it.

I cast Lewis one last, imploring look, then bolted. The Silver, Patterson, stepped into my path but I danced neatly aside, the grace of the movement ruined by a pell-mell swing as I shifted the rifle into a club and struck him across the head. He dropped. I hurtled on.

Like Perry I made for the shelter of a tree, and beyond, a hedge. I tumbled through an archway and into the extensive university gardens, where rows of shrouded hedges and winding pathways were speckled with benches and pavilions.

Instead of taking off towards one of these shelters, I nipped to one side and threw myself down at the foot of the hedge itself, only a few paces from where I had burst in.

Shadows welcomed me. My threads prickled. I had little fear for Pretoria—she had escaped worse, even with another Starlight present. Perry, in all practicality, I had not had enough time to attach to, not to a self-sacrificing degree.

Lewis burst through the hedge, followed by another soldier. They divided, the stranger heading off in one direction while Lewis, pistol lowered, moved cautiously in the other. The two of them exchanged several glances and gestures, then the stranger slipped from sight, and Lewis progressed past me.

I shifted to one knee and levelled the rifle again.

Lewis turned. I stood. Muzzle to muzzle, we faced one another across a row of red-leafed, hip-high bushes.

"Did you betray me?" I hissed.

In the same breath he said, "Run with me."

We stared at one another for an interminable moment, then he holstered his pistol and, instead, offered me an open hand. There was tension in every line of him, awareness that we stood in open view if his companion was to return, but he stood straight and tall and stalwart, fingers extended.

"How can I trust you?" My voice cracked, the question directed to both him and myself.

"The Guild intercepted a telegraph from Mr. Stoke to myself," he said rapidly, pleading in his eyes. "I was shipped immediately back to Harrow, where the Guild was waiting for me."

"Madge?"

"And her new husband. He read our letters, Ottilie. He knows everything."

I stared, eyes so round they ached. "What?"

"Run with me. Ottilie, please."

"Run where?" The question was vast, edgeless, and devouring. "If Moran knows—"

His response was immediate, impassioned, and accompanied by pleading eyes. "Anywhere but here."

Reason swiftly deserted me. I was overwhelmed by the *want* that the sight of him elicited in me. Want to trust. Want to be seen. Want to be held, to belong, and to run, run, run.

A shout rose beyond the gardens. "Illing!"

Lewis's gaze shot from the sound to my rifle, then he leapt the bushes. All at once I was sprinting beside him, out of the hedges and into the university's main sprawl.

Tall, lofty buildings and ancient halls spread around us. We passed a dry fountain, its tall, humanoid statue shrouded for the coming winter. Our footsteps echoed, but there was no help for that.

We reached the university's outer wall, some ten feet tall, half stone, half decorative wrought iron.

"Help me over," I panted, slinging the rifle across my back.

"Still terrible at climbing?" he quipped. It was the first emotion he had shown other than pleading and intensity, and my blood skittered through my veins at his flash of a smile.

The reader may wonder, at this juncture, why I had decided to trust him. Allow me to reaffirm the earlier departure of my reason and the fact that, despite my attempts to distract myself with Harden, I had been in love with Lewis Illing for years. That bond, his simple familiarity, and the desperateness of the situation combined to leave me with no true choice.

Trust, then, is perhaps an inadequate word. I still had questions, questions that required answers. But the bonds between us had reasserted themselves, and I was helpless in their grasp.

Lewis clambered onto the top of the wall and reached back down, his boot providing a foothold and his hands grasping my upper arms. When I straddled the top of the fence he dropped down the other side, landing firmly on the stone ledge, and took me by the waist.

This ostensibly romantic gesture was ruined by the fact that I lost my balance. I dropped straight into him, knocking the pair of us off the wall and onto the hard cobblestones on the other side. The rifle clattered and swung, discharging with a deafening crack.

I was cushioned by Lewis's chest. Lewis was not so fortunate.

He made a breathless wheeze and lay there for a stunned breath. I scrambled to my feet and put an arm under his shoulders, helping him upright.

"Sorry!" I hissed.

"Fine—I'm fine," he wheezed, still doubled over.

"Ho, there!" a voice shouted up the street.

We turned. Despite his breathlessness Lewis stepped partially in front of me, drawing his pistol again. I swung my rifle back up. The chamber was empty, but even after the audible shot, the newcomers wouldn't necessarily know which weapon had fired.

"Guild rat," the voice said, speaking as if to a third party. Several more figures peeled from the night. Then even more. Eight men, four women, armed with clubs and bearing a look that chilled me to the bone. Their expressions were something between hunters and drunkards, giddy and arrogant in their joint purpose. Several had coils of rope over their shoulders.

Zealots.

The speaker leaned out, peering around Lewis towards me. "Aw, and his chit. Better run, love, I've got my eye on you."

The tension in Lewis's posture changed to something else

then. Something more dangerous, more at ease. Something... resigned.

He shot the man in the knee. Before the Zealot could so much as stagger, Lewis fired again and again, each at a different target, each on the heels of one another.

The Zealots did not charge. Instead they scattered with shouts and curses, dragging wounded comrades to safety.

I grabbed Lewis's arm and pulled. For a second he resisted, a pillar of stone, then together we ran.

Shots chased us—the Zealots had more than clubs. One pinged off the stone just behind us before new voices entered the streets, the shouts and whistles of police.

Whether they would have proved friend or foe became irrelevant as we sprinted off, round the university wall and down an alleyway. I did not have Harden's intimate knowledge of the back ways of Harrow, but I knew enough to lead us away from the university and towards the west river. Towards the museum.

My lungs burned and my mind raced. Pretoria and Perry would either head there, as previously intended, or back to the hotel.

I did not consider any alternatives—that they had been captured or killed. No, thoughts of that nature would do no good.

I glanced at Lewis, rifle still cradled to my chest. The streets around us had quietened, eerie and windblown, and the only sounds of life were distant. He was alert, stoic, but with an intensity under the skin that left me uneasy.

I took Lewis by the arm and pulled him into a shadow. He regarded me calmly, as if he had expected this, and put a little space between us.

"I have been in Harrow for ten days," he said. "Madge insisted on keeping me close, believing you would surface. And you did, at the opera. I saw you leave with that man. I did not know to intervene, and I hardly wanted to turn you into the Guild. So I let you go."

Startled as I was, I sensed he had more to confess. I held my tongue.

"Guild spies learned that Baffin had captured an Adept and intended to hand her over to Incarnadine. We intervened, as you saw, and I let you go, again."

"That much I know," I murmured.

"Madge sent me after you tonight," he revealed. "She told me to take you somewhere safe, and keep you away from Mr. Moran." Something else entered his eyes then, something probing. "She did not say why."

I recalled Madge sending me away, so unexpectedly. I remembered Moran's interest, his fixed gaze.

Madge was protecting me. Then, and now. It was more painful than consoling. But precisely what was she protecting me from? What did she fear her husband would do?

It did not bear thinking about, just then. I had to settle matters with Lewis and get to the museum before Baffin.

"Give me your hand." I jerked off my glove and held out my bare fingers. "Now."

He pulled off his own glove and did so. His hand was warm, almost too warm, and patterned with sweat. I barely felt either.

Memories came to me, fleet and clear. Lewis shooting at the Zealots. Lewis shaking the hand of another Guild soldier. Lewis with his hand on the back of Madge's chair at the opera, surrounded by music. Lewis shaking hands with Mr. Moran, standing on a pier with the river wind in his hair.

It was that last I held onto. I felt Lewis's reluctance. I felt a spike of panic too, and dread. I followed that feeling and found another, connected memory—that of him sitting in a carriage across from Madge, her leaning forward.

"We both want the best for her, Mr. Illing," my sister vowed. *"Trust me, in this. And tell my husband nothing."*

Frustration. Injustice. Powerlessness. Indecision. Lewis's raw, unfiltered response to my sister's words were a blazing fire behind a barrier of ice as he calmly replied, *"Thank you, Mrs. Moran. I will not let you down."*

One last memory came, drifting to the surface as the carriage and Madge disappeared. It was Lewis striding down a familiar hallway in Golden House. To one side of the passageway, a Silver Guild soldier saluted. On the other, the door to my prison lay.

In the memory, his eyes drifted to the door. His steps faltered, if only just. And the feeling inside him—the swell of worry, of need, of *affection* he felt at the thought of me on the other side of that door?

I took what remained of my reserve and hurled it into the river.

The alleyway came back to me, along with the feeling of Lewis's fingers in mine. I quickly dropped them and pulled my glove back on, but not before his gaze, which had lingered on my face, dropped to my engagement ring. He seemed startled to see it.

"I believe you," I said, gathering myself. It was not easy. I was shaken. Actually, I was shaking, quite literally, a shiver not only in my hands but in the core of my bones.

Lewis cared for me. It was not quite love, but it was something, and it was powerful and confusing and persuasive.

"I am with you," he assured me. There was a vulnerability behind his eyes just then that prodded at my careworn heart, and I was truly done for when he added, "I still want the future we planned."

"Even if Mr. Moran knows of it? If he will try to stop us every step of the way? We certainly cannot sail out of Harrow or the Sunrise Isles."

"It was always going to be hard," he said, and I sensed he was reassuring himself as much as me. "It changes little. We can leave tonight, Harden will get us out. Where have you hidden our funds?"

My stomach dropped. "About that..."

"Ottilie," another voice drifted towards us. Between one blink and the next Pretoria appeared, shedding a skew of time with a ripple in the air, like hot sun on stone. She surveyed Lewis while, behind her, Perry became visible. He held Maddeson's assistant by the arm.

"Illing," Pretoria said caustically. "What are you doing here?"

I took a half step between them. "Tori, all is well."

Lewis's hand still dropped to his pistol. "Rushforth. I am here for your sister."

"In what capacity?" she asked. "As Guild dog?"

Lewis rankled. "I am no one's dog."

"Let us test that," she said, holding up a finger. With her other hand she dug around in her pocket. "I have a biscuit here somewhere."

"Pretoria, the museum," I reminded her. My own hackles were rising, incensed on Lewis's behalf. "Now."

"Oh, you told the hound about that?" She pulled out a smattering of pocket lint and puffed it at Lewis. "Now, *sit*, boy."

"I was about to," I snapped, brushing stray lint off my shoulder.

Lewis bore all this with a clenched jaw. He picked more lint from his moustache as he said, "Ottilie has verified my story."

"Hm." Pretoria studied us a moment longer, then dusted her hands. "Well, we haven't time to waste. If you betray us, Illing, you will never see the sunrise."

"Unoriginal," he muttered.

"You know Perry, and this is Geoffrey. He is our prisoner." Pretoria flapped a hand behind her, to where Perry and Maddeson's assistant stood. "Shall we carry on? That other Starlight may prove a nuisance if we do not keep moving. Did you recognize her? Loretti. Always a tedious girl, never an original thought. Ottilie, you can apprise Lewis of the situation en route."

I nodded stoutly. "Let's be off."

CHAPTER 30

"I will stuff you in a sarcophagus if you cause any trouble," Lewis quietly informed our prisoner, Geoffrey, as we moved through the service passageway of Ciceley House. He held the younger man by the arm, and Geoffrey tripped along like a reluctant toddler.

"I won't, I swear," the younger man insisted. "W-we ought to check the vaults, first. The detective said it would be stored there. The artifact, I mean."

All of us save Pretoria stopped as one as we reached the café proper. She continued, one hand raised to shield herself in a skew of time, fingers light, head tilted to one side as she listened.

"Safe," she determined. "No sign of Baffin yet, though we must exercise all caution."

We joined her inside, spreading out under the dome of the painted ceiling. The café seemed demure now, ceiling in shadow, chairs empty, extravagant chandeliers and lording windows devoid of light.

"Perry and I will take the puppy up to Maddeson's office," Pretoria said. She was clearly favoring canine insults that evening.

Geoffrey looked startled. "Am I the puppy?"

Pretoria ignored him. "The vaults are below." She gave me a meaningful look. "That is a better task for you."

"Lewis and I will see to them," I acknowledged. I was riddled with nervous anticipation, the thought of finally finding the artifact both intoxicating and taxing.

"You are sure?" Pretoria asked, casting a meaningful glance at Lewis.

I suppressed a flare of irritation. "I am sure."

We divided. Pretoria, Perry, and Geoffrey headed for the nearest staircase, and Lewis and I made for the main foyer.

The museum was deathly quiet save for our footsteps and rustle of heavy clothes. Diffused streetlight trickled through the front doors, illuminating the pillars, courtyard, and high walls beyond the glass. We passed under the gaze of two enormous manticores at the base of the main staircase and paused, looking for our next destination. The others, meanwhile, headed up the stairs to the second floor with quiet feet.

The thin light of the streetlamps faded entirely as Lewis and I entered a central passage. My Eventide eyes took over, separating the gloom into sepia tones.

A meaty thud and masculine "Oof" echoed from up the main stairs.

"Just a guard!" Pretoria whisper-shouted down to us. "Carry on!"

Lewis met my gaze with arched brows. I cracked a smile.

We passed a cloakroom with its empty shelves, hooks, and coat hangers, and slowed at a heavy door marked *Private*.

"This looks promising," I said, just loud enough for him to hear.

"Shall I take the lock?"

"Please."

"Hold this."

He placed a lighter in my hand and crouched—as an Entwined of the Sun, he could not see in the darkness as I could.

Glancing around to ensure we were alone, I clicked a flame into life and bent close to the keyhole.

Light illuminated Lewis's face, revealing pupils dark and wide and fixed on me. Our proximity was a demanding thing, charged and unnecessarily preoccupying.

"You look different," he said, as if to justify his momentary stare, and turned to the lock.

"How so?"

He fiddled obscurely with his tools. "You... ah, tired. I need to concentrate."

"Well," I huffed, and held the lighter close enough to singe his moustache. He flinched back, opened his mouth to say something more, then froze.

Footsteps echoed from somewhere indistinct, accompanied by the drone of male voices. I instantly let the lighter go out.

Thus followed a rather unwieldy series of events in which I knocked into Lewis, who tried to support me and dropped a pick with a clatter. His hand landed, rather pointedly, on my left breast, which, though it happened to be the superior breast, was still mortifying. I stifled a startled sound and, in trying to grab the door handle to support myself, clawed him in the face.

"For all that is holy—cut your nails!" Lewis hissed.

"Watch your hands!"

Before our less-than-amiable banter could continue, my hand closed on the door handle.

Memories leapt out at me. I saw a hand, an arm reaching up to the silhouette of Dr. Maddeson. They had gone through, but not returned yet.

The footsteps, now clearly coming from beyond the door, closed in.

"Cloakroom!" I whispered.

"I cannot see!"

I snatched his hand. Together we scuttled back down the hallway, I lifted a divided section of the counter, and pulled him through.

"...your research," Detective Supford's voice drifted to us, accompanied by the opening of the door. Light flooded the hallway and cut across the countertop.

Lewis and I dropped down, side by side, behind the counter. Just out of reach of the light, we held our breaths.

"If your assistant has already retired for the night, perhaps you can give me a list of what you require?" Supford asked.

"Of course," Dr. Maddeson replied. "Let us go up to my office. The artifact is more than safe in the vaults until the Grand General arrives, I assure you."

The Grand General himself was on his way? That was a nightmarish thought.

"I appreciate your willingness to help, Professor," Supford said. I picked up something in his tone, something displeased but resigned, and wondered if he was glad for the Grand General's imminent arrival. "And your discretion."

The light drew nearer, shrinking our little haven of shadow. We hunkered closer, our earlier conflict forgotten in the need to stay hidden. Lewis's hand brushed my arm, but only to draw his pistol and hold it, ready, beside his head.

We listened until their footsteps mounted the main staircase, passed out into the foyer, and faded away.

"We do not have time to warn Pretoria," Lewis said quietly.

I took a breath to think. "Agreed. She can manage Supford."

Lewis unfolded and offered me a hand, which I took. At the same time, I noticed a scratch on his clean-shaven jaw.

"I am sorry I scratched you," I offered quietly as I found my feet and let him go.

"I am sorry I... ah, patted you," he replied, voice equally low.

I waved the conversation aside. "The lock."

"The lock," he affirmed.

We returned to the door marked *Private*. Lewis made quick work of the lock this time, aided by the lighter once more, and preceded me down a dim staircase beyond.

True darkness wrapped around us. Lewis slowed, taking the lighter and holding it before himself, but my Eventide eyes required no adjustment.

At the bottom of the steps I took the lead. We set off at a brisk pace, passing room after room and turn after turn. The belly of the museum was old, at least as old as the citadel, and the chaos of stones that formed the walls spoke of even more ancient ruins pillaged in the construction. Still, hefty cabling for electricity laced along the walls and here and there a darkened bulb protruded from the ceiling.

The hallway abruptly ended in a huge iron door, set with a large tumbler and an iron bar.

When I touched a finger to the tumbler, I found the memory of Dr. Maddeson's enthusiastic spinning of the dial, the brush of his sleeve, and a whispered exchange with Supford.

"Can you open it?" Lewis asked, stepping back and scanning the vault in its entirety.

"Perhaps." I kept my hand on the tumbler. Images appeared again, vague and indistinct. I heard, felt, and saw the dial spin beneath Dr. Maddeson's touch.

The dial scraped softly as I spun it to the first number. I was rewarded by a soft click and glanced at Lewis with a triumphant smile. He grinned back, genuine and impressed, and I felt a happy warmth from my cheeks to my toes.

I set back to my work. Five turns later, there was a louder clunk, and my task was done.

Together, we heaved on the iron bar. The door ground open, letting out a rush of musty, oddly scented air—old wood, chemicals, and dust.

Rounded arches of ancient stone branched off into a network of cellars in the same style as those beneath The Three Trees, studded with hefty pillars and lined with shelves. Statues stood veiled beneath sheets, hung with labels. Crates of every size were shoved into free spaces, and every shelf was laden with boxes, each marked with painstaking care.

My stomach sank. "It could be anywhere. I hardly even know what it looks like."

"And I cannot see far," Lewis added. He was grim in the little orb of light from his lighter. "You start. I will find a lantern."

I nodded my agreement, and we separated.

I ducked under a low arch and avoided an Ummani coffin urn so large it could have fit both of us inside. Chilled by the thought, I carried on, scanning labels and peering into boxes.

One section of shelving held unrecognizable animal skeletons, empty eye sockets watching me from carved and painted skulls. Another row housed meteorological instruments, discs and dials arching through the gloom.

Still another hosted pottery from every era of human history, depicting hunts and festivals and geometric patterns in age-muted tones. Clay tablets sported pressings from reed styli, and one particular crate, yawning open, held a blank-eyed automaton in Seaussen court garb from three centuries past.

The Sarre—Landsdown Trove.

I darted back and pulled out a small crate. Inside, packed in wool, were several paper-wrapped objects.

"Lewis!" I hissed to the darkness.

I received no answer, but distantly I thought I saw a swell of light.

I set the crate on the floor and brushed my fingers across the bundles. I wanted to tear them open in reckless curiosity but reached for the papers' memories instead.

Dust came off on my fingers, along with distant memories of being packed away. None of this was recent enough to be our artifact. I still unwrapped them, just in case, and found funerary statues of mundane, grey stone. No familiar symbols.

I turned, surveying the shelves around me with the back of one hand to my forehead, dusty fingers crooked and hopelessness welling in my throat.

"Ottilie!" Lewis's voice echoed towards me, just loud enough to hear. "Over here!"

I set off at a run, abandoning the crate on the floor and darting through a regiment of suits of armor into a broader section of the vault. The ceilings were higher here, and several tables were set out between veiled hangings on wooden frames. One table held rows of weapons, unsheathed and carefully oiled. Another held stacks of books.

Lewis stood over the last table with a lantern held high. And on the surface before him, was an orb of dazzling blue stone.

CHAPTER 31

I had the sensation of a great bell ringing above my head, profound and bone-quaking. But the vault was silent; I heard nothing except the rush of my own breath and the shift of Lewis's feet.

I approached the table slowly, almost reverently. The stone, I discovered upon closer inspection, was not precisely an orb. It had twelve sides, each adorned with a symbol like those on the box.

"Have I gone mad, or do you feel that, too?" I whispered, trying not to shatter the weighty stillness.

"I feel something," he mused, leaning down to consider the sides of the artifact. He matched my tone.

I bent to consider the other side of the artifact—a dodecahedron, my memory now supplied. Twelve sides. Twelve surfaces of stone, and upon them, memories and secrets that might unravel not only this entire sordid affair, but the balance of power between humans and Entwined.

Only eleven sides had singular symbols. The final side contained a section of text in neat, tight lines, though their edges ended abruptly. Was this part of the Stele Maddeson had mentioned, the valuable stone carved into this shape at a later time?

I drew a bracing breath and caught Lewis's gaze again,

seeking courage in his eyes. He seemed to understand, and gave a small nod.

I laid a hand on the artifact. It fit neatly into my palm, smooth and cool, the ridges of its many sides smoothed with time.

Memories assaulted me, as strong and vivid as they would have been in the heart of twilight. I inhaled sharply, taken aback, but I did not retreat.

"Are you well?" Lewis asked.

"The stone is acting like twilight. Did you touch it?"

"Not since Sarre, and I noticed nothing at the time."

I fell quiet again, overtaken by a maelstrom of disordered, anachronistic images. There was no order to them, no structure. Just a tempest of power and recollection.

I glimpsed Dr. Maddeson, setting the artifact reverently down. Detective Supford, examining it. Lewis carefully wrapping it in canvas, back in The Sarre. The darkness of its box. Seaussen rebels, their faces covered in brightly colored cloths, bore it through a smoky forest. Then I saw a lavish house, perhaps Lord Stillwell's former residence in Sarre Grand, with pale painted plaster, gauzy curtains, and crashing waves.

Last of all, I saw Mr. Stoke. My sorcery flared and I snatched at the vision like a rider at a runaway horse. The image slowed, broadening and clarifying until I stood in a hotel room. Mr. Stoke cupped the orb in his palms and considered it, speaking to someone I could not see.

"*The only thing I can,*" Stoke said, frowning at the piece. He looked harried and battered, bruises clear on his face. "*If what the professor has told me is correct, I cannot put her at risk, nor any other Entwined. Until I know more, I will ensure this does not fall into the wrong hands.*"

Someone must have spoken, out of contact with Mr. Stoke and the stone, and thus inaudible.

The detective replied, "*Thank you, Jon.*"

Jon. I delved further into the stone's memories, searching for any clue as to who that was.

The last memory the stone possessed of Mr. Stoke was

him tucking it behind a wall panel in what I surmised was his hotel room. Then there was darkness, a tremor of feet here and there. A new light, a hand, a face. A police constable with the name *J. Hopgood* on his breast pocket.

I reeled back into the present. Lewis stood beside me now, one hand resting on my back and his expression writ with concern.

"Ottilie? What is it?"

For a few heartbeats I could not speak, overcome with emotion at the sound of Mr. Stoke's voice and the implications of his words.

"He knew. Mr. Stoke knew what I am. He hid this"—I raised the artifact, voice thick with gratitude and grief—"to protect the Entwined."

"He was a detective," Lewis pointed out, but not unkindly. His brows furrowed. "He could still have warned you about Wake."

I shook my head, shrugging as if the physical movement could detach the pain of my agreement. "He looked injured," I admitted. "Perhaps the situation simply escalated too quickly."

Lewis made a noncommittal sound.

I charged on: "A constable who works with Supford, I saw him, too. He recovered this, the orb, from Mr. Stoke's hotel room. I cannot see precisely when... but the memory is quite recent. Perhaps even today?"

"That would seem reasonable." Lewis nodded vaguely towards the ceiling. His hand was still on my back. "Considering a detective is here now."

I nodded, trying to corral my emotions and focus on the facts. But my eyes burned and I felt, in that moment, sapped of strength.

I had the artifact. I had it, and with it, hope of reclaiming Lewis's and my future. But Mr. Stoke was still dead, killed for his good intentions, for his attempt to maintain peace and protect me.

He clearly had not believed the artifact would be safe from Baffin in Stillwell's hands. Perhaps he was right, perhaps he was wrong, but my excuses had begun to feel both flimsy and selfish.

I clenched my eyes shut, trying to block out my emotions, to steel myself. We would have to find another buyer, one with no connection to Baffin. Pretoria could do that, though it would complicate matters.

Lewis's hand slipped up, cupping my shoulder and allowing me to bury my cheek in his neck. His other hand, however, remained on the table—a statement, a lingering separation, which I could not help but interpret.

Heart aching all the more fiercely, I straightened and put the stone into the pocket of my coat. It sat heavy, but secure.

"We ought to find Pretoria," I said.

A deep, long creak echoed through the vault.

We both snapped our heads around. In the same movement I stepped towards one of the other tables and took up a saber.

Lewis drew his pistol.

No sound came towards us. No lantern parted the gloom of the vault.

"Either we have just been locked in," Lewis murmured. "Or whoever that is needs no light."

"Mr. Wake."

"Or Moran."

"I dislike both options."

Lewis took my hand and tugged me in the opposite direction of the door. I did not protest, the artifact heavy in my pocket as we stepped behind the huge, veiled frames.

As one we crouched, he on one end of the frame and I the other. He nosed the veil aside with the mouth of his pistol and I held my blade low, peering through a narrow gap between a fraying tapestry and the wooden structure.

Before long, a shadow moved at the edge of the lanternlight. A figure, prowling. Surveying the tables, but not committing themselves to the light.

I blinked. From one moment to the next the figure was gone, as if the shadows themselves had consumed him.

A hand seized the back of my neck. I screamed, throwing my elbow back and twisting.

Fingernails dug into my flesh as an awful, bone-aching sensation overtook me—familiar and dreadful. My vision sparked and I felt a nerve, somewhere at the base of my skull, begin to spasm.

"I will kill you," Mr. Wake said. "Where is the artifact?"

"Look for it yourself," I managed.

He tightened his grip and shook me, then looked at Lewis. The Bronze was poised, a predatory calm in his eyes.

"Where is it?" Wake repeated.

"How am I supposed to know?" Lewis growled. "Let her go."

Grey washed over me. My saber barely dangled from my fingers, and one nudge from Wake sent it clattering to the floor. He reached then, patting my pockets. Looking for the artifact.

My focus narrowed. Wake's one hand, moving towards my pocket. His other, on my neck, warm and crushing. Flesh to flesh.

Flesh to flesh.

I shoved one hand into my pocket and grabbed the stone.

Ethereal power roared through Wake's and my connection. I saw a mother's face, soft with love, then cold with death. I saw an angry boy in the shadows, one with bloody knuckles and a mouth full of curses. I saw Moran. He was dressed in hunting leathers, with the boy at his side.

The boy was Wake. He kept pace with Moran with a rifle at his hip and his face angled away. Still in the vision, the muscles of his neck strained as if my power were a physical force, forcing him to face me.

In this world of vision and memory, Wake was fighting back.

We broke apart. I snatched up my saber with all the grace of a drunkard and rounded on him.

"What is Moran to you?" I bit out.

Wake stepped backwards into a shadow and wholly disappeared.

"Where—" I cut myself off. Time for memories and connections to Moran later. Clearly Wake was no simple Silver. Moving through shadows was a Moonless ability—or should have been.

As this realization and its ramifications careened through my head, a gun cracked. I felt the bullet rush past, punching through a hanging right where Wake had been and was no longer. Beyond, there was a sound of exploding pottery.

"He is Moonless—watch the shadows!" I warned Lewis. I retreated towards him, the hangings around us no longer a shelter but a trap.

We reunited.

"We need Pretoria," I panted.

"Agreed."

On the other side of the tapestry something shattered and the lantern went out. My Eventide eyes took a moment to adjust, every desperate second taut with tension, then I seized Lewis's hand and ran.

Through the shelves we sprinted, he blindly following my lead. I expected Wake to unfold from any direction, and my dread mounted as we sprinted alone, uninterrupted.

Wake, of course, waited for us at the door of the vault. He stood calmly, head tilted slightly to one side, revolver in hand.

I anticipated a threat, a demand. But instead, he simply opened fire.

Two muzzle flashes, directly after one another. I threw myself backwards into Lewis at the same time as he fired back, discharging his weapon right beside my ear.

Lewis and I hit the stone floor. I was briefly aware of his body beneath me, a tangle of limbs, then a horrific ringing overwhelmed my senses. I rolled, struggling to gain my feet.

Something struck the back of my head.

I came to in fits and starts. There was light now, distant but expanding, and a cloying scent of smoke.

I pushed myself upright, hair in my eyes and something warm and salty on my lips. Blood. I looked down and discovered I had been lying in a smear of scarlet, glistening in a rising dance of firelight.

The smashed lantern had started a fire. The artifacts, the shelves—the vault was burning. It was a terrible realization, but distant, down a dark and echoing well.

Had I been shot? I felt no pain, felt very little at all. My vision was short and blurry, and my ears still rang, loud enough to make me cringe and clamp my hands over them.

Movement pulled my gaze right. There, Wake perched atop Lewis, hands cinched around his throat. Between us, bloodied and waiting, lay the artifact.

I tackled Wake, snatching the artifact on my way by and smashing it into our assailant's head. It connected with a satisfying *thunk*, jarring my hand and lancing pain up my arm.

We toppled off Lewis's other side and into a row of shelves. A box fell beside us, muffled in my damaged ears, and clay dust plumed. Coughing, half-blinded, and tangled in Wake, I struck at him again with the artifact.

He reeled out of the way and grabbed my wrist. With the contact came Leeching, draining the strength from my muscles and reviving his own.

He pried my fingers apart with terrifying ease and kicked me down. The artifact fell and rolled in a tottering rhythm. I barely managed to bring my hands up to soften his next kick, aimed for my head.

"Lewis!" I cried.

The kick never landed. There was movement around me, a scuffle and an impact against the shelves. Another crate fell along with numerous smaller objects, then hasty hands helped me stand.

I steadied myself on Lewis's arm, partially tucked into his chest, and looked back to see fire spreading through the vault. Heat rolled towards us, scented with the destruction of centuries, millennia, of precious things.

It was an Archivist's nightmare made real. Old wood flared, tapestries turned to ash, and pottery cracked—all bizarrely muffled to my ears.

Lewis turned to stand between me and the flames. He was speaking to me, I realized, his mouth moving as his hands cupped my cheeks. The firelight illuminated him from behind, outlining him like a painted saint.

"My ears," I managed, my throat thick for more than one reason. His hands were tender, his expression urgent, and his concern sincere. It was the rawest I had ever seen him, and to be the subject of his care was a momentous thing.

Then, somewhere to the side, the vault door opened.

The influx of fresh air made the fire flare, surging closer and throwing us into bright relief. A figure rounded the newly opened door, about to lunge through with the artifact in hand.

Lewis lunged, but he was limping. He toppled into the back of the door and discharged his pistol after Wake. I saw the pop of light, but even the gunshot was a distant muffle to my ears.

Wake hurled himself out into the hallway. The artifact fell to the floor and rolled into the smoke, each side glinting in the firelight as it turned. I instinctively flinched towards it.

Then the vault door closed with a swirl of smoke. I saw the mechanisms automatically spin, felt them *thunk* into place like nails into my own coffin.

Lewis threw himself down on the internal lever. I joined him, casting a frantic glance for the artifact as I did. Nothing, just thickening smoke and shelf after shelf, relic after treasure, waiting to be devoured by the flames.

I brushed stray hair, smoke, and dust from my eyes and turned my focus to the mechanism, searching for another way to open the door. Surely, there was some safety device, something Wake had used to open it from this side.

"There must be a secondary lever!" I shouted—or, felt that I shouted.

But if there was, we could not find it. We searched and cursed as my eyes ran with tears and sweat, and the smoke sent us into fits of coughing.

The door swung inwards without warning. A dark, moody blue orb rolled before it, tapping a pattern of blood across the floor.

I snatched up the dodecahedron, and Lewis and I charged through the gap.

There was too much smoke to see our rescuer, or if they were indeed a rescuer. Just then, it did not matter. Together Lewis and I pushed the door closed one final time, blocking off the heat of the fire. Smoke curled across the ceiling.

The closing of the door cut off the light of the fire, but the passage was not dark. It was lit by a lantern in the hands of none other than my dear sister, Madge.

Lewis gave a wheezing, coughing groan.

I felt much the same, and wished quite passionately I had not lost my saber.

The artifact was heavy in my pocket.

Madge raised a pistol. Her voice was still muffled in my damaged ears, but the passage was quiet, and I caught enough to understand. "We have little time, so I shall make this quick. I am here only to warn you. Baffin and his people are on their way to secure the artifact. Do you have it?"

"No," Lewis said firmly.

I conjured a defiant glare.

"You do," Madge stated and stuck out her hand. "Give it to me and run. It is safest with the Guild, you know that. You have no time to waste."

No, we did not. Furthermore, the vault door at my back was beginning to radiate heat and hiss unsettlingly.

"Does your husband have a son?" I asked suddenly. I probably shouted it, which was indelicate, but I did not care.

She looked at me with wide, startled eyes. It was answer— and distraction—enough.

I charged. As I expected, she did not fire her pistol, not at me, and especially not in such a small space. She did try to strike me over the head with it, though.

I dodged and slammed her into the wall. Lewis reacted with alacrity, commandeering her weapon despite his lingering limp.

I took advantage of the momentary press—close enough to an embrace to make my sisterly heart ache—to snatch at Madge's memories.

I saw her slipping into the museum in the shadow of Mr. Moran. Following him with careful, measured distance. I saw a confrontation between the two of them, caught my own name.

"Ottilie," Lewis broke in.

I broke off and shoved Madge ahead of us. "Move," I said, though my voice was not as harsh as I intended.

Madge. Me. Moran. Wake. Lewis. There were conflicts and connections afoot that I could only begin to parse.

With our prisoner, we hastened back through the

basements. Lewis was limping even more now and I was frighteningly weak, but we kept Madge in check and eventually spilled out onto the marble floor of the corridor above ground in a drift of smoke.

Pretoria and Perry converged on us. Wake was nowhere to be seen.

"You!" Pretoria threw out a pointing finger ahead of her, glaring at Madge. Madge glared right back. "What are you doing here?"

Madge did not speak.

Pretoria made an exasperated sound and hastened to look back down the stairs, batting away smoke that now curled up into the ground floor. Lewis grabbed her, giving some warning that slipped past me—likely of Wake.

Now that we were back in Pretoria's company my Leeching-induced weakness came on again in full force, my heartbeat fluttering too lightly in my skull, my ears ringing.

Geoffrey, Maddeson's assistant, was here too, looking pale and haggard. Maddeson himself gaped at us, his bound wrists held by Perry. A third figure, a night guard, was trussed up against the wall at the end of the hallway and appeared to be unconscious. Detective Supford was not present, but I was far more concerned about Wake's location just then.

"Did you see him?" I asked through the confused clamor. I heard myself, finally. "Mr. Wake? He is Moonless, he can use the shadows. And Moran is here!"

Pretoria visibly grimaced—I must still be talking too loudly. She put a hand on my arm and began to speak to Lewis again, then did a double take and stared at me.

"You've been shot!" my sister accused me.

"I have not," I shouted staunchly. "Where is Detective Supford?"

"Tied up in Maddeson's office. Ottilie!" Pretoria tore open the last remaining button of my coat to reveal my blouse and a drooping blossom of blood. "This is dreadful!"

"Pfft, it hardly qualifies as being shot, more of a mild goring," I insisted, squinting at the long wound beneath, scraped across my ribs.

"I, however, have been shot," Lewis admitted.

We all turned on him and I found the source of his limp—a circular, bloodied hole in his trousers.

I gaped. "Lewis! Why did you not say—"

"I did. You did not hear," he returned.

I dug into my pockets, shoving around the artifact as I shook out a handkerchief. I pressed it to Lewis's thigh.

"Can we please run away now?" Perry shouted in exasperation.

That spurred us. Madge crowded in, to help my poor wounded self, I assumed, with the hopeful naivety only a little sister could supply. But it was at this juncture that my eldest sister, with false gentility, slipped the artifact from my pocket. In my distraction, binding the kerchief to Lewis's leg with a belt supplied by Pretoria, it took me far too long to notice. My delayed, "You hag!" rang out only once she was a dozen paces away.

At that moment Wake stalked from the shadows behind the cloakroom desk and seized Geoffrey by the hair.

The young man died in a dazed way, sinking to his knees as the color fled his cheeks. I saw his final moment, when the spark of life left his eyes. My nightmares still paint the image most vividly. A bafflement, realization, and a terrible, crippling sadness—realization of a life unlived, hopes never to be achieved, loves never to be found. Then, nothing at all.

Wake's back straightened. Bleeding burns on his face healed, his shoulders levelled, and he spat blood upon the floor.

CHAPTER 32

Dr. Maddeson turned and fled, emitting a warbling scream that might have been comical in other circumstances.

"Get him!" I shouted.

Perry complied at the same time as Pretoria threw out her hands towards Wake, a skew of time already blurring the air.

He seemed to anticipate the gesture. He darted around her, avoiding the skew, and hurtled around a corner after Madge and the artifact.

Fear and hatred collided inside me, both of them directed towards Madge. My sister was not helpless, but her self-defense capabilities could be described as 'provisional' at best, and she had always been more than willing to hide behind the next, larger mage. Glim magic, too, was little use in physical confrontations. If Wake caught her...

Pretoria seemed to be of the same mind.

"I have them, get out of here!" she shouted, then she, too, was gone in a ripple of skirts. "Go!"

Lewis and I were left bleeding in the hallway with Geoffrey's grey-skinned corpse and the stink of smoke.

I flinched after Pretoria, but in the sudden quiet, I could just about pick out a new sound. The roar of engines.

Headlights cut through the tall windows, beaming

through the foyer and slicing down the hall towards us. Before they had even stilled I heard doors slam, and the light was interrupted by the flickers of running figures.

"Damn," Lewis said, eloquently. "That will be the Grand General."

"Can you walk?"

"I will follow you. Go. Help Pretoria."

For a moment, I almost considered the idea. I had come so far for the artifact, suffered so much.

But I disregarded it all with embarrassing readiness. It was chased from my skull by the image of Lewis struggling through a dark museum, hunted by soldiers. The sadness in his dying eyes, as there had been in Geoffrey's.

"I shall not abandon you," I vowed. I had intended to sound aloof, but there was a softness in my voice that I did not expect—my hearing was properly returning now, though I still endured a constant, distant ringing.

I added, "You agreed to escort me to Ilandrume. And how would I find your forger without you?"

"You would manage."

Not without a penny in our pockets, a quiet voice murmured at the back of my mind. But now, of all moments, was not the time to admit the police had seized our savings.

I slipped an arm under his shoulders and we set off, slipping out of the hallway just as the foyer doors opened and voices drifted inside.

"Ottilie, go," Lewis urged in a low voice. "If Pretoria gets her hands on the artifact first, you may not see it or her again."

I tightened my arm about him, refusing to let go. "I am more concerned with Wake at the moment. Is this your top hobbling speed, Illing?"

"It is."

"Then you will be winning no ribbons, good heavens."

Lewis made a strange sound, and it took me a moment to realize it was a laugh. I looked up at him, an inane, completely inappropriate smile on my face.

"I had forgotten how ridiculous you are under duress," Lewis said as we hastened on, ducking around displays of great hairy elephants and passing beneath several dozen suspended birds, swinging vaguely against the painted ceiling.

A shout came from up ahead, beyond the *Hall of Natural History* with its myriad displays of stuffed creatures: Pretoria, vengeful and frustrated.

"Would you prefer I flew into hysterics?" I whispered.

"Those are your only options?"

Another flurry of shouts and curses came from up ahead, and here and there crashes and twisted bursts of sound.

"Faster, Lewis," I urged.

We rounded one corner, then another, and entered another exhibit—*Weapons of Antiquity*.

Glass-fronted cabinets glinted out at us, their armaments dormant in their cradles, upon their hooks, and within their velvet nests. Several cabinets were already shattered, the floor strewn with glittering shards. A row of cannons I had noticed upon my last visit hulked in the center of the room, facing the windows and the blazing headlights from vehicles in the courtyard beyond. The lavishly adorned ceiling looked down upon it all, its river spirits and imps rapt in their lascivious play.

No one had seen us yet—we remained hidden in the entranceway, watching the scene unfold.

Madge lay strewn beneath the creatures' stone-eyed gazes, struggling and failing to find her feet in a sea of shattered glass. She was covered in blood, streaks and patches punctuating the pale blue of her dress and the gaunt white of her skin. The artifact lay on the floor nearby, surrounded by glittering shards.

Pretoria advanced on her, a saber in hand, glass crunching beneath her boots. Moran stood between them.

The air blurred as Moran threw out a hand. Pretoria shuddered, bracing as the skew hit her. Her whole body froze—every smooth black hair, every ripple in her skirts, every flicker of expression and spark of light across her blade.

Pretoria broke free with a vengeful sound and hurled a skew right back at him—tendrils of blurred air, warping the light and twisting off her sword, towards her enemy.

Moran moved. I blinked, losing sight of the both of them before they reappeared on the run.

If one has never witnessed two Starlight mages duel I must apologize, for I am no Bronze, and I can do the act little justice. Events became nearly impossible to follow. They fought with time, in blurs and skews cast from their free hands, Pretoria's sword, Moran's cane, and the movement of their bodies. They seized one another in their magecraft and shattered one another's holds. Constant distortions of time turned the thud, shift, and skid of their feet into a mind-bending, disjointed trommel, and blurred the thin light into a sheen like frozen river fog on a winter's morning.

A flicker of movement jerked my attention to the side. Wake stepped from the shadows behind a cabinet and started across the floor, making for the artifact, Madge, Pretoria, and Moran.

"Wait here," I urged Lewis, and took off. I cannot say what I truly ran towards. Was it Pretoria, fighting for her life? Was it Madge, wounded and traitorous and perhaps, in the end, just trying to protect me? Or was it the artifact and the ever-thinning hope that, with its acquisition, Lewis and I might finally be free?

Pretoria caught sight of me. Her attention was only divided for a moment, but it was enough to alert Moran. Without so much as turning, he threw a hand in my direction and clenched his fingers.

My lungs seized, suspended outside of time. I staggered.

"Moran!" Wake bellowed.

The hold on me released and I hit the floor on my hands and knees. Mr. Moran spun, something between horror and resignation flooding his face.

"He. Is. Mine." Wake advanced with a sword levelled. "Move, Rushforth."

Pretoria vanished in a skew of time. She reappeared beside me just as I found my feet again.

"Get Madge, I'll get the artifact," I panted. "This is going to get bloody."

She nodded and asked no questions. Instead, she squeezed my hand. "To the hunt."

"The hunt."

We closed the remaining space between ourselves, Madge, and the artifact as Wake and Moran faced off. There was a fresh breaking of glass, and Moran levelled a saber at Wake. The very same sword that had slain Empress Alessandra.

"Do you all know what he did?" Wake bellowed, his voice taking up every corner of the hall and crashing back upon us in echoes. "Do you know what he wants that for?"

He threw out his free hand at the artifact, lying in the glittering glass and the ever-shrinking space between me, Pretoria, and Madge.

"Baffin thinks he can change *them*, the Lusterless, the mundane, into *us*," Wake spat. The intensity of his hate was staggering. "But all it truly does is turn us into monsters."

Moran hurled a skew of time and physically charged. The skew distorted Wake's words but could not stop them, echoing, repeating, and embedding in our ears as the older man threw himself at the younger.

I would not grasp what Wake had said, nor its implications, until later on. Just then, Madge finally found her feet and made to intercept me.

We reached the artifact almost simultaneously. I seized it and dodged. Madge howled in fury and snatched at me, just as Pretoria tackled her.

At the same time, every light in the museum turned on, momentarily blinding the lot of us. I rolled, panting and clutching the artifact to my aching chest. I glimpsed Pretoria dragging Madge away. I saw Lewis, hobbling into the fray as Wake chased Moran—straight towards me.

I lunged to my feet and took off towards the other end of the hall.

"Ottilie!" Pretoria shouted as I passed. She had Madge by the arm, but with her free hand, she tossed me a sword.

I snatched it from the air and bolted through the doors to the next exhibit.

Statues surrounded me. I darted around them, skirting busts and fragments of motifs, a statue of a profoundly naked young man, and threw myself behind a broken façade of warriors in profile. I peered through its painstaking carvings just as Wake sprinted into the room. He held a newly acquired sword, and Moran did not follow.

Was he dead? What of Madge, and Pretoria? What of Lewis?

Wake vanished behind a pillar. I froze, taking stock of the shadows nearby.

Too late. He lunged from a patch of darkness not a pace away, sword flashing—a fine, long rapier.

I batted the lighter blade aside and backed off, my own saber crooked casually between us. Its grip might be unfamiliar but this moment, this confrontation, this I knew.

I slipped the artifact into my pocket and attacked. I moved quickly and sharply, casting aside finesse in favor of driving him back, away from the shadows and into the light, where he might be trapped. He parried every thrust and cut, clearly taken aback by my ferocity. He managed a twisting thrust—I stepped off line and dropped the tip of my blade, catching the other side of his weapon and charging in.

Our hilts met, forearms braced. I held for a skull-pounding moment, then hooked my crossguard under his hands and drove the hilt of my saber into his face. He staggered and I sidestepped past him, already slashing for his exposed back.

He followed me with his blade, dropping it over one shoulder to protect himself as he turned.

I delivered a quick thrust to his sword arm.

The blade, for all its quality, was dull with age. It pierced the sleeve of his coat but only just. I twisted my wrist, snapping the blade down at his forearm instead and beat a swift retreat.

He dropped his rapier. His mouth bloodied, bellowing with pain and blind with rage, he grabbed a delicate bust from a nearby pedestal and hurled it at my head.

I dodged. He snatched up his sword again and delivered a long punch of a lunge. His mouth was crimson, teeth lined with blood, and I was sure in that moment that I had never seen an expression so freely malevolent, so utterly grotesque.

His sword was longer, his arm longer. I parried, barely nudging the tip of his blade to the side. I retreated a tight step, flowing into another guard, then another and another.

Now it was I who had little chance to retaliate. I moved on pure instinct, my muscles remembering, my instincts reacting far quicker than my conscious mind.

But I was tiring and wounded, and adrenaline could not keep the pain at bay forever.

When our blades next locked, I had to yield. My muscles screamed as I disengaged, deflected a wild blow and darted behind a statue. My savior, poised with a pitcher of water on one broad hip, was only saved from a thrust through the throat by the fact that she was, obviously, granite.

I heard a ping, unexpectedly light, as Wake's blade broke. I would have pressed my advantage, but Wake threw himself at the statue with all the forethought of an enraged bull.

It toppled with a *thump* and *crack* that made the floor shake and shattered the tiles. I barely made it out of the way in time, blocked a stunted, graceless stab from his broken blade and tripped on a piece of stone. I caught myself on the edge of an ancient sundial, once large enough to park a carriage atop, and fled.

No footsteps followed. Instead, Wake vanished into the shadow of a hallway.

I sprinted on, avoiding shadows where he might reappear and reaching into my pocket for the artifact.

"Rushforth!" Moran's voice rippled across the chamber.

I ducked behind another lavish façade, hollow with carvings, and watched him stride into the room. He still carried Baffin's legendary sword.

I was not stupid enough to duel a Starlit mage, let alone expose myself to that deadly blade. My head was pounding now, my breathing ragged.

Surreptitiously, I tucked the blue orb into the intricate façade in front of me. Then I burst out with the last of my strength, sprinting for another set of doors. A skew of time grazed me, tugging at my hair and skirt like a wave of water, then I was free again.

Another exhibit, more glass cabinets, a grand doorway guarded by winged stone statues of mythological beings. I avoided the shadows, few though they now were, and—

I burst into the foyer and skidded to a stop directly in front of Grand General Baffin. He stood in apparently heated conference with Detective Supford who, looking as though he had just received a verbal lashing, still had a gag about his neck like a kerchief and was rubbing rope-raw wrists.

Shock flicked across the Grand General's expression, but only momentarily. Supford's own face shifted to something indecipherable, save for the tightness around his eyes that warned he could, or would, not help me now.

A dozen rifles levelled at my chest.

I raised my empty hands.

"Grand General," I wheezed. "So good to see you. I was just beginning to miss my box."

*Doors of rock
and gates of stone
Keys of gold
and iron bone
Threads of ebony
ever entwined
Eyes that open
on a world divine*

INSCRIPTION FROM RIEMONI TABLET O9,
LANDSDOWN TROVE;

TRANSLATED FROM OLD ARASI BY C. C. OGGLECOTHE,
UNIVERSITY OF GREATER LORVA, 1864

CHAPTER 33

Rain splattered a small window as the Grand General situated himself in a chair across from mine. He leaned back, allowing Wake to light the cigarette pinned between his lips. He puffed, set his elbows on his knees, and considered me.

I crossed my own legs at the knees and hooked my handcuffed wrists over them. Wake—his wounds miraculously healed—retreated to the door, leaving the Grand General and I in an open space.

I felt his lingering gaze like a cold draft.

"So?" I prompted. "This is not your house, and I became rather disoriented in the back of the truck. Where are we?"

"The Old Citadel," he replied, tapping off the first round of ashes onto the wooden floor. There was no rug, nor was there any décor on the plaster walls. The room looked as though it had been abandoned until recently, when it had been scrubbed clean. A room without personality, without markers or identification. A prison cell, despite its lack of stone and iron.

Thunder boomed beyond the window.

"Where will your companions take the artifact?" the General inquired.

"That entirely depends on which companion you are speaking of," I said, trying not to show just how deeply I cared about what he might say next. Alone as I had been at my capture, I had no way of knowing whether anyone had escaped. "We are not what you might describe as a cohesive fellowship."

"Your Starlit sister. She certainly has the skills to intercept the artifact between when Mr. Wake saw you pick it up and when we met in the foyer," Baffin said and took another draw on his cigarette. His gaze was calculating. He knew precisely the information he was giving me by inferring Pretoria had escaped, and it made me nervous.

"Well," I said, taking pains to hide my relief. "Pretoria and I are not as close as we once were."

Baffin's expression was grave. Reaching into his pocket, he pulled out a small notebook and a pen, and placed them on the windowsill. "I will leave this with you. What you write on these pages will determine what I do with you. Tell me what you know of the artifact. Tell me about your companions. Judge for yourself what will save your life, or end it."

With that he rose. Wake opened the door, and Baffin stopped on the other side to look back at me.

"A foretaste," he said, and waved a dismissive hand at Wake. "Leave her hands intact."

Cold fear prickled up the back of my neck as Wake closed the door and turned on me. I stood up quickly and put the chair between us.

"Mr. Wake, I am already quite aware what you are capable of, there is no need to demonstrate," I said, palms out to ward him off. "We need not be enemies."

Wake took the center of the room, crowding me back into the window.

"Wake," I said, unable to keep pleading from my voice. "I hate the Guild as much as you do. I am not your enemy. Tell me about Moran, tell me—"

At that, he leapt the space between us and screamed directly in my face. It was a visceral sound, an inarticulate burst of rage that was raw and pure and wholly terrifying.

I am not ashamed to say that I turned away, cringing into my shoulder.

"Why would you hate the Guild?" he hissed, his voice a blanket of fog over a raging sea. "Tell me."

"My mother," I said. I scrounged the courage to meet his eyes again. "She was devastated when the Guild took us. It nearly killed her."

Wake's upper lip trembled in a brimming snarl. His glare was unsettling, raw with what might have been comical intensity—had it not been entirely genuine. "Not. Enough."

"Emeline," I added. "Emeline Rosenthal. They killed her. The Glass Coffin."

Wake continued to glare, but I detected a minute flicker of his expression. Given his age and connection to Moran—obscure though that still was—there was a chance he had known Emeline, or at least of her execution.

"And the children," I added. I found I could meet his eyes again, not because I had in any way calmed, but because the intensity of the moment and the truth of my words had somehow arrested my terror.

There were dangers beyond this room, as this very conversation reminded me. Threats other than Wake. And there was a life I was still determined to claim, though the how of it was increasingly uncertain.

"Because I will not let them take my children," I stated. "I will not be bred. I will not be traded. I will not be broken as my mother was."

"Then allow me to add fuel to the flame," Wake said lowly. The looming threat of him did not lessen, but the rage in his voice shifted, I sensed, away from me. "The Guild has known about the artifacts for thirty years. Yes, artifacts. The Landsdown Trove, and its Stele. A puzzle to which the Guild already has several pieces. Your Mr. Stoke had another, the one which brought us all together. But the pieces are not what Baffin believes."

He had said as much at the museum, but I did not remind him of that. "Then what are they?"

He lowered his voice still more. "Perhaps they do have the potential to turn human into Entwined, in their proper, united form. Dr. Maddeson believes so, with his texts and translations. All I know is that when one of those artifacts is used on an Entwined, it makes us something more. Permanently amplified.

You, for instance, would exist forevermore in a state of twilight."

The thought was unsettling and alluring all at once. "How is it done?"

He shrugged. "I was a child. I could not tell you. Moran could not either, as I burned his laboratory and killed every one of his assistants when I escaped. A decade of research, annihilated."

He smiled at that, a boyish satisfaction mingled with wrathful remembrance.

"It was imperfect, anyway," he added. "Moran would forever speculate on other methods, other uses, and what the complete restored Stele could do, if its individual parts were so powerful."

"That is a chilling thought."

"It is," he agreed. His demeanor was relaxing, but he was still well and firmly in my personal space, and seemed intent on staying there.

"What were you?" I asked, pushing the conversation forward.

"Moonless," he said. "And now I am what a Moonless became. But my mother, she was a Silver. I carried enough of her blood to gain her strength and Leeching too, with Moran's meddling."

I had more questions about him and his abilities, not least related to the manifestation of two kinds of Entwined. But another query seemed more important, particularly when I recalled how simply touching the orb had heightened my abilities, back in the vault.

"Why are you helping Baffin?" I asked. "If you know that the artifact has real power?"

"Because he stands a chance of bringing down the Guild."

"Even if he kills Entwined in the City States in the process?" I pressed. "At the risk of giving him the power to make *himself* Entwined?"

"Baffin has his delusions," Wake said dismissively. "We cannot be made, Miss Rushforth. We are like gods—we have no beginning, no end. Only greater heights of glory. Heights which our masters, *all* of them, would keep us from."

A chill crept over me. "I would not go that far."

Wake did not reply. Instead, he glanced at the window as rain began to patter a little harder on the glass. He seemed to gauge the light, then pulled me into it—the faux twilight of a storm.

My threads awoke, prickling and warm. He pushed my collar down and turned my chin with a thumb, examining my throat, then looking up at my forehead.

"Your threads are already extensive," he observed. "The Guild must have been furious to lose you. I wonder what you would be, if they had done to you what they did to me? Moran intends to find out, I believe."

That struck too close to home. Was that why Madge had sent me away, and released Lewis to keep me safe? Was that the division between her and her husband?

I pulled away and separated myself from Wake by a pace. He allowed it, watching and waiting.

"Did you kill Mr. Stoke?" I asked. "Did you do what you did with Geoffrey, and steal his life to save yourself?"

"I did not kill Stoke," he replied.

There was a knock at the door—three sharp raps.

"I have somewhere to be," Wake said. He looked me up and down, and sucked his teeth in momentary contemplation. "You are not going to confess anything in that notebook for the General, are you?"

"Of course not."

"Then he will send someone less tactful to encourage you," Wake told me. "If he does not lose patience altogether and throw you to the Zealots again."

"Let him. They already failed once."

Wake gave me a look that said, very clearly, that he thought me naive. "Well, then," he said. "Goodbye, Ottilie."

I waited for the door to close, then went to the windowsill, opened the notebook, and picked up the pen.

The Grand General opened the notebook in the door of my cell, blinked, and squinted.

"Try turning it over," I offered from a corner, where I sat with my forearms propped on my knees and my inky fingers dangling. "You are the one on the bottom."

He choked in disgust and flipped through the other pages, then cast the notebook aside. It hit the wall and fell open onto the floor, showing a rather explicit depiction of Baffin and a Kessan imp entangled in one another. My drawing hand is quite good, if I may be permitted to preen, and my imagination liberal.

"Lewd drawings?" he growled. "Have you no sense of self-preservation, woman? I offered you a chance."

"You did not even look at them all," I replied with false disappointment. "The one with the Sirens of Amarto is particularly inspired."

Baffin turned to Wake, who had returned from whatever sordid appointment he'd had and now loitered in the doorway. "Find me another Eventide among our Separatist prisoners and have them scour her memory."

"There are none," Wake said. "There are several Eventide Affinates, but no one with the strength to get anything off her."

Baffin was clearly displeased. "A word in the hall, Mr. Wake."

Wake conceded and the two stepped outside. I watched the closed door, listening, but could not make out their words.

At length Wake came back in and, grabbing my arm, hauled me to my feet.

He did not speak as he led me out of the room, down the hall and towards a flight of stairs. Focused as I was on not falling over, it was not until we walked past a particularly large, lavish mirror that I noticed Wake's face. It was tight and grim, but his ire was not directed towards me.

"Where are we going?" I asked.

"The dark."

CHAPTER 34

Iron clanged. My hair, thoroughly tangled, blinded me as I jerked a bag off my head and hurled it to the floor. I spun around as a key clanked in the lock of a barred iron door, and two nameless jailers strode away.

They took the light with them. I closed my eyes for two breaths, letting my Eventide eyes adjust, and opened them again as I glanced around my prison.

It had a cot in one corner and a grating in the floor of another, where the soft trickle of running water drifted up. There was no window, no source of light whatsoever.

That made the sight of Lewis lying on the cot, flushed and struggling to sit up, all the more terrible.

"Who is it?" he asked, his voice more displeased than threatening. He had been stripped to his shirt and trousers and bore visible bruises. The shot to his leg had been bandaged, but by the fevered look in his eyes, not well.

"Lewis," I said, running to his side. "Have you been down here all this time? Alone in the dark?"

"Solitude has its merits," he soothed. He startled me by taking my hand as I crouched beside him. "I wrote you a poem. I know how you loathe my recitations, but if you will permit me..."

He trailed off, closing his eyes as if to remember. The

moment stretched long and, concerned, I reached to feel his forehead. It was burning up, as was his thigh when I gently put a hand near his bandage. "Damn."

"Indeed," he affirmed, drawing the word out blearily. "I may die soon, Ottilie. You must read my poem. Promise me you will."

"You have yet to write it down, so I cannot. You will simply have to refrain from dying for now," I informed him. "Try not to be so dramatic."

"My darling, we are imprisoned and I have been shot. I have been bandaged by a manic veterinarian with not a droplet of scrubbing alcohol in sight. I believe I have also been poisoned."

At this, he found a cup on the thin mattress and held it up.

I blinked twice in rapid succession, struggling to track his words past 'darling.' I took the cup from him and sniffed. It smelled of damp tin, and nothing more. "Why do you say that?"

He found my hand again, clinging to it and either ignoring or not processing my question. "I am doomed, and of little use to you. I am sorry."

I patted his hand and set the cup aside. "You are delirious. Please rest and let me think. I will get us out of here."

I turned away before the sight of his haggard face could sully my courage. I paced the cell, examining it from all angles and stared down the grate, which was far too small for anyone to slip through, even if it had not been secured.

I went to the barred door and peered as far as I could down the passageway in both directions. I saw other cells, but heard no sounds of occupation.

"Where are the other prisoners?" I asked, coming back over to Lewis. "From the way Baffin spoke, this prison should be packed with Separatists."

"*One and two and three and four, coffins laid upon the moor,*" he canted in reply. His voice faded at the last word, and I realized he had slipped into unconsciousness.

I gently felt for his pulse and leaned forward, listening to his breath. Both were steady, but that did little to soothe me.

For a time, I paced. Hours may have passed, or perhaps

it simply felt like it. I tried to think, tried to soothe myself with the exercise, but both proved useless. I could see no way out of the cell. I could not carry Lewis, and we could not rely on rescue.

Hunger began to gnaw at my stomach and my nerves felt properly fraught. I found no quip, no dry observation to alleviate the gloom.

Once I realized that, my fortitude began to unravel with frightening speed. I stood facing the bars, my back to Lewis, as I battled.

"I am not alone," I murmured, forcing that to the front of my thoughts. "They do not have the artifact. Pretoria escaped. All is not lost."

But what *all* would look like, from here on out, I could not say. I simply would have to survive long enough to find out.

"Ottilie?" Lewis called, sounding vaguely more alert. "Ottilie, are you well?"

I tried to scrub my face with my hands, saw my still-bound wrists, and closed my eyes. Several tears trailed down my cheeks.

"A moment, please. I am thinking."

A stretch of quiet.

"You are crying," he observed softly.

"I do not cry."

The cot creaked. "Come here."

I glanced back, huffing impatiently, but the sight of him sitting there, wounded leg stretched out before him and compassion in his eyes broke the last of my reserve. Some sense seemed to have returned to him, and he looked more alert, too.

I went to him and sat on the edge of the bed. "We will escape," I promised, though I knew it was a lie.

Warm arms enveloped me. I stilled, too tense, too distraught, to take any consolation from his embrace—an embrace I had imagined a hundred times, alone in my apartment with only Hieronymus for company.

Hieronymus. I had lost him. I had lost him, Mr. Stoke, and Lewis's and my hope of a free future. Even if we survived this, what was there for us?

"Lewis," I whispered. "I lost our money. The police confiscated it."

He stilled. I wondered if he had not understood, if the fever had overwhelmed him again.

"No matter," he said. "Perhaps we can... ah, reclaim it."

"Perhaps. But even then... it is still not enough for our escape."

"No matter," he said again, though this time there was a quality to his voice, a forced mildness, that made my stomach sink.

"You are just saying that because you think you are dying," I mumbled.

He drew back a little, squinting down at me. "Pardon me?"

"Earlier, you insisted you are dying."

"Ah. I am sorry. Why are you not embracing me? Would you like me to let go?" He started to pull away.

"No!" I cinched my arms around him, though I felt color rise in my cheeks. I hedged, "I did not want to hurt you."

"I am not fragile, Ottilie."

Slowly, I leaned my head into his shoulder. I relished the solidity of him between my arms, the press of his ribs, the shift of his muscle, the rise and fall of his breaths. Harden flickered through my head, but did not root.

For a time we held one another, there in the lonely dark. As my melancholy began to lift, I loosened my grasp but did not sit up, my forehead in his neck, my breath mingling with his. I began to grow overly conscious of those breaths—a little too fast, perhaps. My blood ran faster too, his proximity taking on a new level of meaning.

If he felt it, he did not comment. We simply remained as we were, each to their own thoughts, until he spoke again.

"Do you have any idea how we might escape?"

I sat up, loath though I was to leave his embrace. I knew, accepted, that such intimacy would not leave this cell. "No. But if you happen to have a spoon, I will start digging."

"There you are," he said, fondness in his voice. "The intrepid Ottilie returns."

I found myself beaming absurdly into the darkness and

pulled myself together. "Well. Did you see anything useful on the way in?"

"Actually, yes," he said, pushing himself a little more upright. "We are in the east dungeons, the pre-imperial section. When there was light, I could see the arches. Can you see them now?"

I looked at the front of the cell, where my Eventide sight cast our prison in sepia tones. "The doorway?"

"Yes. Overtop of it, there was an older, larger entry." He patted the back wall. "This was added, too. The original stone is red granite, imported from the north. You can see the newer stone is grey Harren."

"That helps us?"

"It may," he hedged. "I studied the Revolution a great deal, as part of my military training. There were sections of the dungeons—catacombs—blocked off during the same rebuild. That includes the old siege reservoir. It was fed by the river and connected to the canals of Old Harrow. If we can get in, perhaps we can swim out."

"That is an excellent plan," I decided. "You know the layout?"

"I do."

"Your training was extensive," I observed, grudgingly impressed.

"That I learned on my own," he corrected. "I have an interest in architecture."

"I did not know that."

He shrugged. "I have many interests."

"What else?" I asked, lured off topic by the pleasure of simply talking to him.

He glanced at me—or rather in my direction, since he still could not see. For a moment I thought he would not respond, then he said, "Architecture. Music—orchestral, in particular. The Kessan masters are my preference, though the Basinine are a close second. But anything after Ciollo is popular nonsense."

"Naturally," I said, trying not to smile. "And your poetry, of course."

"Yes. Poetry of any form save pre-imperial Arrentian—how fitting."

"Why?"

"It is boorish and crude and contains far too many references to grovelling."

"To deities?" I asked, sifting through my own knowledge of pre-imperial Harren culture.

"Mm. Yes. And worshipping rulers. And beautiful women... The latter, I will admit, has some merit."

I felt my cheeks warm again. Whether or not I fell into his classification of beautiful women was a question that remained unasked and unanswered, however.

A door clanged off in the dark.

Our eyes locked.

"We must take them by surprise," I whispered. "We do not act until the right moment, when they are inside the cell with us. Then we overpower them."

Though we were both aware of the futility of that hope, he did not question it.

"You must try to look more pathetic," he suggested as footsteps approached. "The more helpless they believe you to be, the better."

I gave him a flat look, which I realized, belatedly, he could not see. "I look exceptionally pathetic, I assure you."

"You do not sound like it. I know you are as indomitable as the tides, but they must not."

"Please stop complimenting me," I requested. I was blushing yet again, and growing weary of it.

The footsteps reached us, and we braced.

There was a clatter. A nondescript guard shoved a tray under the door, tested the lock with a firm jerk, and walked away again.

"Perhaps we should have expected that," I surmised, glad for the shift in focus. I went and retrieved the tray, which proved to have two bowls of bread stew and two cups of water.

"What if it is drugged?" I asked. "You were convinced so, earlier."

We both stared at the tray for a long, long time. My stomach audibly growled, and Lewis rubbed at his chin.

"I will test it," he said. "If all is well in an hour, you eat, too."

"Nonsense," I returned. "It will be even harder for me to carry you out of here if you are senseless."

"Then neither of us should eat."

I stared at the stew and water and swallowed a rush of self-pity. "All right. Agreed."

I set the tray aside and came to sit on the floor beside the cot.

"I am so hungry," I said bitterly. "Tell me about your time in The Sarre. I need a distraction."

"You know a great deal already," he reminded me, rolling onto his side and looking in my direction with a companionability, a lack of poise that I had rarely seen before. "Tell me of your life, here in Harrow."

I hesitated, but the quiet was too loud. "What do you want to know?"

"Something I do not know," he decided. "Your architecture."

I thought for a time, struggling to find something to say that he would not find mundane. Finally, however, the silence grew too thick, and I began to speak.

"One of my neighbors is a cellist," I said, settling back against the stone. It was cold and gritty and unpleasant, but I hid in the memory of my courtyard. "She plays every day, at the same time. Just before dawn, when my threads twine. I lie in my bed and listen. I leave the balcony door open for Ronny, of course, no matter the weather. And it is peaceful, the cool breeze, the chirping of the birds in the wisteria, and the cello."

Lewis made a noise, low and appreciative and prompting me to go on.

I did. I described not the novelties of my days in Harrow, but the mundanities, the common experiences that had been the foundation of my life. The small moments I savored between the work and the plotting and the obligations.

Finally, with the sound of his breathing steady in the dark, my words trailed off. And, head leaning on the cot next to his, I fell asleep.

CHAPTER 35

I awoke to music and shadow and strange plays of light. The swell and lulls of an orchestra drifted around me, melancholy and brimming with emotion. Lewis watched from a doorway, his cap under his arm and his eyes overbright, his focus somewhere beyond the stage where the Kessan Opera from the other night played out.

I drifted past him in my opera gown, my gaze equally distant. Wake strode hard on my heels, a forceful hand on my back, and I felt the surge of Lewis's ire.

"Illing," Madge's voice called.

The music changed, shifting into a faster, more harried movement. I saw Lewis and I at the Guild's engagement ball, dancing with a dozen other couples. Skirts swirled. Backs arched. Lewis's eyes trailed from my lips down the smooth skin of my throat, to the hollow of my collar and the swell of my breasts.

Another shift in melody, simplifying, growing more distant. A gramophone in a tent on the edge of the world. A stack of letters covered with my writing, neatly stacked on a crate beside a perfectly made cot. Lewis shaving at a small, jury-rigged mirror, a sketch of Hieronymus that I had sent him pinned beside it.

"Ottilie?" his voice rasped.

I closed my eyes, but nothing changed. I opened them again and saw a woman standing over me, dressed in the Kessan fashion with a fitted jacket and small bustle beneath her straight skirts.

"She survived," the woman said to someone I could not see. I tried to turn my head, but could not. "Dim the lanterns."

My consciousness flickered as the lights dimmed and the woman disappeared. I blinked, and she was back again, and my threads were twining in an artificial twilight. I felt them rise across my throat, my jaw, down my temples.

But the sensation did not stop there. It prickled across my collarbones, my shoulders, and down across my chest towards my stomach. It felt like trails of water, hot and just on the edge of burning, and as it spread memories whispered to me—not from any object that I could sense, though I understood that I lay on a hard surface. They seemed to cling to the air itself.

My consciousness drifted again, and when I next came to my senses, I lay on a divan.

I squinted around myself, disoriented. I was in a large study, shelves packed with books and tables layered with instruments. There was a desk to one side, illuminated by a green glass lamp, and diagrams were pinned to the walls over bloody red, vaguely floral wallpaper.

Hand-sketched anatomical diagrams of men and women were on the table, just legible from where I lay. Diagrams of threads twining necks and shoulders, some even spreading down backs and entirely across faces. Others were charts and lists. My eyes struggled to focus on the words, but I made out the titles 'Of the Sun' and 'Of the Moon.' Entwined classifications.

I held very, very still. Had I somehow fallen into the hands of the Guild? Had Lewis and I been rescued from one den of villainy, by another?

Lewis.

I looked around sharply. I was alone—no, just then I heard movement. A woman shifted into sight, riffling through a stack of papers.

I closed my eyes again, memory churning. I knew her, but it took me a moment to remember where from.

From my delirium. For I *had* been delirious, I recognized that now.

She survived.

I sat up sharply. Or rather, I intended to. Instead, I managed to throw myself ungracefully onto the floor. Cheek mashed into a serviceable carpet, I wheezed.

Footsteps approached and the woman looked down at me, brows furrowed. "Your sedative has yet to wear off," she advised. "I shall fetch you more. Do not try to move."

With that she moved off, out of my sight but in the direction of the desk.

"Pardon—No!" I croaked. "Where is Lewis?"

I heard riffling in drawers, and the clink of bottles. "Try not to speak, either."

"I demand to know where he is," I persisted, regaining a little more of myself. There was little point in attempting dignity, not prone on the floor as I was, and I squirmed relentlessly, trying to sit up. "I demand to speak to Madge!"

"Who?" the woman's voice inquired curiously. I heard several footsteps as she retraced her steps a few paces, still out of sight.

"Margaret Rushforth. Margaret Moran."

"Oh, your Golden sister? She is still at large," the woman replied.

The meaning of that sank in slowly. Though I had finally regained some control of my arms, I quickly stilled again, hiding my advantage.

"This is not the Guild," I observed.

Her response was distracted. "No, no. I work for the Grand General. You are in his care."

With dawning horror, I took in the study again. From the perspective of the floor, where I still lay prone, I noted the ceiling was of red stone. Pre-imperial. Furthermore, there were no windows. We were still in the Old Citadel dungeons. And this woman's obviously diligent study of the Entwined, combined with my delirium and fragments of memory painted a horrible, unsettling picture.

"What have you done to me?" I asked.

She survived.

Had Lewis?

The woman approached, a cloth in one hand and a bottle in the other. "I have, in theory, nullified your Entwined characteristics," she said as she poured something from the bottle onto the cloth, something amber and thick. She smiled. "Reducing you to a mere mortal, like myself. It was my notion, that the power that creates Entwined might also uncreate them. Securing Adepts to test my theories on has been difficult but... here you are."

She sounded smug, as if she expected me to be impressed.

I just stared. Nullified? But Baffin's intent was to amplify magicless humanity. The Guild's was to amplify already powerful Entwined. Could there be a third purpose?

If there was, Wake had lied to me. Or did he not know?

The woman carried on, "Your threads no longer respond to faux twilight, which is promising. But that may be a temporary effect, of course. We will need to observe you in true twilight before I can draw any conclusions. Now, one deep breath, here we are..."

She crouched and reached to clamp the cloth over my face.

I grabbed her wrist and pulled. She toppled forward, smashing her face on the carved wood of the divan.

I staggered to my feet, jerked the cloth from her grasp and pinned it over her own, disoriented face. She writhed and tried to scream—I clamped her to my legs and held the cloth fast, ignoring how her nails gored my hands and forearms, and how rapidly my body began to quiver with fatigue.

The woman convulsed, scrabbling more weakly, then stilled.

As she fell away from me, I realized my clothing had been changed. I wore something like a sleeping gown, simple and of grey fabric, with buttons all the way down the front. My own clothing, from corset to stockings, was nowhere to be seen.

A sickly, constricting feeling of violation wrapped around me. I furiously tossed the drugged cloth aside and hobbled to the desk, desperate to see what the woman had been looking at when I awoke.

Somehow, I suspected what I would see there. Amid inkwell, notebooks, and bottles was a fresh sheet of paper, newly inked with a diagram of threads on a simplistic but nude female form. The pattern of the threads from her temples to collarbones was unmistakably familiar.

I tore the sheet apart, hands shaking. Beneath was another sheet with the same figure—me—but this time marked with fewer threads, only on her throat. Belatedly, I noticed a time and date in the corner.

I flicked my gaze to the clock on the wall. Five hours ago.

I tossed that diagram aside and looked at the final one. No threads, with the time of notation less than half an hour ago.

I reached up to touch my throat. I felt nothing there. But the lamplight was bright. I would not expect my threads to awaken under these circumstances.

Strengthening, I returned to the woman and put a hand on her bare head. Memories trickled into my mind, but they were gossamer and mist, indistinct in shape and devoid of sound or sensations. That did not bode well. Throat thick, I glanced around and noted the mechanism for the oil lamps, beside the door.

I turned the lamps lower. The sound of my movements, the hiss of flame, and the ticking of the clock were the only sounds. The latter itched at the back of my mind, warning I hadn't much time, that someone would come along soon, or the woman would wake up—though the last seemed doubtful, given how limp she was.

When I was wrapped in faux twilight, I stood over the Kessan woman. Crouching down, I took both sides of her head in my hands, hard enough to bruise—I hoped—and focused.

More memories swam towards me. I saw myself from her perspective, clothing unbuttoned, cold and exposed. I dug my nails into her skin in vengeance. I saw her writing, a stream of notes and diagrams. Then, finally, Lewis, on a familiar cot. He had still been in the cell when this memory was formed. I could not see back far—this was hours ago, at most.

I dropped the woman's head roughly and set to ransacking

her pockets. I would have taken her clothing, but there was not enough time for that. What I needed were keys.

I found none on her. I returned to the desk and searched the drawers. A clatter. I triumphantly took up a ring of keys, and caught my breath at what lay beneath. A Guild medallion. Lewis's Guild medallion.

I pocketed both and glanced around the room again.

My gaze slowed on a case against the far wall, glass-fronted and small. Above it was a plaque reading *Landsdown Relics*, and inside, two pieces of unmistakable blue stone. One was a dodecahedron, though it was not the one Lewis and I had found. The patterns in the stone were signature—just like threads. The other was a palm-sized pendant, covered with small, neat rows of Old Sarren script.

I stormed across the room, snatching up a fire poker as I went. I smashed the case with a single, brutal blow. My strength was truly returning now, and with it my ire.

I shook the artifacts free of glass, clasped them to me, and smashed as many instruments as I could on my way to the door. Their proximity made my altered power hum and my head feel light, but I kept my focus on the task at hand.

A woman's coat hung beside the door, along with a neat bowler.

I took a moment to twirl up my hair, stuffed it under the hat, and pulled on the coat. I settled my shoulders and attacked the buttons, tightening my resolve with each brass fitting. I shoved the artifacts into the pockets and returned to the desk for more destruction—I threw every notebook and paper that would not fit into my pockets into the fire, and gave it a good stoking.

Then, poker in hand, I stalked into a stone hallway.

I immediately turned my head, letting my hat hide my face, and tucked the poker into the folds of my skirts. A man, just about to turn a corner up ahead, called back, "Miss Thera! The riots have passed Communion Square!"

I gave an affirmative gesture, taken aback though I was, and the man hurried on. Well, riots in the city were no good thing, but they would at least serve as a distraction.

I paused for an instant, looking both ways and trying to decide which direction led to Lewis's and my cell. One way was grey stone. The other, red.

I hurried off down the latter and rounded a corner.

A guard in a grey uniform startled, started to salute, then gaped. Her hand dropped to a pistol at her belt.

I slammed my poker into her arm and smashed it immediately back up, at the side of her head. She stumbled, letting out a grunt of pain, and fumbled to draw her sidesword.

I kicked her knee. She went down with a crack of skull against stone and gave a pitiable, drawn-out moan.

I divested her of her weapons—pistol, sword, and shot. Now properly armed, I continued on my way.

Searching the catacombs that night was one of the most distressing experiences of my life, and if luck is with me it will remain unsurpassed. Plagued by worry for Lewis, anxiety over my waning sorcery, and a sickening anger at the situation at large, I wandered. I hid from guards, lost my way and retraced my steps, and engaged in an exceptionally brief but lively duel with a strange gentleman who I kicked into an unoccupied office and trussed behind a desk.

In the midst of this, the ground began to rumble. I disregarded it at first, thinking the quaver the aftereffects of sedation. But the next rumble was more distinct, and dust rained from the ceiling.

I stumbled into a wall and heard, from far up ahead, a chorus of screams and shouts.

I rounded a corner, panting. There, to the sides of a large, circular chamber, were a series of massive cells.

They were packed with men and women from every class, from barefoot beggars to a society lady with a wilting hat perched stubbornly atop her head.

They were crowded against the bars, reaching for and calling to another group of figures dressed as guards. I say dressed as, because they most certainly were not guards. They were attempting to pick the locks, and Emrys Harden was in the thick of them.

"Artha Fucking Thera!" someone roared. A prisoner's

finger stabbed through the bars towards me, its red-faced wielder practically foaming at the mouth. "That's her!"

Separatists rushed me.

"I am not—I am not her!" I protested. I brought up my sword and levelled my pistol, backing into the mouth of the corridor. A bullet chipped at the wall next to me and I threw up an arm, barely keeping stone dust from my eyes.

"Mr. Harden!" I shouted. "Mr. Harden!"

Harden's voice overrode the mayhem, though I could not make out his words. He shouldered through the crowd and pushed someone's rifle down impatiently.

"Miss Fleet," he said. "Thought I might see you here."

The sight of him sent a scurry of ill-fitting feelings through me, but the most prominent one was relief.

"I have the keys," I said, weapons still raised. I continued to the crowd at large, "I am not your enemy. Mr. Harden, use the keys, but I do need them back."

Weapons lowered and I tossed the keys to Harden. He briefly left me, unlocking the remaining doors, then returned to me as his people began to organize into small groups and disperse down the passageways. Several brushed past us, offering apologies which I waved at with forced nonchalance.

"You were captured, and have escaped?" Harden observed, looking me over. "Or are you on a rescue mission?"

"Both, I fear. Have you seen Lewis?"

"No, I'll help you find him." He glanced over his shoulder at his people and called, "Maggie! I'm off!"

The familiar older woman saluted him.

Gratitude momentarily overwhelmed me. I did not resist as Harden gathered me to him with a light touch on the back and we started down the corridor through which I'd come.

"Lead the way," he prompted. His presence beside me was both steel in my spine and a new ease in my step, a natural consolation that I could not look at too closely.

I smiled at him, a tight but genuine thing. "Thank you."

He drew his pistol and we set off at a run.

CHAPTER 36

We found the corridor with Lewis's and my cell by pure happenstance. Running footsteps heralded the approach of guards and we diverted down a narrow staircase, winding down half a dozen steps and twisting into an awkward junction between new walls and old.

I recognized the familiar pattern of grey and red stones and started to run down a fresh corridor. More barred doors. More cells. I glanced into each, resisting the urge to call Lewis's name.

Finally, I found ours. The bag that had been over my head when I was brought down still lay on the floor and the cot—

The cot was empty.

Lewis staggered into sight beyond the bars, blind in the darkness and clutching a bloodied temple. "Ottilie, he's—"

I was slammed into the wall, a hand around my throat, another twisting my wrist. My sword clattered to the floor.

Wake snarled in my face.

Then he was torn away. Harden followed his initial assault with a straight punch to the nose, then took the other man to the floor in a heap. A pistol discharged with a burst of light, momentarily blinding even me.

Wake roared.

"Lewis!" I cried, stumbling around the wrestling forms.

I could barely breathe, my throat aching, lungs struggling to recover. "I have... I have the..."

I shoved my pistol through the bars and waved it wildly. He took it without a word, directing it at the battling pair. Lewis's weight was decidedly on one leg, the other still thickly bandaged and showing signs of bleeding again.

I shoved a key into the lock as Harden and Wake continued to exchange blows. Another gunshot went off and Wake shuddered, but did not go down. Harden did, though. His knees hit the floor.

Harden's face began to turn ashen as Wake Leeched his life away, healing himself.

"Lewis," I gasped.

"No more bullets!" I felt his hand close over mine, taking charge of the keys. "Go!"

I lunged for my fallen sword. In one smooth movement I snapped it up and threw myself at Wake, screaming unintelligibly as I did. My feral attack had the desired effect—he broke off murdering Harden, but that brought his full attention back to me.

Something inside me cowered as he straightened. In the sepia world of my Entwined sight, the blood on his face was black. His rage appeared mindless, his expression grotesque.

I stabbed him. The monster turned, taking the point of my sword to the meat of his shoulder instead of the tender flesh of his throat. He reached out at the same time, seizing my sword by the crossguard and clearly intending to jerk it from my grasp.

I abruptly let go. Wake staggered back, tripped over Harden in the confined space, and went down.

I launched after him, kicking vengefully at his kidney. Though satisfying, this was unwise. He grabbed my ankle and pulled me to the floor. I nearly landed on my own sword and heard a clatter as it was knocked away.

The breath punched out of my lungs and my energy flagged. Gaping like a fish out of water I rolled, scrabbling for my sword. I found Harden instead and commandeered his arms to haul myself upright.

"Em! Move!" Lewis shouted.

Harden hauled me backwards. I toppled into him, kept only from falling by his now firm barrel-hold on my upper body.

The door of the cell slammed open, taking Wake full across the side as he found his feet again. He staggered, stunned, and toppled backwards into the deepest shadows.

He did not reappear.

The three of us stared for a long moment, fists and weapons ready, breaths harried and rough.

Still, the Moonless did not come. Instead of feeling relief I felt increasing dread.

"Where did he go?" I whispered.

"Away to lick his wounds," Lewis replied.

"To steal the life from someone else before he takes another run at us," Harden summarized. Harden hauled one of Lewis's arms over his shoulder. "Hey there. We need to go."

"Emrys," Lewis rasped back with a pained half-laugh. "You know a way out?"

"I do. Ottilie? You hurt?"

"Nothing that will stop me," I said truthfully.

Harden led us through the dark, not deftly by any means, but successfully. The sounds of continued conflict echoed through the passages, along with distant, ground-shaking booms. But we were alone, surrounded by our own footsteps and ragged breaths.

Every moment, I expected Wake to reappear. Every second he did not ratcheted up my anxiety, until I would have set the whole catacombs ablaze just to scatter the shadows.

When the red rock of the old substructure dominated, Harden released Lewis and motioned to a slim hole in the wall. It was flush to the floor and no more than a foot high. It had been covered by a grating, evidenced by the iron mesh set off to one side. But now it yawned open, and the sound of running water came to us. Running water and distant, distorted voices.

"Just my people," Harden explained. "The water isn't deep."

"Go first," I urged. "So none of them shoot us."

Harden hesitated, then nodded. He lowered himself down and dropped through the gap. Lewis cast me a glance, as if he intended to force me to go next, but refrained. More slowly and painstakingly, he copied Harden and vanished.

For a breath I was alone in the passageway, with its shadows and eerie echoes. I checked the pockets of my stolen coat, ensuring the relics were secure, then shimmied after the men.

I dropped down a bare four feet. The tunnel was startlingly low, and Harden and Lewis were bent near in half. Still, my relief at being out of the passageway, on the way to escaping the citadel, left me half-delirious with relief.

Both of them reached hands for me, at the same time, and I cracked a smile. "Gentlemen," I chided. "I cannot hold both your hands."

Harden grinned back at me.

Lewis gave a huff. "I still cannot see a thing."

"I can hold your hand, too," Harden offered him coyly.

"You may have to carry me by end of this."

I slipped my hand into Lewis's. Harden set off, and Lewis and I followed carefully behind.

Voices reverberated eerily off the walls. Their hushed, susurrating nature only increased the strangeness, filling the sloshing quiet with the rasping whispers of spirits and ghouls and Moonless monsters.

Soon, we encountered a knot of Separatists. By the time the tunnel broadened and we could stand, we trailed twenty other escapees.

"We are in the sewers," Harden murmured. "Beneath the old city."

We reached another grating, a massive blockage of thick iron bars. These had been filed down, a task that must have taken a great deal of time to do surreptitiously. We stepped through onto a narrow walkway of stone, clinging to the side of a canal. Distant light could be seen from both directions, and I realized that this was one of the areas where Old Harrow's canals ran under the buildings.

We gathered in the shadow, just before the line of light. The other Separatists had gone the opposite direction after a murmured conference with Harden, streaming off and dissipating into the light. A distant boom welcomed them to the sunlight again, and somewhere off in the city a siren wailed.

Harden, Lewis, and I were alone again in the cool darkness.

Harden looked at me. "Your sister's hotel is on the other side of the city. We'll never make it safely, not with you hobbling, Lewis."

Another explosion shook the ground, affirming his statement.

"So is The Three Trees," I pointed out.

"There are other safehouses."

"Yes, well. We can make our way alone, Harden, you have done enough for us."

He shook his head emphatically. "Bullshit. I'll see you safe."

"We will not be safe until we leave the city," Lewis put in. "Conflict in the streets is one thing. They will be looking for us, specifically."

"I can get you out," Harden said.

"All right, make the arrangements," I conceded. "But I cannot abandon Pretoria and Perry."

"You are not abandoning them." Lewis's response was frustrated and emphatic. "They are probably safer than we are. You are staying alive."

I looked between the pair of them, both watching me, though their expressions varied. Harden's gaze shifted from incredulous to contemplative, eyeing me up and down as if he intended to physically prevent me from leaving, but couldn't figure out how to do it while holding Lewis up. Lewis looked increasingly exhausted, a shadow in his eyes that looked almost... resigned? I couldn't parse that look, not right then, so I focused on Harden instead.

As my eyes met his, he seemed to yield slightly, not sensing my concession, but understanding that my mind was made up.

"I'm sorry," I said, realizing what I had to do even as I spoke. No part of me wanted to go, but there was no real choice. "I'll meet you at The Three Trees."

CHAPTER 37

"Miss! Miss!"

An empty street stretched before me, echoing with hissed shouts. A line of soldiers crouched in an alleyway, half focused on me, half on the street behind me. One leaned out, as if preparing to sprint in my direction. They all looked harried and exhausted, and several civilians huddled in the space beyond them.

Gunshots erupted behind me. I sprinted for the cover of an abandoned streetcar and landed inside just as bullets tore up the street. I crawled the length of the vehicle and peered out the far end.

The soldiers were fully engaged in a firefight by then. I had no choice but to cover my head and hold fast.

When the shooting died down, chased by running footsteps, I peered back into the street. Empty. The soldiers were gone, as were those they had been protecting. Armed civilians advanced up the street towards the streetcar, rifles and cudgels in hand.

I held my breath. If they were Separatists, I could cite Harden's name—as Mayfair, of course. I'd learned my lesson before.

But there was a chance the attackers were Zealots. Baffin might be quietly supporting the group, but here in the chaos of the streets, the lines were far more blurred.

I steadied myself. Slipping back into the rows of seats, I crawled beneath them, flattening myself against the wall, and went still.

Someone boarded the streetcar. I heard others moving past, muttering and reloading rifles and kicking debris out of the way.

Boots approached me. My neck screamed at the awkward angle but I held perfectly still.

One step. Another. The boots came even with the row I hid beneath.

Jasper, the distrusting Separatist from The Three Trees, peered over at me. Our eyes met, clear as day, and he did not seem in the least surprised. Perhaps he did not recognize me. Perhaps he did. Regardless, all he did was sniff, brush at his nose, and continue on his way.

Relief made my stomach weak. As soon as the sounds of their passage faded I scurried from the streetcar to a side street and took off at a mad sprint.

I had been an idiot to leave Lewis and Harden. This was madness, absolute madness.

Somewhere off in the city, a woman screamed. There was such terror in that scream, such horror and helplessness, I could bear it no longer.

No more skulking. No more hiding. I ran to the closest shelter I knew—home. And if Baffin's people came there looking for me? So be it. It was evident that reaching Pretoria would not be possible until the Separatists went to ground and the city calmed.

The front door was tightly locked, but I forced my aching, spent muscles up the wisteria one more time. The balcony door was unlocked. My room was still in disarray. But it was *my* room—my possessions, those I had not carried off with Pretoria or had been confiscated by the police, were here.

This small bit of fortune nearly brought me to my knees. I stood in the clutter with tears in my eyes, surveying the familiar desk, chest of drawers, bed, and cracks in the plaster. It was cold, but the sun through the glass of the balcony door warmed my back.

Hieronymus was not there, of course. But I had not expected him to be.

I quietly found clothes. They were ill-fitting and worn, but better than the horrific gown and Thera's stolen coat. I risked opening the tap in my little water closet and scrubbed myself as best I could with fresh, clean water. I found canned food in the kitchen, though the gas had been cut off. I tended my wounds and bound them—myriad bruises and scrapes, many of which I had not been aware of until that moment. I found no signs of what Thera had done to me, but that was no real consolation. I threw the buttoned gown and her coat and hat into a corner.

Then I went back to the balcony doors. The sun was close to setting over the rooftops and there with a view only of the courtyard, I could believe that the city was not at war. I could tell myself that the last week had not occurred, that Lewis was still abroad, Mr. Stoke was alive, that there were no priceless artifacts set in the jumble on my desk. I could almost believe that I had not been violated and meddled with to unknown effect. Then I saw drifts of smoke rising up into the blue sky, and noted how many of the neighbors' shutters were firmly fastened.

The light waned. Twilight slowly crept up the walls of the courtyard, chasing the last rays of the sun.

I raised a hand to my throat, dreading what I might feel. Or what I might not.

Would my threads twine tonight?

I retreated to the edge of the bed and waited. I waited for the sun to pass over the rooftops. I unbuttoned my collar again as shadows crept across the floor and the last of the sunlight winked out. I turned my throat, bruised and battered, towards the mirror, and waited.

I closed my eyes. At first, it seemed my threads would not come. Tears welled in my eyes.

Then, a tingling awoke on my skin, beneath my jaw. It spread, familiar and warm, behind my ears and down my throat, over my collarbones and up through my hair, across my temples.

I brushed a hand over my skirt. Memories separated from the fabric, shockingly clear. They were recent—me picking them up off the floor, shaking them out and clothing myself in them. But my relief was so strong I sobbed aloud and clasped an ashamed hand over my mouth. I was too tired, too emotional, too...

Somewhere distant, church bells rang a curfew.

Further awareness overcame me. For my threads were still spreading, moving beyond their usual twilight positions. I felt their warmth from my temples across my forehead, from behind my ears over my jaw, and from my collarbones over my breasts, down my spine.

Energy returned to me—a frantic, desperate spark. I untucked my shirtwaist and divested myself of it with hasty fingers, then pulled down the sleeves of my combinations.

Threads covered my entire upper body. I pulled up my skirts, revealing my bare legs, and saw with growing bafflement that threads trailed there, too—prickling and twining and smoky.

Moonless. Wake's voice drifted through my head. *Now I am what a Moonless becomes.*

I closed my eyes. Memories began to come to me, images not connected with this room or my person. I realized with growing apprehension that they were carried *on the air* coming through the cracked balcony door.

Soldiers in the streets. Winds whisking past closed shutters. A body hung from a lamppost against a backdrop of impervious, ever-flowing river and grey-clouded sky.

Thera's attempt to nullify my power had failed. Instead, she had amplified it.

As the Guild had done with Wake.

I will spare the reader a further account of my thoughts that night, for they were myriad, complex, and deeply personal. My plans were in shambles, my future uncertain, and I, it seemed, was irrevocably changed.

Finally, however, my exhaustion was too much. Even once my magnified threads retreated, I could not leave the apartment in such an exhausted and bewildered state. Even fear of the searching Guild and prowling Wake could not convince me to go back out into the turbulent city.

Besides, no one would think me stupid enough to come home.

I awoke to warm sunlight. There was a weight on my legs and I instinctively did not move them, so as not to dump Hieronymus onto the floor.

My eyes snapped open. I cried out shamelessly and seized the warm bundle from the blankets, clutching him to my chest and burying my face in his fur. He mewed disagreeably and squirmed out, landing on the bed and twining around my back before buffeting my fingers for scratches.

He was whole. He was safe. For one sunny, warm moment, all was right in the world.

Then someone knocked at the door.

I froze. Ronny mewed and leapt to the floor, stretching in the sunlight. The balcony door was cracked—good heavens, had I forgotten to close it?

The knock was firm, but not agitated. My first thought was Pretoria, but she would not have knocked. Neither would Wake or the Guild. It was Lewis or Harden then, perhaps.

I debated climbing out the balcony door. But as I stared at Hieronymus, trying to figure out how to carry him down, a key clicked in the lock. There was no more decision to be made.

Constable Hopgood stepped inside. He saw my state and averted his eyes, but entered all the same and closed the door quietly.

"I apologize, miss, needs must," he said, holding one hand over his eyes and looking at the floor.

I found my tongue—and my shirtwaist, which I hastily buttoned. "You? What are you doing here?"

"Mr. Stoke requested I watch the apartment for your return," he confessed. "I came by this morning and saw the balcony door open."

It said a great deal that he would continue such a duty so long, particularly in the state the city was in.

"Did he ask you to do that when he told you about the artifact?" I asked.

Hopgood looked taken aback, but in a pleased way. "He said you might unravel it."

I felt a sad smile cross my lips. "Is that it, then? His confidence in me was so great that he abandoned me?"

"Not at all, miss." Hopgood rested a hand on the balcony door. "If you'll come with me, I'll let him explain."

CHAPTER 38

Constable Hopgood lived in a narrow house not far from my own apartments, on an island in the river. There was little left of the island itself—it was encased in stone. Stone streets, stone houses, stone walls. It was picturesque, with an air of crowded community, but frequently flooded in the spring, and had thus been left to the lower middle-class.

The streets were unnervingly quiet as we went, save for the cry of gulls over the river. We saw only other lawmen and soldiers, and it was obvious from the short words the uniformed Hopgood exchanged with them that if I had been alone, I would have been forcibly removed from the streets.

"I need to understand," I prompted in a stretch of privacy, unable to articulate a more pointed question. I had too many of them. "What happened to Mr. Stoke?"

"He turned up in Farfleet Hospital yesterday, on the west bank," Hopgood said. "He had been unconscious in their care for several days, and reached out to me as soon as he awoke."

I had Hieronymus with me, in a carpet bag for lack of the wicker cage I had never bought, and his irritated mews came through the patterned fabric as I processed this. "Then the body you found was not him, just made to look like him?"

"Yes. It was Lord Stillwell's original messenger, his valet. Mr. Wake threatened the man into hiding, whereupon he connected with Mr. Stoke, who'd also gone to ground. Mr. Wake tracked down the pair of them. Mr. Stoke shot Mr. Wake, and Mr. Wake killed Stillwell's man to save himself—Leeching, as we suspected. Stoke saw an opportunity to falsify his death, and took it."

"But what good would that do, if Wake knew Mr. Stoke was not the man he killed?"

"Mr. Stoke was in no good condition himself. He was looking to buy days, hours even, and never expected the façade to hold up to scrutiny. He was not just hiding from Mr. Wake, you see, but the Guild. Anyhow, his wounds took their toll, and he was found and taken to Farfleet, unnamed and unconscious."

I recalled Mr. Wake's tale of running into Mr. Stoke as he fled a third, unknown party. "By the Guild, do you mean a Starlit mage, Everard Moran?"

"A Starlight, yes," Hopgood affirmed.

Moran, who had learned of Stoke's connection to the artifact through Lewis's and my letters.

I scrubbed at my forehead, overwhelmed. In my carpet bag, Ronny mewed.

"I should let him finish the tale, miss," Hopgood said. We had reached the riverbank, exposed and windy, and his guard visibly rose. "Let's pick up our feet."

I nodded, hurrying along at his side. The day was grey and dismal and the wind that buffeted us smelled of river, smoke, and rain. No one else was about save a military vehicle, prowling across an intersecting street.

Up ahead of us, an old military bastion blocked our view down the boardwalk, keeping its silent, stoic vigil over the city. Great clouds of gulls wheeled from its ramparts, their cries jarring in the general hush.

I eyed the gulls warily as we passed around the bastion and were granted full view of the riverbank once more.

Bodies hung from every lamppost down the grand, open boardwalk. They swung, swollen-faced and limp—men and women, in skirts and trousers, booted and barefoot. Gulls and other scavenging birds swarmed, shrieking and hopping backwards, exploding into disgruntled clouds as soldiers with a cart made their way unhurriedly along, cutting the corpses down.

"Stop, there!" It took several shouts of this before the words penetrated my skull. A group of four soldiers made to intercept Hopgood and I.

"Let me talk," Hopgood muttered.

"Constable, who is this?" one of the soldiers asked. He was evidently an officer, from his bars and mannerism, and the way he looked at me made my sore muscles tense for flight.

Stretched out before us, the bodies of dead Entwined Affinates swung listlessly. Gulls swooped. A soldier hacked ineptly at a rope, making the corpse of a white-haired woman shudder.

"I am escorting this woman home, sir. Found her hiding in an alleyway," Hopgood lied flawlessly.

"What is your name and why were you on the street?" the officer asked. From the way he searched my face, I sensed something more to the interrogation. Baffin's people would be looking for me, after all.

From my carpet bag came a piteous mewling. "Mrs. Emmet Fowling, Dorothy Fowling," I said, lying as easily as Hopgood, with an appropriate quaver and nervousness and shame. "My daughter's cat. He went missing—she's been beside herself, sir."

"The city is at war, Mrs. Fowling. Would you rather your child had a mother or a cat?"

I looked down.

"I've spoken to her quite forcefully, Captain," Hopgood assured with a confiding air. "She understands."

The captain looked me over one last time, then frowned. "See her to her door."

"I intend to."

The soldiers moved on.

"You are an admirable liar," I murmured to Hopgood as we carried on.

"Wish I didn't have to be," Hopgood muttered.

We crossed one of the bridges to the island and soon

came to the constable's house. My heart was in my throat by the time we mounted the stairs and he unlocked the door.

The house was hushed, save for the ticking of a clock.

"I sent my family out of the city soon as matters went south," Hopgood told me, closing the door and locking it again behind us.

"And good you did." A voice came from the parlor and there, through the door, I saw a familiar figure reclined on a worn sofa. He pushed himself more upright as I came in, his face soft and apologetic and saddened all at once. "Miss Fleet, my dear woman. I am so sorry."

There were tears in my eyes as I sank down on a chair across from him. He looked terrible, face swollen and discolored with bruises, one leg heavily splinted. Bulging bandages betrayed other wounds beneath his loose clothing.

Ronny growled from inside his bag and I finally opened it, letting the cat leap out onto the rug, his hair on end, and shoot off into the shadows.

"I am so very glad... very glad that you are not dead," I said, fumbling the words.

He laughed, and I laughed, and for an instant I could imagine us back in his office on a normal, mundane day.

"I owe you an explanation," he said. "It will be thorough, I promise."

Hopgood cleared his throat and excused himself, leaving Mr. Stoke and I alone with the skulking cat.

I looked at my employer expectantly, and the tale began.

Mr. Stoke began to speak. "In making my inquiries about Lord Stillwell's artifact, I did, perhaps, a little more than due diligence. Stillwell clearly did not want to attract attention to the matter, otherwise he would not have come to me, a has-been who owed him a debt. Someone he believed he could control."

I frowned at Stoke's description of himself, but he waved me off.

"I interviewed Professor Maddeson in the course of my research, and he was only too proud to inform me his work on Old Arasi and the Landsdown Trove was funded by Baffin.

He agreed to compile some relevant information for me and sent it to my home address."

"I found that," I said. I felt as though something were bubbling up in the back of my throat, but it was no pleasant thing. My surprise and relief were fading, and beneath them, I was still frustrated and injured. It needed more than facts and a systematic explanation.

It needed to know why he left me alone.

There was a flicker of pride, and a little chagrin, in Mr. Stoke's eyes. "I thought you might."

"Why did you not warn me?" I asked. "The evening you sent me away. The night Wake attacked you, and you fled with the artifact."

Mr. Stoke cleared his throat and tried to sit up a little more. "At first, I believed involving you would do more harm than good. I believed your innocence was your best protection, and that Lord Stillwell would never stoop to threatening my secretary. I did not anticipate Mr. Wake's intervention that night, nor his nature, nor the rapid involvement of the Guild. It is no excuse, but matters escalated swiftly."

I waited for him to go on.

"Mr. Wake appeared that night, posing as Stillwell's valet. I know—knew—Stillwell's valet, however, and immediately realized something was amiss. I made the mistake of voicing my suspicion. We fought, and I was given reason to suspect he was a Silver—a Guild agent, I surmised—and feared for you."

"You had realized I was Entwined," I observed.

Mr. Stoke nodded. "Some months ago, though you hide it well."

"Not well enough," I said wearily.

He did not comment on that, but filled the silence with continued explanation. "Now, at this juncture, I suspected the Guild to be puppeting Mr. Wake and making a play for the artifact, but I could not rule out that Stillwell had hired a Rogue mage to ensure my cooperation. And in light of what I had learned of Baffin's interest in relics, like the artifact I then held—I realized turning over the item was about far more than money. I needed time, so I went into hiding."

"Yet you still did not warn me," I added, unable to swallow my bitterness.

"By the time I realized innocence would not protect you, I could not find you," Mr. Stoke said. "I did try."

I rubbed at my forehead. "I see. Mr. Hopgood has told me the rest, I believe. You found the valet, and Mr. Wake found the pair of you. As did a Starlight mage."

Mr. Stoke watched my expression for a breath or two, evidently trying to read me. "Yes. I encountered the Starlight mage when I attempted to return to my office for supplies. In fleeing him, I crossed paths with Wake again, and was saved only by that other mage's approach. The next time I saw Wake, however, I was not so lucky. Nor was the valet."

I found myself nodding slowly. "Wake must not have wanted Moran to recognize him. They have a history."

Mr. Stoke's interest piqued. "Moran?"

"Everard Moran. I have much to tell you, as well," I said, sitting back finally and folding my hands in my lap. I wrote dignity into my posture, but my fingers laced a little too tight. "I had my share of adventure while you lay in hospital. But you have not mentioned Mr. Harden, nor what you did with the artifact itself."

"Yes," Stoke acknowledged. "After fleeing both Moran and Wake in one night, I realized more drastic measures were required if I intended to keep the artifact safe. I had devised how to open the box. So I sent the box itself to Mr. Harden, while I removed the contents, a stone dodecahedron. I hid it in the wall of the room I had rented."

"Took me days to find," Hopgood griped. He had reentered the room with a tray, set with a teapot and cups, and a tin of biscuits. He set the service on the table and sat down in the last remaining chair. "'Course I hardly had the time. With the city in this state, one dead man, even a former Detective Sergeant and military man, was not priority. Supford gave me what time he could."

"When you found the artifact, you told Supford, and he reached out to Maddeson," I noted.

Hopgood nodded and poured three cups of tea with no

saucers. He then popped the tin of biscuits open and took two for himself. "Didn't know not to. Also didn't know the Grand General was keeping tabs on our investigation."

I watched Hopgood, momentarily struck by the calmness of his movements, the nonchalance of the way he took up biscuits and tea. He exuded safety, finality, as if something were at an end.

Perhaps it was. He had found me, as Stoke had asked. He had found Stoke, as he and Supford had set out to do.

But just because Mr. Stoke was alive and the pieces of the puzzle were coming together did not mean that *my* part was over.

Pretoria. Madge. Lewis. Harden. Even Dr. Maddeson himself. I had to find them.

I gave Mr. Stoke and Constable Hopgood a brief account of my part in the last week's tumult. I held nothing back, save details that might risk other parties, like Pretoria and Harden and the Separatists, and did not touch on the unexpected efficacy of Thera's meddling.

I also did not speak of the artifacts in my pocket, noting only that the one from the box was now missing.

When all was laid bare, we were quiet for a time. Hopgood had eaten half the tin of biscuits. Ronny had crept out and settled in my lap, and I petted him with gratitude, calming both my nerves and his.

"Oh," Hopgood said suddenly. He reached around the side of his chair and picked up a box, large, but evidently not heavy. He handed it to me. "These are yours."

Inside I found all my possessions confiscated by the police, including my hat with its yellow silk flowers, and my picture of my sisters and I. My throat felt thick at the sight of it, and I hoped desperately that Pretoria was safe and that Madge... Well, that she was not dead, at least.

The last thing Hopgood handed over was my envelope of money. I stared at it, my eyes, my mind, suddenly full of all it represented. Renewed hope of a new life, a new name. A momentous step towards freedom. A journey with Lewis, and the chance to begin and end each day in quiet and safety. To have a simple, unobtrusive existence.

My imaginings still warmed me, but now my mind kept turning, and more thoughts came to the forefront. I considered how I would feel months from now, after Lewis and I had parted ways in Ilandrume and my life had fallen into routine. Day after day of waking, rising, tending to whatever new employment I found, then returning to bed alone. Would it not, eventually, feel mundane? Lonely? Could I forget, as I lay in bed in that new world, that Harrow was in turmoil, that Harden and Stoke might burn with it? Could I truly accept that I might never see Pretoria again, and that she remained under threat from a Guild that, itself, was on a precipice? And Madge...

I thought of the artifacts in my pockets. Of Thera and her research, of Lewis and I and the uncertainty before us. Of Wake, his power, and his madness.

There was no real decision, at the end of my pondering. I simply knew, then and there, that I could not have the life I had hoped for—at least not yet. There was no heroism in that conclusion. It was a fact, and a burden.

I could not let Baffin, or the Guild, unlock the secrets of the Landsdown Trove. I could not close my eyes and walk away.

Ronny, as if sensing the direction of my thoughts, leapt off my lap in disapproval and meandered out into the hallway.

"He's making himself at home," Hopgood remarked.

I eyed him, considering the thought.

"Ottilie, if I may," Mr. Stoke interrupted. "This city is no longer safe for you. I have a friend in Mittleport who would gladly take you in, once we get you out of Harrow."

I almost rejected the offer immediately, but asked instead, "What about you?"

Mr. Stoke looked at Hopgood briefly. "There is a great deal to do here, in Harrow. I intend to keep a weather eye on Mr. Baffin, and I must speak with my old friend Lord Stillwell. He has been conspicuously quiet, this past week, and I struggle to believe he has no notion of the power of the artifact."

"It would be best if you let the matter lie," I urged. Sudden, deep-seated concern overtook my thoughts and plans, my reserves and resentment.

"I do not believe I can," Mr. Stoke said with a half-smile. "This is my city, my home. And this mystery is undeniably entangled with the conflict."

"I see." I leaned forward to clasp his hand. I had meant the gesture perfunctorily, but found I held his hand a little more tightly than I intended. He held my gaze as I continued, "Thank you for your offer. But I have a plan, sir. You need not worry for me."

He searched my face and, as the seconds passed, I saw his protests fade. "I will not ask you the details, for all our sakes. But the thought of you alone does not sit well with me."

I said, smiling consolingly as I took half the money from the envelope and tucked the rest back into the box of my possessions, "I will not be alone. Constable? Do you mind keeping my cat for a short time? And keeping my things here?"

He blinked at me. "I suppose?"

"Thank you." I tucked a thick fold of bills into my pocket. "Now, one last question. Do you have a spare uniform I might borrow?"

CHAPTER 39

I kept my constable's helmet low as I surveyed the wreckage of the Grand Museum. It had begun to rain quite heavily, and thunder rolled across the city as a proper autumn storm settled in. It cooled the air, cooled my skin, and calmed the last of the conflict in the streets. I had made the journey relatively unaccosted, dropping Detective Supford's name to the singular patrol who had questioned me.

The success of my journey did not encourage me, though. Not as I watched the rain pool in the museum courtyard, glistening puddles smoothing away broken glass and washing smoke stains from piles of rubble.

Half of the museum's magnificent windows were blown out and the remainder were cracked and blackened. Scars of smoke licked upwards from these, memories of the flames that I had had such an integral part in sparking.

My heart broke. So much beauty, so much history. Gone. I felt it on the air, tasted it on the wind. It held memories of licking flame and crumbling stone, all that remained of so many treasures.

That alone was enough to sadden me, but a thought came with it. Even if the artifact had not been cracked or crushed, how could I find it in this destruction?

A museum guard, armed with a night stick and a rifle,

met me at the gate. At mention that I had been sent by Detective Supford, he admitted me inside, if only to get back out of the rain.

It was dark within, the gaslamps long blown. Several lanterns illuminated the scarred foyer, and a table full of more guards off down the passageway towards the café. They seemed demoralized by their task, guarding a gutted museum from further ravages in the restless city, and paid more attention to the meal they were sharing than to me.

The air stank of smoke, burned varnish, and singed hair.

"Brought in the cadets, I see." The guard from the gate looked me over. "Well, lad, I can't allow you past the foyer, but tell me your business and I'll see what I can do."

"A file in the offices, upstairs," I said. I was aware I was treading a little close to the truth, but needed the legitimacy of a known name. "Dr. Maddeson's office. If it... survived?"

"Got the fires out before it reached the third floor." The guard waved this aside. "What file?"

I fluffed a random description and watched the man leave, climbing the stairs carefully to the second floor. Then, cautiously, I made for the doors to the exhibits, opposite to the hallway and the other guards.

I glanced back, once. One of the guards was looking my way, so I made a show of stretching and sitting down on a fallen chunk of masonry, slightly in the shadows.

He looked away, and I continued on.

As soon as I was out of sight, I started to run. My Eventide eyes unfolded the darkness with little effort, and though what I saw in their sepia tones was grim, I did not falter.

Collapsed sections of floor. Toppled chunks of roof. Bracing had been placed everywhere, and far off I saw the light and heard the sounds of men at work, erecting more scaffolding and pillars, beams and supports.

I came to the room where I had faced off with Wake, fingers twitching with tension and urgency. Half the floor was gone, but, miracle of miracles, not the section where I had hidden the dodecahedron.

I skirted the collapsed section, passing charred statues

and cracked façades, until I came to the right one.

The little stone orb for which we had all fought and suffered slipped into my fingers. The moment felt... not momentous, but horribly insignificant. There was no great satisfaction, only an awareness of all the suffering it had caused, and the suffering it might yet produce.

I slipped it into my trouser pocket to join the others, beneath the protective fall of my constable's jacket, and left the museum before the guard returned.

A feeling of unreality overtook me as I returned to the rain and headed straight across Old Harrow, for Dockside and Pretoria's hotel. It was not a short walk, but time seemed to skew around me, my only thoughts of my next step, the next street. Before I knew it, I was in sight of the Old Citadel, before the statue of Lady Honoria Grey and her children.

Chanting wafted up the street as I approached. I slowed at the edge of a sudden and unexpected crowd, my skin beginning to crawl. There were dozens of people here, converging as I watched.

The citizens nearest me startled, pointing at my uniform. They carried clubs and guns, and did not seem to care for the rain slicking their hair and dripping from their hats.

Zealots. I instantly diverted. No one moved to stop me, though they watched me with caution—apparently they did not consider a lone, boy-faced constable a threat.

Suddenly a great shout tore all our gazes up. Up. Up.

A man swung up over the heads of the crowd, under the mournful eyes of the statue, isolated on her little island. He jerked and clawed at the noose about his throat. The more violently he struggled, the louder the crowd cheered, jeered, and screamed. It was a manic sound, a primal sound, and it terrified me to the core.

Run. The word leapt to my tongue and clotted there, souring and turning fetid. *Run.*

I did not. Could not. I watched as the man was hauled higher, as his struggles lessened, as his strangulation truly began.

Copper threads sparked and lit and spread—the Zealots had stripped him to the waist. They twined across his collarbones, where a Guild medallion was plastered to the sweat-slicked hair of his chest.

A Guild mage. They were hanging not an Affinate, vulnerable and accessible, but a *Guild mage*.

A second rope was slung up and a second figure hauled into sight. She screamed as she rose, a middle-aged woman with her upper body similarly revealed, her clothing torn and corset exposed. Her threads spasmed into manifest—fiery, like the afterburn of lightning. A Gaslamp Entwined.

A hand dug into my hair, beneath the back of my helmet. No sooner had I cried out than I was barrelled under a massive arm and hauled forward. The crowd parted. I could not breathe. Could barely see. There was more shouting, more laughing, a clamor and a chaos that melded into ringing in my ears.

Then there was a noose, pulled tight, holding me in place on my knees. I felt the hands that tore the constable's jacket from my upper body. I felt them tear open the top of my shirtwaist, buttons popping. I felt the helmet torn from my head and my hair skew down.

Incarnadine's face filled mine.

"We got here eventually, Miss Rushforth," she said, her eyes full of gentle satisfaction. "So kind of you to turn yourself in."

Thunder boomed. Lightning latticed the sky, followed by another clap of thunder.

Another rope—my rope—was slung up over the lamppost. I was prodded and dragged into place, already half-strangled by the damp noose. Above me the man swung, limp. The woman was still twitching, though that was more likely due to the jerking of the rope itself than her final exertions. Those that held the rope had not tied it off to the balustrade as they had with the man. They still held it instead, tugging and jerking and making her body dance.

"No bravado now," Incarnadine observed, smoothing the wet hair back from my face. "As I expected."

I could not reply. The rope was too tight. Too tight for pleading and begging, for last words and the bravado she was so satisfied to have killed.

I heard a gunshot, then another, then the blare of horns. Headlamps pierced the stormy gloom and people began to scatter, shouting warnings and grabbing comrades as they went.

Incarnadine turned. The Zealots holding me—a man and a woman—froze.

Their leader's distraction was momentary, but it was enough for me to flail forward, tear the hatpin from her head and plunge it into the torso of one of my captors. They howled and dropped me. The other recoiled, confused, and I broke fully away.

The noose went tight. I toppled backwards and might have snapped my own neck, if I had not made a flailing grab for the nearest person.

I never saw who it was. Headlamps blinded me and a speaking horn roared over the crowd. "Zealots, stand down by order of Grand General Baffin! You are under arrest!" There was more to it, but I did not care.

The noose finally slackened. I shoved aside whoever I had caught myself on and jerked the thing over my head, panting, wheezing, and sobbing as I did.

And then I ran.

CHAPTER 40

I pounded on the door of Pretoria's hotel room. There was no sound of movement beyond, but I sensed I was being watched through the peephole. I pounded again, desperate.

The door opened and Pretoria stood there, her expression aghast.

"Zealots," I croaked with what little voice I had left.

I was immediately folded into a desperate embrace, and held my sister tightly in return. We clung to one another until my trembling slowed and the ferocity of her grip softened to a gentler, cradling hold.

Someone, meanwhile, closed the door behind us. Through misty eyes, I saw Lewis. He supported himself with a walking stick for his bandaged leg, and his eyes had a haunted, near-maddened quality to them. I saw no outright evidence of Thera's work, but there was something hidden in the way he looked at me. A conversation yet to be had.

"Your Mr. Harden and Perry are searching the streets for you." Pretoria stole my attention again. She was pawing at my cheeks, my throat, taking in my injuries. "Are these marks from—"

"Yes," I rasped.

Lewis moved, and the next thing I knew, I had a blanket wrapped around my shoulders. His arms came with it, and Pretoria yielded to his larger frame.

Lewis held me, properly held me, with both arms and a gentleness I felt through my bones. When I pulled away and looked up at him, the expression on his face was cobbled from unanswered questions and battered stoicism.

A muffled sound came from the bathroom. I looked sharply to the side and saw Dr. Maddeson tied to a chair on the tiled floor, his hair mussed, and his cheeks puffed around a gag.

The sight was so unexpected that it shattered my fugue. "How did you manage to keep *him*?"

She sank down on the edge of the bed. Lewis, transitioning his hold to one arm, led me over and I sank down at her side. He hovered above us, weight on a cane.

"The professor swiftly realized that staying with Perry and I was safer than being alone on the streets. Until we got to the hotel, of course. Then he attempted to run." She leaned forward to shoot the professor a long look. "You will not be doing that again, will you, sir?"

Maddeson shook his head defeatedly.

"What..." Lewis brought my gaze back to his face. He had one hand in his hair, raking it back as he fought an internal battle.

"Not yet," I said. "I cannot explain... not yet."

They accepted that. Pretoria found another blanket and some water, and as I sat under their ministrations, my hammering heart finally slowed.

Perry returned soon after, with Harden in company. Both wore immaculate soldiers' uniforms and greeted me with obvious relief.

"You know how to worry a man," Harden rebuked. He took me in in one sweep, seeming to see far more than the blankets and my pale face. He exchanged a glance with Lewis.

Too many unspoken things hung in the air. I gathered my courage, and my voice, and spoke. "I have decided on a course of action."

"We can discuss what to do later—" Lewis started to say, but I cut him off with a shake of the head.

"No," I said. "Let me speak."

They let me.

"Baffin has made his move against the Zealots," I stated. "That means either they broke from his control, or he no longer needs them. Either way, Baffin's plans to cement his hold on the city and oust all Entwined are succeeding, and in their final stages."

I looked at Harden, an apology in my eyes. "We cannot save Harrow. *We* cannot. But we can prevent Baffin from pursuing his research into the artifacts. I know it seems like the least of our concerns, but if he succeeds, as I believe he will"—I did not say why, just then, but I shifted my gaze to Lewis—"his power will become absolute. He believes the artifacts can be used to grant humans the power of the Entwined. I think, perhaps, he is not far from the truth."

Lewis and Harden stood side by side, their expressions varied arrangements of incredulous, irate, and guarded. Given the angle at which I sat, I could not see Perry's face clearly just then.

Pretoria started to speak, but quietened as I took her hand. Neither of us wore gloves and the contact came with a whisper of memories, formless feelings, and glimpses of moments past. They came to me without effort, and stowed away in my mind.

In my pockets, the artifacts seemed to hum in response.

I went on, "I know you have questions. I will answer them. Simply understand—both Baffin and the Guild are after a truth, a power, that could unhinge and reshape our world. But we can stop them. Both of them. All we need do is retrieve all the items from the Landsdown Trove. We find them, and destroy them."

There was a muffled cry from the bathroom.

"Oh fetch him, would you?" Pretoria asked Perry.

Perry complied and Maddeson joined the council, gaze flicking nervously from party to party.

"You cannot destroy them!" he raged as Perry pressed him into a chair. "Aside from the Stele itself and unlocking the Old Arasi language—you would have to destroy the work and persons of multiple scholars the world over to truly erase this.

You cannot do it. I will not let you. You are overreacting, Miss Fleet."

"Rushforth," I corrected.

He frowned in consternation and plowed on, "When I have finished my translations, when the world understands that Entwined and humans are one and the same, there will be *peace*."

"He is an idealist," I explained to the company, rubbing my face wearily. My skin was damp and sweat-slick, and I longed for a bath. For solitude, security, and fresh beginning.

But more than that, I longed for action. I had found a purpose, a drive. A noose had cinched it into place. And the artifacts in my pockets were my ballast.

Maddeson's face reddened. "Now, see here—"

From there, my monologue and Maddeson's assertions gave way to a general discussion. I revealed more details, including Wake's and Moran's connection, though I did not mention Lewis's or my potentially altered condition.

"The professor may have a point," Lewis said cautiously, into a lull. "The Guild has succeeded in amplifying Entwined in the past. Documents burned may have redundancies. So we must even the field, as it were."

Harden watched him, agreement in his eyes. I wondered, passingly, what the Separatists would do with the artifacts and their power.

"I agree with Illing," Pretoria said. She looked to Maddeson. "You would, of course, come with us."

"Pardon me?"

"You will come with us to collect every artifact in the Landsdown Trove. You will be our scholar," she said. "We will carry you about in search of the relics, and you can decipher them."

He blustered. "But that is impossible. Many pieces are in private collections. I have been refused them before, not to mention those in the Museum ju Palnicas, the paperwork and permissions alone... And those lost to the criminal underworld—"

"I will acquire them for you," Pretoria said stoutly.

Maddeson had drawn breath to continue his rant, but at this he hesitated. "Pardon me?"

"Anything you need, you will have."

"But the permissions?"

She gave him a level look. "I need no permissions. Nothing will stand in the way of your research."

Maddeson sat back in his seat, looking suddenly contemplative.

"So you are proposing we gallivant about the world stealing antiquities?" Perry summarized, speaking to me. "With the aim to stop both the Grand General and the Guild? We are all to give ourselves to this, out of charity?"

"Out of self-preservation," I corrected.

Perry did not look convinced, but turned to Pretoria. My sister was pensive, in a brooding sort of way.

I left them to their silent conversation.

"Details need not be ironed out now, not until we are safe," I said, and turned to Harden. "Can you still get us out of the city?"

"Out of Arrent," Pretoria added. She broke Perry's gaze. "As I have wished to be all along."

"I can get you out of the city," Harden affirmed. There was something in his voice, something he was holding back, and he did not look at me. "Be ready, tonight."

True to his word, Harden reappeared that night. We heard the rumble of an engine and looked down to see a canvas-backed military truck in the streets.

Soon after, we sat in the back of the transport. It was long past twilight and the ringing of the curfew bells. My threads had twined again, as extensively and powerfully as before, but I had endured it hidden in the bathroom. I could not hide the change from my companions forever, but first, I had to find a chance to speak to Lewis privately.

The vehicle rumbled and bucked beneath us as Harden and Pretoria, seated in the front, plied the guards at the edge of the city with forged papers and impeccable bluffs.

"Have you felt... different?" I asked Lewis under the cover of the engine. We sat together, with Perry and Maddeson opposite. The professor looked startlingly convincing in his military uniform. "Since the cells?"

Lewis gave me an odd look. "What do you mean?"

"Your threads."

"They have not twined since."

I stared at him, aghast. "Are... are you saying your power is gone?"

"I am saying they have not twined since," he repeated in an undertone. "But nor have I had a chance to test them."

I would have said more, but just then Harden pulled the vehicle over. He appeared around the back with Pretoria and we disembarked, just out of sight of the city and its smoky skyline.

"Here is where I leave you," Harden said, looking between us. He nodded to Pretoria. "It will not be easy to get word in or out of the city for some time, but if I hear from you, I'll do what I can."

"Thank you," Perry said, shaking his hand.

Harden took my hand and pulled me aside. I was all too aware of everyone looking after us, including Lewis's obscure gaze. Then Harden and I were out of sight around the other side of the truck.

"I'll not have you leave before I say this," he said, still holding my hand. "They say war is no time for... these things, and I'd thought to let you go in peace, but—I wish we'd had time to see what we could become."

My fingers twitched in his. I thought of Lewis, only just out of sight, but the longer Harden's gaze held mine, the narrower my focus became. My hand relaxed in his. Lewis could not see us, and what if he did? The only affectionate words he had ever spoken to me were in delirium, and though he had shown me greater kindness in the last two days, that could not erase years of romantic disinterest.

"We would have enjoyed ourselves," I admitted. "If that one kiss was any indication."

His lips turned up at the memory and his eyes glinted. "Another, then? For our goodbye? A good kiss will keep."

I surveyed his lips. There was a moment then, a brief impulse, when I almost consented. But he was right. War was no time for such things.

"Thank you, Mr. Harden," I said at last. "For your help. Your friendship. And that kiss."

He relented with a wry, but nonetheless disappointed smile. He raised his hand between us, and I took it in a firm, lingering shake.

"Be safe, Ottilie," he charged. "Keep Lewis close. And when you've collected your Trove, when you uncover all those secrets? Remember me. Remember Harrow."

EPILOGUE

The first snow of winter clinked against the windowpane. It blended into a shy, constant rustle, matching the passage of Madge's brush across her canvas. She sat in a loose robe, her hair bound into a braid over one shoulder as she formed each contour, each highlight and shadow of her subject's face. Her face.

The eyes of her painted reflection fixed on the snow, the window and the white-dusted world beyond, an unread book resting open on her skirts. Beyond the cold glass, the hills north of the Guild fortress of Kesterlee were barren of trees, but ridges of black rock and ice-girded waterfalls decorated their austere heights. Guild soldiers patrolled outside, rifles slung across heavy wool jackets, their horses' manes dusted with snow.

The right half of Madge's face could just be seen beside her canvas. Her gaze was focused, her lips slightly parted, and one could almost smell the magic in the room—the sweetly absent, dusty scent of dried roses in a forgotten vase.

Madge paused her brush mid-stroke. Her expression—the perfect half of it that could be seen—was caught between her social mask and a flicker of the girl who had once led her little sisters through sleepy hallways and soothed their nightmares.

Then her expression shuttered again. She set her brush aside on her palette and scrutinized the painting. Her gaze was calculating, professional and detached, looking for flaws and judging its quality. Still, one hand drifted to her stomach, and one paint-smudged thumb brushed at her sash.

The portrait was objectively beautiful. She had captured herself in perfect profile, early winter light turning the few hairs that had escaped a pompadour into soft, luminescent strands. She had harnessed the nuances of the way her own hand rested on the imaginary book, her long, graceful fingers smudged with paint. She had intricately rendered the lace edges of her blouse, broad across the shoulder and revealing collarbones and throat.

And, above all, she had captured her threads. They were delicate and gilt, lacing across the portrait's collarbones, jaw, and temples like the seams of a once-broken vase.

One might have sworn, standing there on the lavish carpet next to Madge Rushforth, Golden Mage, that the portrait's threads undulated and thrummed with life. And with that life, something of her subject's memory, emotion began to fade. In fact it was already half gone, like fragments of a dream.

Madge brushed stray curls from her eyes with the back of one hand and looked directly into the portrait's icy-blue irises. As she did, she exhaled her magic across the canvas, slowly and steadily. She held the portrait's gaze all the while, shuddering at how they could be so full of emotion, of pain and love and regret. Emotions that she, herself, could not show.

Finished, Madge moved to a side table where a cloth and water basin stood, leaving the portrait alone in the center of the room. The gentle splash of water joined the shush of snow on the window as she washed the paint from her fingers and fought to keep her breathing even, her expression as still as the hushed, cold room.

With each moment that passed, each drop of water, a little more of herself settled into the drying canvas. The portrait's expression writ deeper with anger and loneliness, both raw and vivid. Simultaneously, as Madge plied white and brown and black and blue from the creases of her nails, her own face became composed. Her breathing eased. Her lips ceased to purse, and her posture settled.

When the magic was finished, Madge dried her hands on a delicate towel and turned to the door, where two suitcases sat ready to depart, next to a neat pile of travelling clothes. She passed the portrait of herself without a glance, dressed efficiently, and picked up the suitcases.

Then she left the room to its eerie, snowy silence. She left the tear-stained portrait behind; her own, perfect likeness locked into eternal misery.

She did not look back.

ACKNOWLEDGEMENTS

I wrote *Entwined* in a short, tense window between signing my first agent and selling my debut novel, *Hall of Smoke*. It was the distraction I needed, quick and fun and just for myself, and it kept the anxiety at bay as I waited for word that *Hall of Smoke* had sold. It saved my sanity, but more than that, I fell in love with it.

I watched *Entwined* sit on the shelf for a few years after that, gathering dust while I published other things. But all the while my mind was working, remembering and refining, and when the time came for *Entwined* to shine, I was ready. I know the book (and its coming sequel) is a hundred times better for the wait!

I want to extend a heartfelt thanks to my editor, George Sandison, for being such a champion of this book, along with being so insightful and patient. To the whole team at Titan including Elora, Katharine, Charlotte, Kabriya, Julia, and Natasha, you are wonderful, and I'm grateful for all your efforts on behalf of *Entwined*, and all my books!

Thank you to my agents, Naomi Davis and Laura Crockett. Naomi, thank you for securing *Entwined*'s path into the world. Laura, thank you for your continued support, for championing *Entwined*'s foreign rights so passionately, and for jumping on board with such friendliness and enthusiasm.

Thank you to my author buddies, for sprint writing with me, screeching over cover reveals with me, for talking me off the edge, and just being there when I need a friendly ear. You are splendid human beings.

Thank you to my family for supporting me through yet

another book, for loving and cuddling my son while I snag a few hours of work, and for never ceasing to cheer me on. On this note—thank you particularly to Grama Janet. Back in the day, you read the very first draft of *Entwined* and wrote down your favourite lines. You read them to me, and it was the first time I had ever heard someone read my own words aloud. It impacted me so much, stayed with me and buoyed me through the years. From then on, I knew—this would be the book I dedicate to you. Thank you, GG.

And finally, thank you so much to my readers. Without your support, none of my books would be! I dearly hope you loved Entwined, and will be as excited as I am to dig into Book 2!

ABOUT THE AUTHOR

H. M. LONG is a Canadian author who inhabits a ramshackle cabin in Ontario, Canada, with her husband and dog. However, she can often be spotted snooping about museums or wandering the Alps. She is the author of *Hall of Smoke, Temple of No God, Barrow of Winter,* and *Pillar of Ash,* along with *Dark Water Daughter, Black Tide Son,* and *Red Tempest Brother.*

For more fantastic fiction, author events,
exclusive excerpts, competitions, limited editions and more

VISIT OUR WEBSITE
titanbooks.com

LIKE US ON FACEBOOK
facebook.com/titanbooks

FOLLOW US ON TWITTER AND INSTAGRAM
@TitanBooks

EMAIL US
readerfeedback@titanemail.com